New York Times bestselling autho[r]
a life of extraordinary danger…
three sons, a husband, a menage[r]
of sw

Writing as Sherrilyn Kenyon and Kinley MacGregor, she
is an international phenomenon with more than twelve
million copies of her books in print, in twenty-eight
countries. She's the author of several series including: The
Dark-Hunters, The League, and Lords of Avalon. Her books
always appear at the top of the *New York Times*, *Publishers
Weekly* and *USA Today* lists.

Visit Sherrilyn Kenyon's websites:
www.darkhunter.com | www.sherrilynkenyon.co.uk

www.facebook.com/AuthorSherrilynKenyon |
www.twitter.com/KenyonSherrilyn

Praise for Sherrilyn Kenyon:

'A publishing phenomenon…[Sherrilyn Kenyon] is the
reigning queen of the wildly successful paranormal scene'
Publishers Weekly

'Kenyon's writing is brisk, ironic and relentlessly
imaginative. These are not your mother's vampire novels'
Boston Globe

'Whether writing as Sherrilyn Kenyon or Kinley
MacGregor, this author delivers great romantic fantasy!'
New York Times bestselling author Elizabeth Lowell

No Mercy

Sherrilyn Kenyon

piatkus

PIATKUS

First published in the US in 2010 by St. Martin's Press, New York
First published in Great Britain as a paperback original in 2010 by Piatkus
This paperback edition published in 2011 by Piatkus

A CIP catalogue record for this book
is available from the British Library.

ISBN 978-0-7499-4245-8

Printed and bound by CPI Mackays, Chatham ME5 8TD

Piatkus
An imprint of
Little, Brown Book Group
100 Victoria Embankment
London EC4Y 0DY

An Hachette UK Company
www.hachette.co.uk

www.piatkus.co.uk

To my readers, who mean the world to me and who have given me countless hours of laughter and smiles online and at appearances. Thank you so much!

To my team at SMP, who works so hard to get the books out, and especially Monique, whose insights and support are the stuff of legends.

To my friends, who are always there when I need them, especially Kim and Dianna, who never shirk at the proof-reading and brainstorming sessions.

And to my family, who never complain about eating a lot of pizza and who understand why Mom has to spend so much time locked in her room. Most of all to my hubby, without whom I could never do what I do, and who really is the wind beneath my wings.

God bless and keep all of you.

PROLOGUE

The Legend of Sanctuary

You can take my life, but you'll never break me.
So bring me your worst. . . .
And I will definitely give you mine.

Those words, written in French, still remained on the top of Nicolette Peltier's desk where she'd carved them with her bear's claw after the death of two of her sons. It wasn't just a motto, it was her angry declaration to the world that had taken her sons from her. A ruthless tragedy that had spurred her on to create the most renowned of the shapeshifter havens.

Sanctuary.

For over a century, she'd owned the famed Sanctuary bar and restaurant that rested on the corner of Ursulines and Chartres in New Orleans. There she'd reigned as the queen of her kingdom. The mother bear of her remaining twelve cubs who struggled hard every day with the grief over the sons she'd buried.

Not a day had passed that she hadn't mourned them.

Until the day war had come to their door. True to her nature and the words she'd carved as a permanent reminder of her spirit, she had done her worst and she'd protected her children with everything she had.

But that love for them had cost her her life. When her enemies moved to kill her daughter's mate, she'd protected the lycanthrope with the last of her strength and she'd given her life to save her daughter Aimee the agony of burying the wolfwere she loved.

The tragedy of her loss was felt throughout the entire Were-Hunter counsel. Nicolette had been as much a legend as the club she'd owned. A club that had welcomed all creatures and promised them safety and protection so long as they obeyed her one simple rule:

Come in peace.

Or leave in pieces.

Since the night of her death, her cubs have sought to carry on without her support and guidance. No longer an official haven recognized by the Omegrion council, Sanctuary now stands outside the laws that had once shielded them and her patrons.

And that was fine with Dev Peltier. He'd never liked rules anyway.

But the war that had come to their door wasn't over.

They had only fought the opening battle. . . .

Chapter 1

"Is it just me or has the entire world gone stump stupid?"

Dev Peltier laughed as he heard his brother Remi's voice in his ear while he stood outside the front door of the Sanctuary club his family owned. He and Remi were half of a set of identical quads . . . and that comment was so out of character for his surly brother that Dev had to shake his head. "Since when you channel Simi?" he asked into the headset he wore so much that it felt weird whenever he didn't have it in his ear.

Remi snorted. "Yeah . . . like I'm a friggin' Goth demon chick dressed in a corset, frilly skirt, and tights trying to eat my way through the menu . . . and staff."

That was definitely Simi to a T.

But Dev couldn't resist ribbing him. "I always knew you were a freak, *mon frère*. This just proves it. Maybe we should rename you Frank-N-Furter and throw little wienies at you whenever you walk past."

"Shut up, Dev, before I come out there and make myself a triplet."

As if. Remi had obviously forgotten who'd taught him how to fight. "Bring it, punk. I got a new pair of boots itching to head up someone's—"

"Would you two stop fighting over the open channel? ...And grow up while you're at it. I swear I'm going to make bear stew out of both of you tonight if you don't stop." Aimee broke off into a round of French, their native language, so that she could continue insulting and emasculating them.

Dev bit back a smart-ass response to his sister's hostile tone that was punctuated by several cheers of approval from the rest of the crew, whose headsets allowed them to overhear every word.

To be honest, he and his family didn't need the headsets to communicate. Part of being shapeshifting bears was that they could project their thoughts so long as they were within a reasonable distance from each other—though some of them were better at that than others. But that tended to raise suspicion among the mundane humans who worked for them and especially the ones who patronized their business. So they wore the sets in an attempt to at least appear normal.

Yeah, right. Normality had waved bye-bye to his family and his species a long time ago. But what the hell?

He rocked the headset look.

Even so, Dev pulled it off his head as his sister's ranting in French reminded him of his mother's and an unexpected surge of grief tore through him. How he missed the sound of his mother bitching at him in French....

Who would have ever thought? Of all the things to miss.

I must be sick in the head. And yet his mother's sharp voice haunted him from the past.

You need to grow up, Devereaux. . . . You're not a cub anymore. Haven't been one in over two hundred years. Why you bait your brothers so and make me lose my mind? Mon Dieu! *You are ever my bane when you misbehave. Just once, can't you counsel your tongue and do as I ask? How can we rely on you if you insist on acting like a boy child? Did you learn nothing?* Dev flinched as he saw her face in his mind while she read him his daily riot act.

It was a face he'd never see again and a voice that would one day all too soon fade completely from his memory.

How he hated change.

For over a hundred years, he'd taken his post at Sanctuary's door, watching as all manner of beings came and went. A sentinel in more ways than one, he'd let the humans pass without stopping them. But to the preternatural patrons who came here, he always explained the rules of Sanctuary and interrogated them to determine how much of a threat they'd be if they attacked—as well as determine who their allies were.

Just in case.

Now he stood post to make sure their enemies didn't finish destroying the club they'd only just put back together from the fight that had scarred them all.

I miss you, Maman. He missed his father just as much.

Stuff they could replace. Boards could be nailed back in place and counters remade. Smoke damage repaired.

But his parents . . .

They were gone forever.

And that made him furious as more grief racked him. It'd taken all of his strength not to go after the lycanthrope pack that had attacked them. If not for the knowledge of it causing the Omegrion—the ruling council for the werebeasts—to hunt down his remaining family and kill them in retaliation, he wouldn't have hesitated. But that he could never chance. He would not be responsible for the death of a single family member.

Not even his brother Remi.

He'd seen too many of his family killed in front of him. . . .

I really want to leave.

It was a thought that was becoming more and more appealing. Ever since they'd reopened Sanctuary after the battle and fire, he'd been struck hard with wanderlust. The only reason he'd stayed here as long as he had was that his mother had asked him to remain with the family and help protect his younger sister.

Now that his mother was dead and Aimee was mated . . .

Staying wasn't as necessary as it'd been before. Every day he felt the pull to leave and make his own way in the world. He was a bear and it was the nature for most males to find a mate and start their own pack.

What am I doing here?

They didn't really need him. When the battle had come to their door, they'd learned fast just how many allies they had. And that number had been impressive. Sanctuary would stand forever. He didn't have to stay here to protect the door.

And yet . . .

I really hate change.

You're just restless. You'll get over it. You'll see. Besides, he didn't want a mate. Ever. Life was difficult enough trying to please himself. Gods help him if he ever had to try and please someone else.

It was just so much had happened over the last few months that it'd shaken his foundation. He felt lost . . . like his moorings had been sliced and he was left adrift without an engine or paddle. He'd never dealt well with change and so many changes had been thrust on him that he just wanted to leave it all behind and start fresh somewhere else.

Find someplace where he felt like he belonged again—even if he had to go to the past to do it. Someplace where he wasn't looking for his parents to come around the corner or be sitting in their favorite seats. Where memories didn't haunt him.

Or more to the point, hurt him.

The roaring sound of a racing bike broke through his melancholy thoughts as it approached from down the street. It was a Busa. He could tell by the throaty groan of the engine—they had a unique sound that was unmistakable to anyone who knew their bikes. Many of his Were-Hunter brethren used motorcycles as a means of transportation, including him and his brothers. Unlike a car, it was easier to teleport with their powers, and on the street, there was nothing faster that could maneuver out of the way of their enemies.

Or after them.

But this one growled with a specific tone that said she'd been modified for maximum speed and performance.

Expecting to see the Dark-Hunter leader Acheron on his black Hyabusa heading in, Dev frowned as a red one came up the street so fast, he was surprised it wasn't leading a few squad cars. The driver went past the entrance, then slammed on the brakes, sliding the bike sideways and leaving a cloud of burned rubber in its wake. The front wheel popped up before it headed toward him. Just as it reached the curb, the front tire slammed down and the rider parked it right in front of him with a jerking bounce that caused the rear wheel to lift up.

Even though the rider was tall and stoutly built, Dev could tell by her shapely curves that were covered in protective leather she was a woman.

Most likely a hot one too, and that definitely got his attention.

Unwilling to show her he was impressed with her biker skills, Dev crossed his arms over his chest as she pulled her helmet off and set loose a cascade of unruly honey blond curls that fell just past her shoulders. Curls that framed an adorable face. Not stunning or perfect, but exotic. Different. Most of all, her features were beguiling and he couldn't help wondering what she'd look like first thing in the morning with that riot of curls spilling all around her naked body.

She held an air of fierce joie de vivre and it was infectious—as if she savored every heartbeat she was lucky enough to have. However, she rode the bike like a person with a death wish. "You keep driving like that, you're going to kill someone."

She slung one long leg around the seat before she sauntered up to him with a hot, seductive stride he was sure had sent a few men to their graves from heart attacks. She wore a pair of flat New Rock biker boots with flames

8

coming up the sides. Her dark brown, almond-shaped eyes glowed with mischief as she unzipped her jacket and gave him a heated once-over. "I only kill the ones who deserve it, and those I gut with relish."

Damn, she was about as sexy as any woman he'd ever seen. His body reacted to her instantly. And it made him wonder if she'd be so open in the bedroom.

She shrugged her jacket off and slung it over her shoulder to hold it there with one gloved hand, showing him a tight black knit shirt before she leaned in closer to him. The warm scent of woman and leather made the bear inside him sit up and purr and it was all he could do not to nuzzle that soft neck that seemed to invite him in for a taste.

"To answer your question, Bear . . . I *am* as fierce in the sack as I am on the street. Just so you know." She winked at him.

Those words caused his cock to jerk against his will as he made a mental note that she could read his thoughts. His gaze fell from her eyes to the deep cleavage that was pushed up by her black bra. And at the swell of her right breast was the double bow-and-arrow mark that told him exactly who and what she was—not that he hadn't guessed that from her powers or the small glimpse of her fangs when she spoke. Damn, it looked like not even the goddess Artemis had been able to resist copping a feel of that hot body when she brought her over. "I'm not familiar with you, Dark-Hunter."

She straightened the layered row of black skull necklaces that hung around her neck. "We've met before. Very briefly. Not even enough time to exchange names."

Dev scowled as he tried to recall it.

No, definitely not. He'd have remembered this particular Huntress had he ever laid eyes on her before—even if it'd been centuries ago. Even if he'd been dead. She wasn't the kind of woman a man easily forgot meeting. "You must have met one of my brothers." Most people couldn't tell them apart. It went with the whole being identical thing and both Cherif and Quinn took turns at the door when Dev had time off. No doubt she had him confused with one of them. "We're identical quadruplets and I look a lot like my other brothers too."

She shook her head in denial. "I know. I met all of you. I was here the night the wolves attacked." Her gaze went up to where the roof still bore a small trace of fire damage from their fight and her eyes darkened with sympathy. "I'm really sorry about your parents . . . and that we didn't do a better job of protecting them."

He didn't know why, but that touched him. "Thanks for the assist. I know all of you did your best." They all had. But the number of their enemies had been overwhelming. In all honesty, it was a miracle any of them had survived.

But for the Dark-Hunters and their allies, they wouldn't have.

A shadow of pain masked her expression as if she had her own demons buried in those words. "Yeah, but sometimes it's just not good enough and no amount of sincere apologies ever makes it okay. That being said, I really am sorry. For everything." She glanced inside the bar before she recovered her earlier zest. "Name's Sam Savage."

Samia Savage . . .

That was a name he'd heard bandied about by other Dark-Hunters over the centuries. She was one of their fiercest—hence the surname the other Dark-Hunters had given her several hundred years ago as an homage to her brutality in a fight. As immortal slayers who protected humans, all Dark-Hunters came from horrific backgrounds. Each one different, they all had one thing in common: Someone had betrayed and killed them in a manner so foul that they sold their souls to the Greek goddess Artemis for a single act of vengeance against their betrayer. Not something someone undertook lightly and he couldn't help wondering what had happened to Sam to make her sell her soul.

Who had killed her and why had that event turned her into something so brutal even the stoutest male Hunters tended to cut her a wide berth? All the stories he'd heard about her had never answered that. They only said that this woman lived for the thrill of the fight.

The bloodier the better.

"You were an Amazon general at the end of the Trojan War." The granddaughter of their greatest queen, Hippolyta, Sam was said to have been the one to escort Helen home after the war. Something that had been extremely difficult given how many Greeks had wanted to kill Helen for causing the war that had kept them away from home for over a decade.

One corner of her mouth quirked up. "You say Amazon like it's a bad thing."

Dev laughed. "I've met a few of you over the centuries. Not bad, just . . . interesting."

The Amazons were the goddess Artemis's chosen people. It was why there were so many who were Dark-Hunters.

When Artemis had set up her army to fight for humanity against their preternatural predators, the Amazons had always been her first choice and were rumored to be paid ten times more than the rest of the Dark-Hunters. A little favoritism that led to hard feelings from some of the other Hunters toward any Amazon in their bunch.

For Dev, it just meant he had to watch her since the Amazons tended to be ferocious partiers who liked to brawl.

"So what brings you here tonight?" he asked her, changing the topic to a pertinent subject.

Sam paused before she answered. "Don't know really. I had a feeling that something wicked this way headed. So I thought I'd beat it here in order to grab it by the throat and hurt it before it did any damage."

He tsked at her. "Ah baby, don't you know I'm the only thing wicked here?"

She wrinkled her nose at him. "Are you flirting with me?"

"Depends. Is there an ass-whipping in it and will you be naked when you do it?"

She gave him an arch stare. "So you like to have your ass whipped?"

"Not really, but so long as you're naked when you do it I could take it quite happily. . . ."

She laughed. "Kinky. I like that."

He had no idea why he was flirting with her. While he was as much of a manwhore as any of his unmated brothers, he didn't normally waste time on women he knew were off his menu. And sleeping with Dark-Hunters was a key no-no in their world . . . for many, many reasons.

But he couldn't seem to help himself. There was something about her that invited him straight to suicide. "More horny actually. It's been a while."

She sucked her breath in sharply. "Brutal honesty. Nice change of pace. Most men would try flattery first."

He shrugged. "I would say life's too short to beat around the bush, but I'll live for centuries and you for eternity so for us, not a concern. So I'll just say that I don't like to play games or sugarcoat things and leave it at that."

"A bear after my own heart, but don't you know we're not supposed to fraternize?"

He shrugged. "I don't like following rules."

She dipped her gaze down his body with a heated look that set his hormones on fire. "Me neither."

"Yeah, I can tell by the way you drive."

Sam really didn't want to be charmed by the werebeast in front of her, but honestly she couldn't seem to help it. There was something about him that made her smile. And it wasn't just that he was hotter than hell. Or that he had a smile that should be illegal.

He just seemed to be the kind of person who was fun to hang out with and in her world such people were few and far between. His long, curly blond hair was pulled back from a face that appeared to be chiseled from steel. Blue eyes teased her with their intelligence and humor.

And his body . . .

She could lick on that all night long. Even more disturbing, there was something about him that reminded her of Ioel and the way he'd always been able to make her smile no matter how bad her day had sucked. Even after thousands of years, she still missed him.

Trying not to think about that, she dropped her gaze to Dev's arm, which bulged with well-defined muscles, then frowned as she saw the tattoo peeking out from under the short sleeve.

Was that . . .

No. Surely not.

Before she could stop herself, she pulled his sleeve up with her gloved hand to find a double bow-and-arrow mark just like the one Artemis had given her on the night she'd been converted into a Dark-Hunter and brought back to life to fight against the vampiric Daimons. The only difference was that Sam's was a brand and his was definitely ink.

She arched a brow at him. "Should I ask?"

He grinned roguishly. "I like yanking the chains of the gods."

"You must. From what I hear Artemis doesn't have much of a sense of humor."

"She hasn't killed me for it yet."

He definitely had guts. "Are you that brave or that stupid?"

"My mother used to say the two walk hand in hand."

That amused her. Her mother had once said something very similar to her as well.

Shaking her head, she sought to change the subject to the real reason she was here and to remind herself why she shouldn't find this man interesting in the least. "Have any Daimons shown up tonight?"

"You know I'm not supposed to tell you if they do." That code of honor between the Daimons and the Were-Hunters had always annoyed her. The Were-Hunters had been created out of the same race as the Daimons and so they tended to share a bond with their "cousins."

"You guys are as much human as you are Daimon."

"And we don't feed the humans to you either." He winked at her. "But to answer your question, no. No Daimons have been near the club in weeks."

That was hard to believe. Touristy places such as this were known Daimon hunting grounds and hangouts. "Really?"

"Yeah, it's weird, I know. It's like they're on hiatus or something. We've never been this long without at least a group or two visiting. The last one we saw was before we reopened. . . . And that bastard showed up here in broad daylight."

She scoffed at his words. "You're so full of it." What he was saying was absolutely ludicrous. "Daimons can't walk in daylight, everyone knows that."

"I hear ya, but I'm telling you he was here in the flesh and the sun was bright and shining. He walked right out into it like he didn't have a care in the world."

She still wasn't sold on what he was saying. It didn't make sense. "And none of you thought to tell us?"

"We filed a report with the Squires"—they were the human employees who helped the Dark-Hunters and who protected them during the daylight hours when the Dark-Hunters couldn't be out in sunlight without bursting into flames—"and we've been telling every Dark-Hunter we see. But since no one else has seen a Daimon in daylight, they think we're on meth and dismiss the warning as some kind of mass hallucination brought on by too much honey-drinking."

His words amused her. "Are you on meth?"

"You know that stuff won't work on me any more than it'd work on you." Dark-Hunters and Were-Hunters were all immune to most drugs.

Sam still couldn't buy it. "Did you tell Acheron?"

"Again, he said there was only one Daimon who could walk in daylight and that he'd personally destroyed that one. There was no chance in hell we have another Daywalker."

And yet Dev believed unequivocally that they'd seen a Daimon in daylight. She could sense it with every power she possessed. "Maybe it was some Goth kid with fangs screwing with you."

"Yeah 'cause I can't tell the difference between a human and a Daimon. I really suck at this job."

She laughed at his dry sarcasm. How could he be so cute and annoying all at once? "All right. I believe you. But—"

He held his hands up in surrender. "I hear you and I agree it's whacked. I know it makes no sense. I'm just telling you what we saw so that you know. You draw your own conclusions from there."

"Well, if you're right, let's hope this is just an anomaly and that he burned up three seconds after he left here."

"Here's hoping for miracles." He picked the headset up from his shoulders and placed it back over his ears. It was peculiar to her how any man could look so sexy with that contraption on his head, yet he somehow managed.

Totally weird . . .

Dev gestured to the door. "You're safe to go in. There aren't any other Dark-Hunters inside."

She appreciated his warning. Not that she needed it. While being around another Dark-Hunter would drain her powers, hers were so great that the depletion was basically a joke. Not to mention she had serious battle skills that few could touch with or without her Dark-Hunter powers to back them. That was what made her one of the machiskyli ... the Dogs of War. The Daimons had their elite fighters and the Dark-Hunters had the Dogs. Men and women who lived for battle and who took their only joy in cutting the hearts out of their enemies.

It was a badge she wore with honor. And tonight she felt the Daimon presence deep in her bones. She just had to pinpoint it, grab it by the throat, and strangle it until she felt better. Which meant leaving the enticing bear at the door and heading in to do her job.

"I'll catch you later, Bear."

He inclined his head to her as she walked through the doors into the dark interior. Since it was only seven in the evening, there weren't many people in the club. A few humans eating at the front tables. Two more sitting at the bar that was being tended by a wolfwere (so called because he was a wolf in human form) and another bearwere who bore a striking resemblance to Dev. It must be one of his identical brothers.

She sauntered over to the wolf and ordered a longneck.

"You want any food to go with that?" he asked as he popped the top on one and handed it to her.

Sam shook her head and ignored the curious stare he directed at her gloved hands. Food wasn't really her thing and she hoped that she could sip this beer in peace. She started to pull out her wallet, but the wolf stopped her.

"I remember you from the fight. Your money's no good here."

His pain reached out to her as she had a flash in her mind of his past. A past that left him with a profound sense of guilt. He was the one Nicolette Peltier had died protecting and he felt like he'd taken the mother from the woman he loved—it was a bitter ache that stayed buried deep inside him and burned like a coal. He was a good man to care so much about his wife. "Thanks . . . Fang." His name popped into her head as clearly as the images from his past. Images that would be heightened to a brutal level if she touched his body in any way.

He inclined his head to her. "Anytime."

Sam moved away before she took in any more residual emotions and images from him. She hated that power so much. It might not be so bad if she had some kind of control over it, but she didn't. Instead, other people's emotions often tangled with hers until she had a hard time deciphering her feelings from theirs. It was why she tended to avoid people as much as possible. And why she couldn't touch anyone with her bare hands or flesh.

If she did . . .

It was horrifying.

Why couldn't I have the ability to fly? Or something really useful like pyrokinesis?

But no. She had the wienie powers of empathy and psychometry. . . .

For that "gift," she'd like to choke slam Artemis. But she also had telekinesis, which definitely came in handy, especially in a fight. So it wasn't a complete knicker twist since she'd had remote control long before Eugene McDonald at Zenith had ever conceived the first clicker.

Sipping her beer, Sam wandered through the club that was nice and dark—easy on her light-sensitive eyes. And as she passed through, she caught glimpses of a thousand different events that had taken place here over the last century and a half.

While there were unhappy moments, the overwhelming base emotion for Sanctuary was warmth and homecoming. No wonder it was so popular among the preternatural community. While most wouldn't have her powers to see what she did, they would still pick up on the sensation of love and safety that emanated from every object here. This entire place was filled with the care and devotion of the bear who'd built it.

"May the gods bless and keep you, Nicolette," she whispered. As a mother herself, she knew the absolute agony of losing her children. The pain that no amount of time ever healed. It was something no one should ever experience.

She flinched as an image of Agaria's face flashed through her mind. Even now the thought of her daughter could bring her to her knees and it brought a tidal swell of potent rage that still wanted to be appeased. That fury was what made her such a great fighter. The Daimons had taken everything from her and no matter how many of them she killed it just wasn't enough to make up for what they'd done.

To make up for the life that had been brutally cut short.

"You look pissed off tonight."

She cocked her head as she recognized the softly accented voice behind her.

Chi Hu.

Sam turned around slowly to face the delicate Chinese woman whose long black hair was secured into a tight braid down her back. But that fragility was extremely misleading. While Chi barely broke five feet in height and was as thin as a pencil, she was a skilled warrior who could take down anyone dumb enough to mistake her for an easy mark. Dressed in a tight pair of jeans and a black shirt and vest, Chi was exquisitely beautiful. The kind of perfect beauty Sam had ached for when she was human. But over the centuries she'd learned that that kind of beauty was as much a curse as a blessing.

Hence why Chi was now a Dark-Hunter.

Sam smiled. A fellow Dog of War, Chi was the only friend she'd allowed herself to have in the last five thousand years. She still wasn't sure how it'd happened, but Chi was a hard person not to love—once you broke through her icy defenses. "What are you doing here?"

Knowing better than to touch her, Chi gestured around the club. "Same as you. Scoping Daimons. Looking for a good fight to take the edge off. Did the bear at the door tell you about their great hallucination of a Daywalker?"

"He did indeed."

"What do you think it was?"

Sam shrugged. "Maybe a demon they mistook for a Daimon."

Chi nodded in agreement. "Makes sense. They are sometimes hard for the untrained to differentiate." And Chi would know since she was an expert in demonology. "There are several subspecies of demon that are very Daimon-like. One of those could be mistaken by a Were."

Maybe, but Dev had seemed pretty sharp. Then again, Chi was the expert, which made Sam wonder why Chi was here in New Orleans. "When did they relocate you?"

"Three weeks ago."

Sam cocked her brow at that. "Why didn't you tell me you were being relocated too?"

Chi tsked at her tone. "Ditch the suspicion. I wanted to surprise you, *jie jie*. Nothing more. Nothing less. Had I not come across you tonight, I would have called. This is my first trip in to look around and I was hoping I'd stumble on you, which I did." She grinned. "I wanted it to be a surprise. That's all."

Sam inwardly cringed as Chi called her "big sister." In her world "sister" was an insult. And she knew Chi was being honest about the moving and not telling her— another blessing of her powers. Sam was a walking lie detector. "It's really good to see you again."

Chi wrinkled her nose. "Let's just hope this time is not as bloody as the last."

Sam laughed. "Like you don't relish the fight as much as I do. Some days I think more so."

Chi joined her laughter. "True, very true."

Sam narrowed her eyes as she noticed the shiny silver sticks at the top of Chi's braid. Reaching out, she touched one with her gloved fingertip. True to her intuition, it was sharp as a talon as it snagged the leather on her glove. "Nice weapon disguise."

Chi took a sip of her own drink. "You have to be creative these days. Humans are more suspicious than ever. If you want, I can give you a set."

21

"Love to have them. But I should probably pass." Wearing them on her body could be a major hassle since she'd pick up on the emotions of whoever had created them. It was why everything she wore, drove, or used had to be created by Acheron specifically for her—untouched by the hands of another creature. Thank the gods their fearless leader had the powers he did. Otherwise she'd be completely screwed. It was why she didn't like food. Beverages weren't so bad since most of them were done by machines.

Meat for her was out of the question. Gods, how she missed eating steak. . . .

Pushing that thought away, Sam took another swig of beer as she considered what Chi had told her about her latest assignment. "So how many of us have been relocated to New Orleans now?"

"Last I heard, Acheron has eight of the Dogs here."

The number was impressive. "Eight? Isn't that overkill?"

Chi shrugged. "I guess the Atlantean is expecting something big to happen." They'd all been sent here to guard one man in particular. Nick Gautier. That was the extent of what they knew.

Nick had to live even if it meant they had to die.

"But of course Acheron isn't telling anyone what that is." There was more venom in Sam's voice than she'd intended. All things considered, she loved Acheron. She just wished he'd be a little more open with all of them.

Chi held her bottle up in silent salute. "Exactly."

Typical Acheron. He lived for secrets and it made Sam wonder what exactly was up in the preternatural realm that the Atlantean would risk bringing in so many of the Dogs of War at one time. They weren't exactly friendly and most of them were highly territorial. The last time there had been two Dogs in one city, they'd almost destroyed it.

And contrary to the online rumors, it hadn't been her and Ethon going at it.

Chi narrowed a curious stare her way as if she picked up on that thought. "Have you seen Ethon yet?"

Sam grimaced at the reminder of the ancient Spartan general who, after a night of battle, had been forced to take refuge in her house centuries ago. "Not yet, but I did see Roman on the street a few nights back." She spat his name with all the disgust she felt scalding her throat. Roman was a gladiator and while she could appreciate his skills, she despised everything he stood for.

Chi gave her a gimlet stare. "You planning a rematch with Ethon?"

Sam shuddered at the thought. "Do I bring up your old flings?"

"He's really gorgeous."

"And so not what I'm looking for in anything. Even for a single night." Not to mention Dark-Hunters were completely forbidden from sleeping together. She and Ethon had gotten caught up in a moment, spent one night together, and had regretted it ever since. If Acheron ever found out what they'd done, he'd probably kill them.

Artemis definitely would.

And that night had taught her to stay away from lovers forever and Ethon in particular. She still couldn't get the images of Ethon's brutal past out of her mind. Never again did she want to be that assaulted by someone else's damage. She had enough of her own.

Guilt tore through her. She winced, shoving it away before it did any more harm to her.

Chi passed an amused glance over to the bar where the Dev lookalike was pouring a drink for another customer. "What about the bears?"

Sam forced herself not to react in the slightest. "What about the bears?"

"Oh c'mon, don't tell me you haven't thought about being a cub sandwich with them. Especially with the quads. Oh my God, the one at the door is absolutely droolicious."

"Droolicious?"

Chi playfully rubbed up against her, making sure not to touch her skin. "Don't play coy. I know you better than that. Dev is definitely worth a brush of emotions."

Sam snorted. "Yes, you do and yes, I thought about it."

"But?"

"I'm having Ethon flashbacks and throwing up in my mouth as a result. I don't want to relive that damage. Ever." Not even for something as scrumptious as Dev.

Chi snorted. "One night won't kill you."

"Isn't that what Geitara said right before the Battle of Tortulla? As I remember, it didn't go well for her when they slaughtered her and all her troops." Sam jerked her chin toward the bartender. "If you're so hungry, why don't you take one home?"

"One? Honey, I'm waiting for the whole six-pack."

Sam laughed. "You are evil."

Chi sobered instantly as she jerked to her right and scanned the club with her gaze. "Did you feel that?"

Sam turned her head and lowered her chin, listening. There had been a strange sensation that cut through the air around them. Inhuman and feral. It'd gone down her spine like a razor. "I did." It was similar to a Daimon tremor, but different. More powerful. She looked around the club to see if anyone else felt it.

If they did, they didn't react.

How weird.

She met Chi's narrowed gaze. "I'll take the back."

"I'll head out the front."

Sam used her powers to search the ether around them as she headed for the back door of Sanctuary. The Dark-Hunters also had an electronic tracker for Daimons, but she'd never needed one. Her senses and powers had always allowed her to hone right in on them.

But not tonight.

Tonight she lost the scent almost as soon as she walked outside.

How was that possible? And yet there was no denying what she felt. Or more to the point, didn't feel. The air was crisp with a hint of autumn in it. She smelled the gumbo and steaks that were cooking in the kitchen and the scent of the river that was only a few blocks away. But there was nothing here to do with the Daimons.

With all her senses fully alert, she crept around the outside of the building, trying to locate what had called out to them.

Nothing was here. Everything appeared normal and yet in her gut she knew it wasn't.

Chi doubled back to cut her off. She met Sam's quizzical stare, then jerked her chin up toward the sky.

Sam followed the line of her gaze. The moment she focused on the sky, her stomach headed south. Above their heads hung a moon so red and cloudy, it appeared to be washed in blood.

Hunter's Moon. Scientifically, she knew it meant nothing more than the way the sun's light was bending around the earth to illuminate the lunar surface. But she'd lived long enough to know it wasn't just that simple—that science didn't explain everything. Mostly because science didn't know about everything.

It definitely didn't know about the protective veil that separated the worlds from each other. A veil that thinned during a blood moon. Most of all, it didn't know that sometimes ancient man had feared ill omens with just cause.

In the heart and in the soul,
Evil takes its wicked toll.
When moonlight shines like flowing blood,
Over the earth the demons will flood.

The old Amazon poem went through her head. A moon just like that one had once shone down on her home. She'd dismissed it then as unfounded superstition.

And she'd died regretting that stupidity.

"I'll call Acheron," Chi said, pulling out her cell phone.

Sam nodded as she felt the hand of evil slide over her. Something was coming for them, she could feel it. The only question was, what was it?

26

Chapter 2

After texting the other Dark-Hunters in New Orleans about what was going on, Sam spent the next eight hours on patrol while keeping in touch intermittently with Chi. Neither of them found anything unusual. Not a single Daimon seemed to be out tonight. The only predators on the street were human and while Sam had chased the ones away she found, they weren't the biggest threat in the world.

They just thought they were.

How she'd like to feed them to some of the things she'd killed over the centuries. Let them see what a badass really looked like up close and personal. They had no idea how insignificant and weak they really were. A dose of reality might serve them well.

Her phone buzzed. Looking down, she saw it was Chi. She flipped it open and answered.

Chi let out a long sigh. "Still bust. I'm heading back to my house to rest my feet and grab a bite. I'll catch you later."

"All right," Sam said into her phone while she glanced back at the evil moon. A shiver ran down her spine. "See you tomorrow night. Sleep tight and don't let the Daimons bite." She hung up the phone and checked the time.

Three A.M. Almost three hours until dawn. On the one hand, Chi was right and they were wasting their time out on the street. On the other ...

She just couldn't let it go.

Something was here and she wanted to beat it into the ground. The only clue to what it might be had come from Dev.

Deciding to question the bear again, Sam headed back to Sanctuary.

It didn't take long to reach the red brick building where the Sanctuary sign—a dark hill silhouetted by a full moon with a motorcycle parked on it—hung over the doors. A couple of drunken human men staggered out and got into a cab while laughing and joking with each other.

She paused in the shadows to watch Dev leaning against the wall, ignoring them. He had a jacket on with his arms crossed over his chest. A casual observer might think he was catnapping on the job. But Sam recognized that his eyes were at half mast. Still open. Still alert. He was aware of everything around him and while he seemed to be in repose, he was tight and ready to spring into action in a single heartbeat.

Impressive. The warrior in her could appreciate how hard it was to look that relaxed while keeping all senses sharp. But that wasn't the only thing that impressed her. There was an undeniable aura of power that clung to him.

One that told everyone who came into contact with him that he was lethal when crossed. All of his humor aside, Dev was a predator to the core of his soul.

And a nasty one at that. He was the kind who could kill and feel no remorse.

Like her.

A muscle flexed in his sculpted jaw making her wonder if he was hiding a yawn. More than that, the sight of that working muscle sent a shiver of heat through her. She didn't know why he was so irresistible, yet something in her wanted to walk up to him and rub against that long hard body and feel every inch of it on her naked skin.

If only she could.

There had been times in the past when the loneliness had gotten to her. Times when it outweighed her common sense and she'd given in to that need for companionship . . . Oh, who was she fooling? Companionship she could do without. It was the raw, animal sex she'd craved.

That was what she really missed.

But each time had been a brutal mistake. Being that close to another person overwhelmed her with their emotions, insecurities, and memories. She saw things from them that she didn't want to see. Old girlfriends and wives, low self-esteem, narcissistic egos, sick fantasies . . .

Sex never worked out when you could see straight into someone's thoughts and hear them.

Even worse, she didn't like lying to get laid or having to hide her fangs and other nocturnal habits. That was the real reason she'd slept with Ethon. He'd known who and what she was both past and present, and honestly, it'd been nice to be completely open and honest with a lover again.

If only his ego hadn't taken up half the room. . . .

Not to mention the other things she'd seen. Things about him she'd never suspected that haunted her to this day. Poor Spartan. No one deserved his past. She'd had no idea how bad his human life ate at him too. No wonder even as a Dark-Hunter, he was hell-bent on suicide. As a human he'd loved in a way few people could and in a way no one who knew him now would ever suspect.

How she ached for him.

But the bear wasn't Ethon. And she wasn't here to find a bedmate. She was here for information. . . .

Dev felt the hair at the back of his neck lift. Someone was watching him. He could feel it with every animal instinct he possessed. Even though he wanted to go find them, he forced himself to remain perfectly still. Let them think he was completely unaware. If they decided to attack, they'd get the business end of his claws.

At least that was his thought until he caught a scent in the air that made him instantly rock hard.

Samia Savage.

Gah, what was wrong with him that the mere scent of her skin could raise his blood pressure? Probably the fact that she was off-limits to him. The lure of the forbidden fruit. It'd ruined many a man and even more bears.

"I see you, Dark-Hunter." It was a lie. He had no clue where she was, but to say that he smelled her might offend her. Women could be weird that way.

"I see you too, Bear. Hard to miss since you're standing under a light."

She was to his left. Straightening, he pushed himself away from the wall as she walked slowly toward him. Damn if she wasn't the sexiest thing he'd seen in a long time. The way she moved . . .

It was criminal.

She had her jacket back on as well as a pair of opaque sunglasses. Even so, he remembered how pretty her eyes had been and it made him wonder what their real color was. All Dark-Hunters had dark brown eyes. No matter what eye color they'd been born with, the moment they were brought back to life, in addition to being extremely light sensitive, their eyes were so dark as to be almost black. If they were ever lucky enough to get their souls back from Artemis, their eye color would revert to their human color and they'd become mortal again.

For some reason, he had an image of Sam with bright green eyes.

You're being so stupid.

Yeah, he was. He'd never been the romantic kind of guy. It went with that whole half animal thing. Romance was for men who had to beg for women. Something that had never been his problem. Part of the blessing, or curse depending on your viewpoint, of being a shapeshifter was a deep magnetism that caused humans to seek them out and want to pet them. That allure definitely came in handy.

"I thought you'd be home by now," he said as she neared him. Then he realized how stupid that comment was since he was standing right in front of her motorcycle.

Der . . . He might as well be wearing a sign that said *I'm a moron. Please help me remember where I live. Oh yeah, it's right behind me.*

In my defense it's late and all the blood has fled from my brain to the central part of my body.

She didn't comment on his blatant stupidity as she stopped just in front of him and gave him a tight-lipped smile. Those sunglasses kept her eyes shielded from him, but he could sense her gaze on his body like a physical touch and it made him ache for her to brush her hand against his flesh. "I wanted to ask you more questions about your hallucination."

"Please tell me it's the one I have where you mistake my body for a popsicle."

She let out a short laugh. "Where did that come from?"

Easy. The image he had in his head right now of her naked in his bed. "A bear can dream, can't he?"

"A bear *can* dream. But those dreams can also get him skinned."

"Will you be naked when you skin me?"

She shook her head. "Does everything come back to being naked?"

"Not everything. Just when a beautiful woman's involved and only if I'm really lucky. . . . Any chance I might get lucky tonight?"

She let out a short "heh" sound. "You sure you're a bear and not a horn dog?"

He laughed. "Believe it or not, I'm not usually quite this bad."

"Why don't I believe you when you tell me that?"

"Probably because I've been *really* bad tonight." He winked at her. "I'll stop. You said you have a question that unfortunately does not involve nudity?"

Sam had to force herself to keep a straight face while he continued to tease her. *Don't let your guard down.* Men like

32

Dev only wanted a woman for a few hours and then they were done with her.

No matter how cute he was, he was not her type and she was definitely not interested in learning the inner haunts of his mind.

"That Daimon you think you saw . . . did he say anything to you?"

"Not really. Just asked when we'd reopen."

"You remember what he looked like?"

He gave her a droll stare before he answered in a flat tone. "Blond and tall."

Sam rolled her eyes at his description. All Daimons, unless they dyed their hair, which was rare, were blond and tall. "Anything else?"

"He had fangs and dark eyes."

Like every Daimon she'd ever seen. "You're really not helpful. . . . Would you mind if I touched you?"

His right eyebrow shot north before that familiar teasing light came into his blue eyes. "Touch me where?"

"Stop being a perv for three seconds. I just want to see what you saw that day."

He stepped away from her. "I'm not going to let you into my mind, girl. You might steal my passwords or something."

"I don't want your passwords."

"Uh-huh." The doubtful expression on his face was actually adorable. "That's what they all say, then the next thing you know they're in your bank accounts, stealing money, and using your Facebook account to sporn others and getting you banned for life. No thanks."

"Sporn?"

33

"Porn spam. Don't get that innocent look like you don't know what I'm talking about. I know all about you and your Amazon buddies. . . . I've heard the stories. Seen the news and all that. I'm not letting you near my brain such that it is. Last thing I want to do is forget what Ms. February looks like in all her glory. I went to a lot of trouble to memorize that page and I want to keep it."

Sam wanted to be angry at his ridiculous outburst, but he was too funny about it. "Stop being a baby and give me your hand."

He took another step away from her. "No."

"You're serious?"

"Of course I am. I don't want you in my head. Last time a woman read my thoughts, I got bitch-slapped so hard, my ears are still ringing from it. And as a guard bear, I need my hearing intact. Could be fatal to lose it."

"I'm going to bitch-slap you again if you don't stop being a baby."

He growled like a caged grizzly. Impressive sound. But she'd once worn shoes made out of the hides of tougher animals than him and that had been before she'd had her Dark-Hunter powers to back her skills.

"I'm not intimidated."

"You should be. 'Cause that's the only warning I plan to give." Dev really didn't want to do this. He'd never been one to let anyone see inside him. It was intrusive and rude. "I can't stress enough how much I don't want you in my mind."

"What's in there that you're so afraid of sharing?"

"My dirty underwear."

She scoffed as she tried to touch him. "I don't want that. C'mon, Dev."

He shied away again. "C'mon Dev nothing. My thoughts are my own and I don't see you letting me mind meld you."

She kept trying to touch him, but he was really quick and darted just out of her grasp every time. "That's 'cause I have nothing to show you that's important to you. I just want to see what the Daimon looked like. That's the only thing I'll take. I promise."

"Yeah, right. Can you honestly control your powers that well?"

She blushed.

"Ah, see, I knew it. You're going to go digging in there and I'm going to forget how to do origami or something. Or worse, I'll start peeing in corners and burping at inappropriate times."

"Like you don't do that anyway."

"Are you profiling me because I'm a guy or a bear?" His tone was highly offended. "Lady, you don't know me well enough to make that comment and for the record, I have a lot of unbearish habits. I even drink tea in a crappy pink-flowered cup. Have I said how much my sister annoys me?"

She ignored his tirade as she brought him back on task. "It won't hurt."

"Yeah, and the flashy thing is just an eye test."

What in the world was he talking about now? "The what?"

"Flashy thing? Haven't you ever seen Will Smith in *Men in Black?*"

"Uh . . . no."

He sighed. "You're so deprived."

"And you're so peculiar. Is there anyone else who saw the Daimon who isn't afraid of me?"

"I'm not afraid of you. I'm afraid of the brain damage you're going to give me. No offense, but I need my last three working brain cells."

"I've never given anyone brain damage by doing this."

"Uh-huh." He wrinkled his nose. "That you know of. Have you done CAT scans on everyone you've done this with? No. Do you know whether or not you took out their long-term or short-term memory portions of the brain?"

No, but that really wasn't an issue. She wasn't going to radiate him or anything. "Paranoid much?"

"Absolutely. You watch this door for a hundred years and see some of the shit that comes through here. You'd be paranoid too. I don't want no mojo hocus pocus stirring in my head. If I want to play head games, I'll download Sudoku on my iPhone."

Sam held her hands up in surrender. There was no use arguing with someone who was this stubborn. "Fine. I'll do it without touching you."

"Ah, now that's just rude." He narrowed his gaze on her.

Sam knew he had something in mind and when he spoke again, she gaped at his intentions. "Fine then if that's what you want. You go digging in my head and I'm going to stand here and undress you with my eyes until you're buck naked. Just so you know, I'm putting you in a sheer red thong. No bra . . . maybe a pair of red pasties . . . no, better yet, strawberry-flavored nipple paint and I'm coating your entire body in honey."

Sam grimaced. "You're a male pig."

"I'm a bearswain and you're lucky I'm tolerating you to pick through my brain. Last person tried that, I ate their head, and besides, I should get something out of this before you destroy my frontal lobe and make me drool on myself and relearn how to use eating utensils. Have you ever tried doing that when you're a bear? It wasn't easy the first time. Last thing I want to do is relearn it at my archaic age."

She had to roll her eyes again at his unwarranted hysteria. "I don't think that's the part of the brain that controls your drool."

"But you don't know for sure, now do you? No, you don't. 'Cause you're a Daimon necrologist, not a Were-Hunter neurologist. You don't know what damage you're going to do until it's too late and then an I'm-sorry-Dev-I-burned-out-your-brain ain't worth squat. Probably won't even understand the apology because you'll hose my Wernicke's area of the brain and set me back to infancy."

Ignoring him, she closed her eyes and reached out to him with her powers. "If it makes you feel any better, I don't like doing this."

"For the record, it don't. But while you're in there if you happen to see where I lost my nano, let me know. Been looking for it for days now. And the least you could do, Ms. Intrusive, is tell me where to find it."

He was so strange.

Sam drew a deep breath and while he was distracted, reached out and wrapped her hand in his hair before laying her bare fist on his neck. She laughed triumphantly while he cursed. But she had him now and he couldn't pull away without losing hair. She had no idea why getting something over on him made her feel so good, but it did.

Until she realized that she wasn't reading anything from him.

Nothing.

What the . . . ?

It wasn't possible. She touched someone and they bled out thoughts. But not this time. Dev was completely blank to her.

She had nothing.

He snatched her hand away from his neck and grimaced as he lost some hair. "That was a dirty trick."

She ignored his anger. "You're empty."

"Well, you ain't so great yourself, lady."

She shook her head at his offended tone. "No, that's not what I meant. I can't read you. At all. It's like . . ." Like she was normal.

Not possible. She buried her hand in his soft hair again. Still nothing.

Dev started to push her away, but two things kept him from it. One, he didn't want her to snatch out another handful of his hair and two . . .

She felt really, really good this close to him. The scent of her skin filled his head and all he could see was the image he'd told her he was going to imagine. Every nerve in his body fired as he stared at his own reflection in her sunglasses and saw her naked in front of him. Before he could stop himself, he pulled those sunglasses off and tilted her chin up.

Don't do it.

Asking him to stop was like asking a rock to swim—an impossible task. His body hungry for her, he dipped his head down and sampled heaven. Her soft lips met his and she breathed into him.

Sam's senses fired as she tasted the heat of Dev's kiss. Raw and demanding, he ravished her mouth and left her breathless. But it wasn't just his kiss that ignited her, it was the fact that she couldn't feel his emotions while he did it. Hear his thoughts. For one moment and for the first time in over five thousand years, she heard nothing but the beating of her own heart. She felt only her sensations.

Not his. Not even a smidgen.

That reality ripped through her and made her hungrier than she'd ever been before. She could sleep with him and not be haunted by it.

Her heart pounding, she deepened their kiss, wanting to savor every lick and touch the way she'd done when she'd been human.

Dev's hormones kicked into high gear as she ran her hands over him, pulling him closer and closer . . . like she wanted to crawl inside him. She reached down between them to cup him in her hand through his jeans. Nothing could have made him hotter. Well, not entirely true. Had they been naked with her on her knees, it would have definitely made him hotter. But this was damn close.

He turned with her and pressed her against the wall. She lifted her legs to wrap them around his waist and squeezed him tight between her strong thighs.

Oh yeah . . . If they were naked, he'd be in complete ecstasy and right now all he could think about was being inside her.

"Dev! Fight!"

Dev jerked as he heard Colt's voice over the headset—this time of night, they worked a skeleton crew which meant he and Colt were the sole awake muscle in the bar—the rest of the men were off the clock and most likely asleep. The only other staff in the bar was Aimee and their new human waitress who was the size of an emaciated twelve-year-old. Since he didn't know if the threat was human or preternatural, he couldn't ignore the call.

Damn it. He could kill them for the crappy timing.

He met Sam's startled gaze. "Sorry, love. Gotta go."

She nodded as her legs fell away and she freed him.

Whoever had done this, they better be dying 'cause if they weren't, they would be. Grinding his teeth in frustration, he dodged through the doors to head for the ruckus.

Sam cursed in frustration as she took off after him to see what was going on.

Okay, I'm really not this big a slut. It'd just been so long since she'd touched a man without having to deal with his issues, that her hormones had swallowed her common sense. And honestly, she wanted him back for another round. . . .

One that lasted a whole lot longer than three minutes.

Trying not to think about that, she went to help with whatever was happening.

Sure enough, there was a massive fight in the bar between two biker humans. Dev grabbed the biggest one and pulled him away from the smaller man he'd been pummeling while another shapeshifter male got between the combatants.

The bigger human slugged Dev hard across his face.

Dev didn't even flinch as he grabbed the human by the shirt and shoved him back. "Boy, you knock on the devil's door and he will head slam you through the wall."

"Fuck you." He moved to strike Dev again.

Dev ducked, spun the man around, and threw him so hard into the wall that his head left a dent in the Sheetrock. The human staggered back two steps, then crumpled to the floor.

"Dev!" Aimee Peltier snapped, coming around a table to check the human's pulse. Tall and slender, her long blond hair was pulled back in a ponytail. She glared up in fury at her brother.

Dev's face was a mask of innocence. "What? He was warned. Not my fault he's too stupid to know when to shut his mouth and keep his hands to himself. I ain't a saint, baby. They hit me. I hit back. You know the Sanctuary motto."

The bear who held the other human laughed. "So Dev, you want to escort this one out?"

The human held his hands up in surrender. "I'm leaving. Right now. I don't need to kiss a wall first." He bolted for the door.

Aimee rose to her feet with a lethal glower. "He's breathing, but damn, Dev . . . You know better. You could have killed him."

Honestly, Sam considered Dev justified in what he'd done. Like Dev said, he'd warned the human.

A weird groan came out of the man before he rose to his feet. He narrowed his gaze on Dev. "You're going to die for that, Bear." He swept his gaze around at the other

41

male bear and Aimee, then turned that soulless stare to Sam. "All of you are going to die, including you, Dark-Hunter." Throwing his head back, he laughed maniacally.

This guy was definitely *not* human....

Dev grabbed him. "Enough of that crap. You're—"

The man exploded all over him.

Dev cursed as he was soaked by something light yellow that had the viscosity and properties of snot. It went all over him, even into his mouth, eyes, and ears. "Ah, gah, it's a slug demon. Aimee, mindwipe the humans. Colt, get me a towel and Lysol and Listerine." Spitting out some of the mucus, he slung his arms, which caused the snot to fly in all directions.

"Hey!" Sam snapped, ducking the sticky shrapnel. "Keep your snot to yourself."

Dev scoffed at that. "Oh, so now you don't want to touch me, huh?" He tsked. "What is it with women? The instant you put a little slime on them, they get squeamish and have no more use for you."

As he stepped toward her, she backed up. "Don't make me have to hurt you."

"You're such a tease. I knew it. Fine, I'll take my slimy self upstairs and deslug. Definitely brushing my teeth first. Then gargling with boiling water and straight rubbing alcohol."

She shook her head at him. How could he have a sense of humor about being coated in slug juice that smelled so bad? She couldn't imagine how a Were-Hunter with heightened senses could tolerate it and not toss his cookies. Though she'd never been hit by demon snot, she knew from others that it was nasty and that it burned.

"I think you'll forgive me for my rudeness?" Dev vanished instantly.

Sam turned to see Aimee "visiting" the handful of humans in the bar to erase their memories of the demon and Dev. She met the other bear's gaze and couldn't help asking, "This happen often?"

"Not usually. Demons don't normally come here, except for Simi and on rare occasion her brother Xed." He glanced toward Aimee. "May the gods help them. Aimee's not real good at that. Hope she doesn't burn out anything they need."

Ahhh, that explained Dev's paranoia. Made her wonder what Aimee had taken from him with her ineptitude.

The bear extended his hand to her. "Name's Colt."

"Sam."

He dropped his hand when she didn't take it and scowled at the mess on the floor. "Could you tell he was a demon before he exploded?"

"Not even a little bit. You?"

Colt shook his head. "Acheron moves all of you in here. We have a Daimon walk into the bar in broad daylight, and now a demon sliming Dev. I don't know about you, but that doesn't seem coincidental to me."

"I agree. Snot funny."

Colt rolled his eyes. "I can't believe you went there."

"Me neither, but I couldn't resist." She jerked her chin toward the demon remains on the floor. "What would make a demon threaten us, then kill himself?"

"Stupidity? Slugs aren't real smart. Maybe he thought he was teleporting and exploded instead. Or maybe even a bad case of indigestion. There's no telling what he ate before he got here."

"But why threaten us?"

"I'd say shits and giggles, but I'm with you. Something about this isn't right." Colt held his arm out toward her so that she could see his forearm. "Look . . . chill bumps."

Yeah, right. Sam let out an annoyed breath. There wasn't a chill bump on him.

Fang came running from the kitchen door with another blond man—a dragon shapeshifter—following a step behind him. He went straight to Aimee to make sure she was okay while the dragon took over mindwiping the humans.

Sam scowled. "Does the mindwipe happen a lot here?"

"Not as much as you'd think. We do a pretty good job keeping a lid on the unnatural around the humans. Max is the resident containment expert. He can clean out anyone without their knowing it."

For some reason she heard Dev in her ear talking about stealing passwords again. The memory made her smile.

Colt frowned. "What?"

"Nothing." She didn't want to share it with him. She liked having it as something between her and Dev.

I have lost my mind. Dev was impossible and annoying. And right now, he was covered in demon mucus.

And still he'd been sexy.

I am a seriously sick woman. Only the deranged could think a man covered in paranormal snot was hot.

See what happens when you go a couple hundred years without sex. You lose your mind and all perspective.

She turned her attention back to Colt. "You know, I mentioned to Dev earlier that I wondered if the Daimon you guys thought you saw might be a demon in disguise. . . ."

"No," Aimee said as she joined them. "He was a Daimon. No doubt about it. Believe it or not, we can tell the difference."

Sam still wasn't convinced. Demons and Daimons weren't really that far apart on a subspecies scale. "Let's pretend for a minute that I'm right and he was a demon messing with you. Wouldn't all of this"—she gestured toward the demon remains—"make more sense?"

Fang laughed low in his throat like he had a secret none of the rest of them knew. "Yes, but he was a Daimon. Trust me. I *do* know my demons."

Why was he being so stubborn? "Some aren't that easy to spot."

Fang snorted. "For *you* people. I happen to be a Hellchaser so trust me when I say I can tell when a demon is nearby. Spot over there is what woke me up out of dead sleep a few minutes ago. I knew the minute he changed from possessed human to demon and manifested his powers. It makes my skin burn and Daimons don't do that to me."

Sam was unfamiliar with the term he'd used to describe himself even though he'd said it as if she should know. "What's a Hellchaser?"

Fang flashed a cocky grin. "Dark-Hunters hunt Daimons. Hellchasers hunt demons. No matter what they do to disguise themselves, they can't hide from one of us for long. The minute they use their powers anywhere near us, we feel it. Just like you guys with your prey."

He was right about that. As a Dark-Hunter, she could sense anytime a Daimon was anywhere near her. So it stood to reason that he'd have a similar power with his targets. "Then do you know why Spot was here?"

"My job is to police them. I'm not their therapist or parole officer. He could have come in to harass me or just for a drink. With a demon, there's no telling. He might have even followed someone else in here for who knows what purpose."

Sam gave Fang a droll stare as she mentally came to terms with the inevitable fact she'd been trying to avoid. Daimons walked in daylight and Fang was psychotic.

"Fine." Disgusted with what she was forced to do, she pulled her glove off and went over to the snot that Max was in the process of cleaning up.

Nice dragon to mop up without complaining. Though he did pause to give her a puzzled frown.

"Don't ask." She knelt down and touched a small spot of the demon's remains. It was so cold and slimy . . . uuug-gghhh! Trying not to think about that or the fact it was burning her fingertip, she closed her eyes and used her powers to conjure an image of the demon in his true form.

Oh yeah, that was a face even his mother would cringe over. Slug demons weren't attractive. They looked like fat humanoid boars complete with tusks coming out of their chins and foreheads.

But the things she saw playing through her mind were baffling. They made no sense whatsoever. . . .

She saw a place without daylight. Not a city in this world, but it was a city where the sun didn't shine—she had to force herself to ignore *that* obvious pun. It was like the sun didn't exist in that realm . . . and it had to be an alternate realm. There was nothing about it to say it was the human world and it looked completely different. An odd combination of an ancient civilization and a modern one.

Suddenly the demon was in a hall where Daimons gathered in a number she would have never thought possible for them. There had to be well over a thousand Daimons and they spoke in a language she couldn't identify.

Crud. She spread her palm deeper into the ick on the floor to get a better immersion into the demon's last memories.

The room around her spun until she was in the body of the demon. She could hear what he heard, feel what he felt, and see everything through his bloodred eyes. The roar of the Daimons made her ears hurt as she tried to wade through them.

Her master was summoning her and she was desperate to reach him. He was in pain. She could feel it and it made her own body ache. It was her duty to release him. To fight and protect him ...

A male Daimon grabbed her brutally by the scruff of the neck and pulled her forward to a dais where two black thrones were set. Each one was heavily carved to resemble human bones—something no doubt meant to intimidate all who saw it and boy did it ever work on the demon as he faced the throne's occupants. A gorgeous man with short black hair sat in one and in the other was a beautiful blond woman whose eyes were so cold they seemed brittle.

"Can we eat this one, my lord?" the Daimon holding him asked.

The man on the throne shook his head. "Slugs are soulless. Servants. They're not worth our time. Besides, he'd give you indigestion."

The Daimon made a sound of disgust before he flung the slug demon away. It was then the demon saw his master. . . .

He was on the floor a few feet from him, being drained by two Daimons.

"Help me!" his master called as he reached out toward him, but he knew it was useless. There was nothing he could do against so many. The Daimons were killing his master. . . .

He would be next.

The woman on the throne laughed. "Look at the poor creature, Stryker. I think you've scared him to death."

He had, but it was more than that. His master no longer wore a human skin. He was in true winged demon form and still he couldn't fight the Daimons. . . .

The Daimons were far more powerful than all of the demon's kind.

Terrified, he teleported away from the Daimons, back to the human world and to some semblance of safety.

No sooner had he arrived than he felt the unleashing— the sensation of his master's death.

I'm free. After all the centuries of serving under his master's cruel fist, he was now his own demon. Forever free. Joy filled him.

Until a Daimon appeared to his right. "What do you think you're doing?"

"I—"

The Daimon lunged at him, cutting off his words.

The slug demon ran.

"Come back here, you worm! Die like your master."

Terrified, the slug teleported again, but just as he flashed out, he felt something hit his chest like a vicious battering ram. Unable to breathe for the pain of it, he'd headed to the only place he could think of where the Daimons couldn't kill him.

Sanctuary. It was the one establishment that protected all preternatural classes equally. The bears would make sure no one hurt him.

He flashed into the third story of the building where humans were forbidden to go and stumbled down two levels to the bar. At this hour, only a few patrons were in the club, along with a bear at the bar and a bear waitress. It appeared safe. There were no Daimons at all. With that thought foremost in his mind, he went to the bar to order a drink all the while he watched for the Daimon to come for him and finish him off.

Seconds ticked by slowly.

No Daimons. No one approached him.

I'm safe.

His heartbeat slowing, he took his drink and sipped it, grateful that he'd escaped his near death in Kalosis at the hands of Stryker and crew. At least until the pain built inside his chest. It was unbearable. Agonizing.

What's causing this? Was it something to do with the body he'd stolen before he'd gone to Kalosis? Did the biker have some kind of internal defect?

He staggered away from the bar, trying to find some way to make it stop hurting. He accidentally brushed up against a grubby human.

"Hey! Watch where you're going, dick."

He growled at the pathetic human waste.

The human stood up and shoved him. "You wanna fight?"

Was that a trick question? The demon rushed him as they locked horns. . . .

Sam pulled back emotionally from the sight as it intersected with what she already knew. Dev breaking them apart and the demon dying after the pain in his chest burst apart.

She opened her eyes to find Fang, Max, Aimee, and Colt watching her with curious expressions. "He came to Sanctuary because he was running from the Daimons. He thought he'd be safe here."

Max snorted. "Epic fail."

Ignoring him, Fang crossed his arms over his chest. "Why run from the Daimons? Any idea what they wanted with him?"

Not really, other than the Daimons were twisted freaks. "They ate his master and then they shot something into him. That was what made him explode after he got here. There was one Daimon who wanted to kill him in particular, but I don't know why."

Aimee grimaced. "Why would they eat his master? They can't feed off the blood of a demon . . . can they?" She looked up at her mate.

A tic started in Fang's jaw as he considered it. "If a Daimon takes the soul of a Were-Hunter they get the Were-Hunter's powers to use as their own."

"But it's only temporary," Colt said. "When the Were-Hunter's soul dies, they lose those powers."

Max narrowed his gaze on where the demon had died. "I thought they kept those powers."

Fang wiped his hand across his chin. "Whatever. It doesn't matter. We're not talking Were-Hunters. We're talking demons. And those rules could be entirely different."

"The power to walk in daylight," Aimee whispered, bringing them back to what was the most important part in all of this.

Fang gave a grim nod before he locked gazes with Sam. "Now that they're not tied to the night, they'll be coming for you guys when you're most vulnerable."

In the daytime when they couldn't run. The Dark-Hunters would be trapped in their homes and if the Daimons broke out the windows of their bedrooms to let daylight spill in . . .

They were dead.

Or worse, just burn down their homes while they slept. The Dark-Hunters wouldn't be able to evacuate. A bad enough fire would kill them too.

With the Hunters all gone, no one would be here to stop the Daimons from killing any human they wanted to.

It would be open season on humanity.

Bon appétit.

Chapter 3

Dev was toweling off his hair, heading back to his room when Aimee met him in the hallway.

She handed him a piece of paper. "Sam wanted me to give you this."

He scowled at the folded-up scrap of Sanctuary letterhead that still held the Amazon's scent on it. "A paper note? How quaint. I haven't seen one of these in a long time."

Aimee laughed. "Yeah. It reminds me of the days when women would leave their numbers on napkins for you and I'd have to bring you a stack of them every night. Now it's all about sending the text and digits over. Just wait until they release swipe technology."

It was true. And that technology was just around the corner.

He met her gaze and held up the note with an arched brow. "You read this?"

She screwed her face up. "Oh God, no. Last thing I want is to read something I need eye bleach for. Learned my lesson a hundred years ago when that baroness left a note for you. I'm still traumatized . . . and nauseated by it." She headed to her room.

Dev draped the towel over his bare shoulder before he unfolded the note and read the clean, feminine script.

> *Hey Bear,*
> *I know I shouldn't do this, but if you like to live as dangerously as I do, head over to my place before you go to bed.*
> *6537 St. Charles.*
> *It's the white three-story with the black gate.*
> *Don't worry. No strings. No demon slime. Just lots of hot, naked sex.*
> *Sam*
> *P.S. Destroy this immediately. Better yet, eat it.*

He laughed at Sam's orders. It was a real good thing Aimee hadn't read it. . . .

And again, his body went rock hard. What was it with the mere mention of Sam's name or the scent of her skin that drove him into mindless sexcapade mode? Yeah, okay, so the last line probably had more to do with his heated blood than anything else. But that was beside the point.

You don't need this. Your life's screwed up enough. Not to mention, you want to move on without any entanglements.

Yeah, but Sam knew the score as well as he did. Like she said, it was without strings. Mindless. Two adults pleasing each other.

As long as no one found out, it'd all be good.

He balled the note up, then froze. *What if you mate with her?* That thought made his blood run cold.

Anytime a Were-Hunter had sex, it came with one really bad gamble and it wasn't the fear of pregnancy or disease. They couldn't make a woman pregnant unless they were mated to her and Were-Hunters were immune from most human diseases and all STDs.

The horror was, they didn't choose who they mated with for life. The Greek Fates did that and those bitches had a nasty sense of humor. Case in point, his bear sister was mated to a wolf husband. His sister was a human with the ability to shift into a bear. His brother-in-law was a wolf who could become human. Two entirely different animals. When they went to sleep at night, Aimee remained human and Fang was a dog.

If Fang and Aimee ever had kids, which would be a major miracle given the fact they were practically different species, the screwed-up things would look like some messed-up Chow. He shuddered at the thought.

So if he had sex with Sam—even mindless, sweaty animal sex—there was always a chance he could end up mated to her. And mating was something you couldn't fight. If they didn't fulfill the ceremony, he'd be left impotent for all eternity. Literally, since she was a Dark-Hunter.

He would never have sex with a woman again. . . .

I'd rather have an acid enema followed by living mummification.

C'mon, Dev. Don't be paranoid. What are the odds? Sam was a Dark-Hunter. Surely the Fates wouldn't piss off cousin Artemis by mating them together. Dark-Hunters were forbidden from having significant others—the risk

to their partners was too great. They had too many enemies for that.

Yeah, but . . .

Oh, what kind of wuss are you? She was offering him
free, uncomplicated sex and he was second-guessing it?
Yeah, that was totally messed up.

Shaking his head at his own stupidity, especially when
he'd never once in his entire life been a coward, Dev
teleported the towel on his shoulder to the bathroom,
manifested a T-shirt to wear, then jumped to Sam's front
door. 'Cause it would just be in poor taste to show up
shirtless on her doorstep even if it was only for a booty
call. Contrary to popular opinion, he wasn't a totally
unsophisticated animal.

He could have driven over on his motorcycle, but he
wasn't willing to chance sense or anything else overriding
his hormones. He wanted this and he wanted no delay.

Dev knocked on the black, wooden door of the
pristine, rebuilt antebellum mansion. One of the weird
things about Dark-Hunters, they couldn't live in a home
that had any kind of ghost. Since they were soulless beings,
ghosts tended to want to take up residence in their bodies.
So each place they lived in had to be carefully reviewed
by the Squire's Council to ensure the Hunter wouldn't be
possessed. Made him wonder what would happen if one
of the Squires had a grudge against a Dark-Hunter and
lied about their report.

That could get ugly. . . .

For several minutes he heard nothing. But then the
house was huge and if Sam was upstairs, it might take her
a little bit to get to the door.

Or she could have changed her mind.

That would really suck. He'd be left out here looking like a giant bear goober on the front doorstep. *Just don't let the neighbors see me.* That would suck even more. Especially given the obvious hard-on in his pants.

He looked over his shoulder to where the sun was just dawning. The warm rays were quickly spreading up the lawn and street. Could Sam be asleep already?

I should have moved faster.

Damn.

Suddenly the front door opened into the house.

Assuming that was another invitation since he was pretty sure the door didn't do this on its own for no reason, Dev walked through it. At least until he was inside the small foyer and saw Sam waiting for him on the bottom step of the winding, ornate mahogany staircase. Dressed in nothing but a sheer black robe that hung open to show off her naked body, she was exquisite. Every inch of her was ripped from exercise and it made his mouth water for a taste.

Holy gods . . .

The door behind him slammed closed, then locked . . . without anyone touching it. That might scare most people, but since he had a degree of telekinesis himself, he was used to weirdness.

What he found unusual was her state of undress. "You always answer the door like that? You must have the happiest UPS driver on the planet."

She laughed as she walked toward him. "I wasn't sure you'd come."

He arched a brow. "You dress like that to wait on just

me? I don't think so. My God, woman, how many men did you invite over?"

"Just you, baby. Just you. No one else could ever ... well, I won't feed your ego. I have a feeling I really don't need to." She didn't hesitate with her contradiction and by that he knew she was telling the truth—another bonus of his powers. He could smell a lie a mile away. People, mundanes and others, had an odor they let off whenever they lied. "But you took so long to get over here that I was beginning to think you intended to stand me up."

Dev put on his best "aw baby" stance. "You leave a man an invitation like that ... he'd have to be dead to decline. I am definitely not dead. Although rigor has definitely settled into at least one part of my body with a vengeance." He glanced down at the sizable lump in his jeans.

She paused in front of him to run her finger down his chest, raising chill bumps the whole way. His body was absolutely on fire, especially when she bit her bottom lip and looked up at him from under her lashes. "Can you do that Were-Hunter trick where you conjure clothes?"

"Yeah."

An enticing smile broke across her face. "Good."

Before he could ask her what she meant, she reached out and ripped his shirt from neck to hem. Then she attacked him like he was the last steak at a dog kennel.

Dev couldn't have been more floored had she set him on fire and toasted marshmallows over his boys. She ran her hands across his entire body while she licked and sucked his skin until he thought he'd go blind from ecstasy.

Never had a woman been so brazen and forceful with him.

He loved it.

Sam grazed Dev's throat with her fangs. Part of her was dying to sink them in and taste his warm blood. It'd been so long since she was able to actually enjoy sex for herself that she wanted to completely devour him.

"I'm so glad you decided to join me."

He breathed against her ear as he cupped her breast in his hand and toyed with her nipple in a way that had her wet and aching. "I wouldn't think getting laid would be that big a problem for you."

She nipped his chin while she splayed her hands over his muscular back and pressed her bare body against his. Gracious, his skin felt so good. She wanted to cry at the peace she felt touching him. It was truly nirvana.

"It's not getting a guy that's difficult, Dev. It's getting a guy whose thoughts aren't in my head. That's always been impossible . . . until you."

Dev laughed. "Guess I am brain-damaged."

"No. Definitely not." She kissed him, reveling in the silence in her head. She had no idea what he was thinking or feeling. None. She could shout in happiness at the blissful peace. "I could just eat you up."

"I'm here to be your popsicle."

She laughed as she nibbled his neck. "Did you really have that fantasy?"

He sucked his breath in sharply between his teeth as he cupped her head in his hands. "Depends. Would it be a buzzkill or turn-on?"

"Definitely makes me hot."

"Then I am a banana-cherry pop, baby. Lick me to your content. I am yours to play with."

She laughed, then nipped his chin, which was a lot smoother this time than it'd been outside Sanctuary. In a weird way it disappointed her. She'd always loved the prickly feel of a man's face. "You shaved?"

"I scoured myself with lye soap from head to toe to get the evil funk of demon snot off me. I have flossed things the gods never meant to be flossed and used things that would be toxic to most living organisms. All to sanitize my body for your chewing pleasure."

She laughed at his quirky humor.

Dev groaned as she slid her hand down his pants to touch his cock. He felt his powers surge through him. Oh yeah, that was sweet. Capturing her lips, he pressed her hips closer to his.

"Get naked for me," she whispered in his ear.

Dev used his powers to remove his clothes.

She wrinkled her nose as her eyes twinkled in hungry satisfaction. "There's definitely an advantage to having a Were-Hunter for a lover, eh?"

"Woman, you have no idea."

She gave a low whistle of appreciation as she took him into her hand. "You're even hung like a bear."

He laughed at her pun. "You just don't know, baby. You ain't ever been loved till you're loved by a Were."

"I thought Kattagaria didn't like to be called Weres." Kattagaria were the animal branch of the Were-Hunter race. Like Fang, they were animals who could shift into human form and as such they didn't want to be called human in any way. To many, it was considered an extreme insult.

"I'm not Kattagaria." Dev dropped the shield on his face so that she could see the tribal symbol that marked one entire side of his face. It was unmistakable and it designated him as one of the most powerful of his kind. A Sentinel. "I'm Arcadian."

She traced the pattern of his Sentinel markings with her fingertips. "They're beautiful. Why do you hide them?"

Dev glanced away as old memories surged. Because his mother had been Kattagaria and had despised the Arcadian branch of their people, he'd chosen at puberty to hide his true nature from her as well as the rest of the world.

Now that she was dead . . .

"Habit. Everyone assumes all the Peltiers are Kattagaria. I let them have their delusions. Far be it from me to attempt to educate the ever shortsighted, small-minded morons who happen into our bar."

Sam frowned as she heard the undercurrent in his voice. For the first time, she wished she could see inside him to find what had hurt him about that. "Do you count me in that group?"

"Not at all. You haven't tried to kill me for being something I'm not . . . at least not yet."

She ran her hungry gaze over his tawny body. Every muscle was a study of sinewy grace and perfection. All man and all hot. His chest was dusted by golden hairs. Not too thick, just enough to be manly and appealing. Goodness, how she'd missed touching a man and being close to one like this.

A part of her was still timid to touch him for fear that her powers would kick in, but the other part of her was desperate to be held. Just for a little while.

"You don't like false people, do you?"

He narrowed his gaze at her. "Are you reading my mind?"

"No. It's strictly from what you've said. I told you, I can't read your thoughts right now and I don't know why."

He gave her a cocky grin. "It doesn't take much to read them right now." He gave her a scorching once-over.

Sam laughed until he dipped his fingers into the part of her that craved him most. Her legs turned to Jell-O. "I haven't had anyone touch me there in centuries." She gasped as she realized she'd said that out loud.

Dev didn't blink or stop as he stared down at her. A wicked light came into his eyes as he kissed his way down her body. He paused to lave her breasts. Ribbons of heated pleasure burned through her while his fingers continued to tease her.

Then ever so slowly, he continued south until he replaced his hand with his lips.

Sam had to lean one hand against the wall for support as her body twitched and ached in response to his masterful touch. Before she could draw another breath, her body shattered as one of the most intense orgasms of her life claimed her.

Still he continued to please her until he wrung another one from her spasming body. She sank her hand in his soft hair, tugging at it as he continued to tease her.

Dev growled at how good she tasted. It'd been way too long since he last had a woman. Hell, he'd had so little interest in them lately that he'd even begun to fear he was broken. But there were no inhibitions or hesitation with her even though he should have them in spades.

He was sleeping with a Dark-Hunter. Who would have ever thought?

Unable to stand it anymore, he pulled back from her. He lifted her hips to brace her against the black marble-topped table in her foyer before he drove himself deep inside her body. She cried out his name.

Smiling, he thrust against her, seeking solace in her softness.

Sam balled her fist in Dev's hair as she buried her face in his neck to inhale the warm masculine scent of his skin. There was so much power in him, so much skill in the way he filled her and touched her. It was like he knew every way to wring as much pleasure from every thrust as he could. And to be able to have him and not have his emotions overwhelm hers . . . it was incredible.

For the first time in centuries, she felt human.

"Harder, baby," she purred in his ear, wanting him to love her with everything he had. This was the most incredible moment of her life and when he finally came, she joined him.

Completely spent and sated, she leaned back onto the table while he was still inside her. Her breathing ragged, she kept her legs wrapped around his waist while he stared into her eyes and toyed with her belly button. "That was incredible."

He flashed a devilish grin. "Glad I could oblige." He ran his hand around her breast, traced the line of her bow-and-arrow mark, then gave it a light squeeze as he brushed her hardened nipple with his thumb.

She picked his hand up and lifted it to her lips so that she could nip his fingertips.

Dev shivered as her tongue darted between his fingers. He didn't know why, but it brought out a tenderness inside him. Something protective and scary.

What the hell was that? It was like the animal in him wanted to claim her and kill anyone who came near her. Anyone who hurt her or even looked at her wrong. It was feral and powerful.

Right now all of his paranormal powers were charged to their fullest. He felt like his entire body was made of thrumming electricity that needed to ignite and explode. Sex for Were-Hunters always heightened and strengthened their psychic abilities, but this was different.

He'd never felt anything like it before.

She nibbled his knuckle. "Is what I heard about Were-Hunters true?"

"Yes, it's true. We all have a third eye hidden in our shoulder blade."

She laughed out loud. "Where did that come from?"

"The bowels of my imagination and my desire to hear your laughter. You have an amazing laugh and I have a feeling you don't do that much."

Sam swallowed hard. He was right. She very seldom found anything amusing. Life was hard and she was hit with the reality of that fact every time she went near another person who was suffering. Which some days seemed to be everyone she came into contact with.

But Dev was different. He saw beauty and humor even when he had to dig it out of crap.

Or demon snot.

That, too, made her smile. "I meant that you guys can go all night and have multiple orgasms."

He pressed himself deeper inside her so that she could tell he was already hard again and ready for more. "Oh, yes ma'am. Definite perk for my species."

She tightened her thighs around him. "You telling me you're at ready?"

He kissed her lightly on the lips. "Baby, I'm ready to go until neither of us can walk."

She sucked her breath in sharply as he teased her nipple with his tongue. Oh, he felt so good. That tongue of his should be bronzed. "I intend to hold you to that."

"Then let the marathon begin. . . ."

Over the next few hours, he more than made good on that promise. Sam's head swam from exhaustion and endorphins.

After starting in the foyer and working their way through the downstairs and staircase, they'd finally made it to her bedroom where they lay entwined in her light yellow silk sheets.

She was so sated and sore, she didn't want to move at least for a week. "I think you've killed me."

Dev laughed as he peeled the wax shell away from a mini Babybel piece of cheese—she didn't know why she'd bought them since she normally couldn't eat cheese without having farm flashbacks—which weren't bad, just annoying to listen to cows mooing while she ate. But it'd looked so good on the commercials and in the store that she hadn't been able to resist it. He offered her the first bite.

She hesitated, but as she sank her teeth in, she realized that it, too, was safe. It amazed her that she could eat it. There was just something about Dev . . . if he touched it first, it was like he cleansed it and removed whatever funk would attack her.

"You could have sent me away at any time," he said as he ate his own little Babybel.

"True. But I'm just as bad and horny as you are."

"Nah, you're not . . ." A wicked light came into his beautiful blue eyes. "You're worse."

Laughing, she choked on the cheese.

Dev quickly handed her his glass of wine so that she could clear her esophagus. "Sorry about that."

Sam froze as the domesticity . . . the normality of this moment hit her hard. It was like the realization knocked her out of her body and she floated above them, looking down. Dev was lying on his back with the sheet pooled at his waist while she lay beside him on her stomach. They were relaxed and enjoying each other's company— like two old friends. She hadn't been this way with a man since the night Ioel died.

Grief racked her entire being. *How could I do this to him? How could I ever be so comfortable with another man after all he did for me? Gave me?* Ioel had been loyal to her from the first moment they'd met. He'd never even looked at another woman. More than that, he'd almost caused a war within his own clan when he'd refused to marry the woman he was betrothed to so that he could marry Sam instead.

And he'd died protecting her and their children.

Images of that night ripped through her, shredding what little sanity she had as she saw him die in front of her eyes. Even after all these centuries, she still wanted him back. Still missed everything about him. The way he smelled. Felt. Kissed . . .

Oh God, Ioel . . .

How could he be gone?

Dev frowned as he saw the terrified look in Sam's dark eyes. It was like she was reliving a nightmare. "You okay, baby?" He reached out to touch her.

She pulled away instantly. "I need you to leave."

"Yeah, but—"

"Now!" she barked.

Dev held his hands up in surrender. "Fine. But if you need me—"

"I won't. Now get out."

Her tone offended him to the core of his being and it took everything he had not to lash back at her. If it wasn't for the fact that he knew something inside her was hurting, he would have. But he wouldn't be that cold. He didn't believe in kicking anyone when they were down.

If there was one thing in life he understood, it was concealed pain. That core part of the soul that hurt so bad all it knew to do was lash out against anyone unlucky enough to be there when it snapped out of control.

Guess I was nothing but a booty call after all. He didn't know why that thought cut him, but it did. He felt used. How weird.

Whatever. He wasn't about to sit around here and beg. It wasn't in him.

Sam watched as Dev vanished from her bed. Part of her wanted to call him back and apologize. The other part wished she could return to the night Ioel died and have stayed dead instead of making her bargain with Artemis.

66

Yes, it'd given her vengeance against the ones who'd killed those she loved. But her family was still dead. And eternity without them was brutal. Their pain had ended. Hers went on to infinity. There was no hope of it ever ending and that was what had made her a Dog of War. That rage and fury over the injustice of it all that screamed out for some semblance of solace when there was none to be had.

Trust no one. Not even blood.

In the end, everyone had a price and for the right amount, anyone would betray even those they loved most. It was harsh, but true.

Dev had been a nice distraction for a few hours. Now real work began and he wasn't part of her world. Her life was her job. She didn't want any kind of emotional attachment. She didn't want to be normal or have anything like other people.

She was a Dog and she bled their spirit.

A fronte praecipitium a tergo lupi.

Age. Fac ut gaudeam.

Between a rock and a hard place.

Go ahead. Make my day. Loosely translated, but the meaning was the same. When cornered, the Dogs fought until they died. No one touched them.

They were the ultimate killing machine. The ultimate protectors of the world. She would stand and she would fight.

Forever alone. To the death.

Ἡ Τὰν Ἡ Ἐπὶ Τὰς—either with her shield or upon it.

Those words resonated deep inside her as she went to shower. But as she let her mind wander, she saw a new enemy appear. One far deadlier than any they'd ever faced before.

And this particular one would be coming for *her*.

Things were about to get bloody and she would be in the very center of it.

Chapter 4

"We have a problem."

Sitting in his leather chair in front of the fire in his study, Stryker looked up from the book he was reading to find his newest High General and second-in-command standing in front of him. He didn't like for his soldiers to materialize without warning. If she wasn't his daughter and if she didn't look so much like her mother whom he loved more than anything, he'd kill her for the intrusion.

Irritated at her, he turned the page slowly before he responded to her emotional outburst. "I don't have a problem, Medea. Care to tell me yours?"

With an annoyed expression that twisted her beautiful features into a fierce scowl, Medea glared furiously at him—another trait she shared with her fiery mother. "The demon who escaped your party that Phrix blasted with your latest toy? He went from here to Sanctuary where he exploded all over one of the bears."

He had to keep one corner of his mouth from quirking up in amusement. Too bad he'd missed seeing the bear doused with demon entrails. That had to have been entertaining. "And that concerns me how?"

"The Dark-Hunters now not only know for a fact, but *believe* we walk in daylight. The proverbial cat has escaped his bag and taken a dump all over your carefully laid plans ... Father."

Oh, now that was truly upsetting and it made him want to rip out someone's heart. Lucky for Medea, he loved her enough to curb that impulse.

For the moment.

Stryker cursed at their lost advantage against their enemies. It was one they really couldn't afford. "And you know this how?"

"I have a spy in the club who heard the bears and wolves talking about it. Congratulations, Father. We're officially screwed."

He ignored her sarcasm. "*You* have a spy in Sanctuary?" He was impressed by her drive and resourcefulness. That was one of many reasons he'd replaced Davyn with her. Davyn had yet to say a word about being replaced. Of course he had no choice except to live with it.

If not, Stryker would kill him for daring to protest. Though to be honest, Davyn had seemed rather relieved to be removed from command. But that was neither here nor there.

Medea crossed her arms over her chest. "I have a lot of friends in low places." She gave him a look that was definitely inherited from her mother's mostly acerbic personality. "Family too."

And he couldn't be prouder even though it was an obvious dig. Another reason he'd promoted her. Unlike Davyn, he didn't get the impression she was about to wet herself every time she had an audience with him. "Good girl. Did this spy tell you anything else pertinent?"

"Acheron's wife is three months pregnant."

Stryker went completely still as raw anger overtook him. One cause was jealousy, pure and simple. It wasn't fair that Acheron could breed while that ability had been taken from Stryker and his fellow Daimons over something none of them had done or even participated in. As Apollites, they could have children—for a brief period during their seriously truncated lives. But the moment they refused to lie down and die horribly at age twenty-seven, when they crossed over to being Daimons that right ended.

Bastard Apollo. For that, among many reasons, he wanted to hold Apollo's heart in his fist and feast on it.

The second cause of his anger was that he couldn't touch Acheron's wife no matter how much he might want to. Gods how alliances sucked.

Acheron's mother, the goddess Apollymi, was their benefactor and Stryker's adoptive mother. But for Apollymi, he'd have a way to cripple the Dark-Hunters forever. Take out their weakened queen—Acheron's wife—and their king would follow. Pregnant women were always an easy target and Acheron loved her to such an extent that he'd never get over losing her. It was such a twofer that it was hard to resist.

But Stryker had enough self-preservation to let it go. Killing Soteria would anger the goddess he served and no one with a brain angered Apollymi. As the Atlantean goddess of destruction, she wielded a nasty tendency to disembowel anyone who irked her.

Even Stryker.

Damn.

Yet not completely bad. If Soteria was pregnant, Acheron would be distracted and wouldn't venture far from home. He'd be too worried about his enemies, especially Artemis, coming after his wife to harm her or the baby. And given what had happened to Acheron's sister and nephew when he'd left them alone and his own guilt over their deaths— The Atlantean would be semi-neutralized by that fear. . . .

Stryker could work with that.

"What's that grin mean, Father?"

"It means he's plotting something, dearest. Something bloody and foul. The only question is who is his target, and pray to the gods the answer isn't you."

Stryker smiled wider as Zephyra joined them. She was without a doubt the most beautiful woman to ever live. The mere sight or scent of her made him so hard that it was all he could do not to strip her naked and take her no matter the audience.

That woman moved like a flowing breeze, graceful and slow. Seductive. And just as quick to turn vicious without warning. Her long blond hair made his fingers itch to touch it. She stopped beside Medea to give her a hug and the sight of them together made his heart rush. His girls. They looked more like sisters than mother and daughter and they were the only thing in the universe that meant anything to him.

Except for his son.

Pain lacerated his happiness as he tried not to think of how much Urian hated him and why.

But that wasn't the focus of this. He had matters far more pressing than his son's abject hatred over something he couldn't change. "The Dark-Hunters are now acutely aware of our newly acquired powers."

Zephyra growled in anger as she moved away from Medea to stand in front of his chair. "That puts a crimp in our plans. They'll be fortifying now. Rotten bastard scum."

Medea scoffed. "Their protectors are pathetic humans. Since when do we concern ourselves with cattle? I say we feast on them and massacre the Hunters while they sleep."

Ah, her bloodthirsty, fighting spirit made him proud.

But Zephyra shook her head. She knew the same lesson Stryker did. "Don't get cocky, child. Never underestimate a human in survival mode. They can be quite resourceful when cornered. Capable of anything."

Stryker concurred. "The key is to not attack them yet. They'll be looking for it right now. Keep them guessing and eventually, they'll drop their guards. It's just too exhausting for them to stay tense. Not to mention the fact that we're still in the process of converting our army."

Speaking of resourceful and highly aggravating creatures, the demons they had to use to make their people walk in daylight were now hiding from them.

Cowardly bastards. Why couldn't they just lie down and die for them? Not like the demons had anything to live for anyway. They were disgusting and had no real use in the world. He and his people were doing them a favor by slaughtering them so that the ugly buggers would no longer have to look at themselves in the mirror.

Stryker turned his attention back to his daughter. "Once our numbers are strong, we'll ..." He paused as her earlier words went through him again and it jarred something in his brain. "Medea ... how do the Were-Hunters know about us? Did the demon talk before he exploded?"

"No. I was told there was a Dark-Huntress there who was able to touch his slimy remains and see what happened."

"Really?" Now that was interesting. Stryker fell silent as his mind kicked into high gear. A Huntress with psychometry ... That was an extremely rare talent. So rare that he'd never heard of a Dark-Hunter with it before. Oh, this could be a blessing in disguise and then some. "How deep do her powers go?"

"I don't know. Why?"

He met Zephyra's gaze. Like Medea, she was scowling at him. "We need her."

Phyra's eyes darkened with irate suspicion. "What exactly do you need her for?"

He bit back a laugh before he offended her and she attacked him over it. His wife was ever jealous. Not that she had any worries where he was concerned. There was no other woman in the entire universe who was her equal in his eyes. "If she can touch someone or their belongings and pick out secrets, she could very well have the ability to tell us how to capture Apollo. Or better yet, uncover a way to break our curse and free our people."

The new light in her eyes told him that she not only understood but agreed. "I'll get our best on it."

Stryker nodded. If what he suspected was true ... they'd not only be able to kill all the Dark-Hunters, but the father of his race.

Then the world would be theirs and nothing could stop them. At long last, he'd make Apollo bleed the same way Apollo had bled him.

And all the Dark-Hunters would die.

Τω Ξίφει τον Δεσμόν Έλυσε. By the sword, he would untie the knot. And the Apollites and Daimons would take their place as the rulers of all subspecies— which was everyone.

He couldn't wait.

Chapter 5

Sam stifled a yawn as she sat at her computer. She'd posted notes to every Dark-Hunter and Squire message board, loop, Twitter, MySpace, and Facebook account she could think of. Even the sites that on the surface appeared to be role-playing games but in reality were their people hiding in plain sight. She'd been texting and leaving messages for hours, warning her brethren and their employees what was brewing.

The Daimons would be coming for them. And they were pissed off.

On the one hand, she could understand their anger. The Daimons were born as Apollites—a race of superhumans that had been created by the god Apollo. Then, because of the actions of their jealous queen who'd ordered the death of Apollo's human mistress and son, they'd been cursed by him to die horribly at age twenty-seven—the same age his mistress had been when the queen had her killed.

Their only hope to live past that date was to start sucking human souls into their bodies, but the problem with that was that souls weren't meant to live in them. As soon as a Daimon took the soul, it started to wither and die and if a Dark-Hunter didn't find and kill a Daimon before that soul expired, it would cease to exist.

Forever.

But on the other hand, having watched the Daimons slaughter her entire family, Sam wanted them completely wiped from the earth. They were disgusting animals with no regard for human life and for that they deserved total extermination. And if it was by her own hands, then all the better.

"You want a war, Stryker ... I'm ready to give you one."

Just not until the sun went down. Damn the gods for that restriction on the Dark-Hunters and Daimons alike. For the next few hours, there was nothing she could do except wait.

Sam ground her teeth as she saw the tiny rays peeking in through the slats in her blinds. She was on the other side of the room, safe from their reach.

For now. But one well-placed brick or baseball and those dangerous rays could pose the ultimate threat to her. If they touched her skin, she'd burn up like a B-grade movie vampire.

Not wanting to think about that, she glanced at her clock, and sighed. It was just after noon. Way past her bedtime.

You can't kill Daimons if you're too tired to think. Go to bed, Sam. There's nothing more you can do until dark.

She hated that. It wasn't in her to withdraw. As a soldier, her mentor had beaten that into her. Amazons don't back down. Sometimes you might want to. Sometimes you ought to. But Amazons never backed down.

Except for sunlight.

Aggravated, she glared up at her ceiling. "You know, Apollo, if you wanted us to keep humanity safe, you shouldn't have banned us from the daylight too." Then the advantage would be with them, not with his cursed race.

Why are you wasting breath? Even if the Greek god heard her, he didn't care. She knew that better than anyone. The gods had more important things to do than listen to human complaints.

Still, she felt better for having said it.

She reached for her glass of water and headed to the stairs that would take her up to her bedroom on the third floor of her house. The only thing she really hated about living in New Orleans was that you couldn't have a basement, which was much safer than an upstairs bedroom. Unfortunately the sea level here was such that a basement would flood constantly. Since she lived alone, if a fire or hurricane struck, she'd be at its mercy.

For that reason most Dark-Hunters had a human Squire who stayed in their house as a personal secretary and guardian during the day.

Sam didn't.

You should have let Dev stay with you.

That would have been a mistake in more ways than one. Plus she didn't know if his shield—whatever it was— would hold the same if she was asleep. Since the moment she'd become a Dark-Hunter, she couldn't allow anyone near her while she slept. Once she was unconscious, she had no way to block them. Her dreams tangled with their thoughts and she'd spend a restless day seeing and hearing everything they did.

She'd tried once to have a pet dog and then a cat, but their thoughts were even stranger than the humans'. So she was relegated to eternal solitude. Not that it mattered. After all these centuries, she was used to it.

At least that's what she told herself.

Yawning again, she entered her room and dropped her robe. A few hours of sleep and she'd be as good as new.

And if that damn bird that kept thinking about eating worms parked its butt on her windowsill again today while she was sleeping, she was going to shoot it even if it did flood sunlight into her room.

DEV WOKE UP with a start. His heart pounding, he used his heightened hearing to listen carefully and see what had awakened him. He heard Aimee's soft snore from her room down the hall. The normal house activity of the day crew working . . .

Nothing out of the ordinary. Just another typical day.

After one hell of an incredible morning that had ended with him getting mentally bitch-slapped at the end.

Not wanting to think about that, he turned to look at the clock. It was just after two P.M. He cursed. He'd only had three hours of sleep.

Go back to bed.

He rolled over and closed his eyes. But no matter how hard he tried, he couldn't manage to go back to sleep.

Worse, he was being haunted by the scent of a certain Amazon frustration.

"What is wrong with me?"

Sam had made it clear that she was done with him. Her play toy had been shoved back in the drawer and she didn't want to see it again. And yet he couldn't get the thought of her out of his head.

She's aggravating. Frustrating. Off-limits.

And sexy as hell.

I should never have imagined her naked. . . . Never gone to her house and spent the best damned morning of my life with her.

That was like willing himself not to breathe. Some things a guy just did automatically and when a woman like her offered him a full morning of rampant sex, he took her up on it.

Groaning, he pulled the pillow out from under his head and laid it over his face. *Go back to sleep.*

Screw it, suffocate yourself.

At least then he'd be out of his misery.

But it was useless. He couldn't do either one. He was up. Fully awake. So was his cock. . . . Damn it to hell. He'd be cranky as all get out for the rest of the day and night.

There was nothing he could do. His body refused to doze back off.

It was still thrumming from the incredible sex he'd had, the charge to his powers, and an insatiable desire to repeat what they'd done all morning. He was lucky he'd been able to go to sleep the first time.

Now . . .

Useless.

Disgusted, he got up and went to the bathroom to get dressed and try to put some sanity in his brain.

When have you ever been sane?

Well, there was that. . . .

It didn't take long to shower, shave, and dress. He went downstairs to find his identical brother Quinn in the kitchen, bitching about Remi from the night before. It was a familiar sound and a rant he'd had a time or two himself.

Dev gave him a lopsided grin. "You know, I could put him down while he's sleeping if it'll make you feel better."

Laughing, Quinn set his armload of dishes next to the sink. "Don't tempt me. Not like I didn't have the same thought myself. Worthless bastard."

Dev stopped next to the sink. "What'd he do?"

"Screwed up the paperwork from last night again." Quinn growled low in his throat. "How can he not read a register receipt after all these years? I swear to the gods . . . Maman would have a stroke if she saw it."

They both went silent as those words hung between them and they were faced with the reality that their mother would never have a fit about anything ever again.

Gah, when would that pain stop hurting so much? It was only second to the guilt he had over not having protected his parents. Had he been quicker on the draw, he might have saved his mother's life.

Shoving that useless regret aside, Dev twisted his hand in the chin strap of the helmet he was holding. "Let Aimee sort it out. She's better at that than us anyway."

"I'll tell her you said that."

Quinn probably would too, and Aimee would be highly offended even though Dev meant nothing by it, other than she had more business sense than the rest of them. Women. They were always getting pissed off over nothing.

Just like Sam throwing him out of her bed for no real good reason. The gods only knew what he'd said that had ticked her off.

Quinn started rinsing the dirty plates before putting them in the dishwasher. "So what are you doing awake? You don't normally get up till dinnertime."

"Couldn't sleep."

Quinn wiped his forearm across his forehead to brush back a stray piece of curly blond hair. "You're off tonight, aren't you?"

"Yeah."

His brother let out a long sympathetic breath. "Man, sucks to be you."

Dev didn't comment on his sarcasm as he left the sink and headed toward the door that opened into the club. His older brother, Alain, manned the bar of the almost empty place. There was only a tiny number of humans playing pool in back and eating at the tables at the front of the club.

Alain paused as he caught sight of him. "What are you doing up?"

That was the drawback of being nocturnal. If he ever rose before sunset, his family ragged him over it. "The apocalypse cometh. Thought I ought to be awake for it."

Alain snorted. "You know, to most people, that would be a joke. But around here . . ."

He had a point. Dev probably shouldn't kid about such a likely scenario. "Not very busy, huh?"

"You missed the lunch crowd. We were actually short-handed."

"Why didn't you call up for help?"

Alain shrugged nonchalantly. "You guys were up too late dealing with the demon mess. Didn't want to disturb y'all. We handled it without too much of a tragedy."

"You didn't eat any of the tourists, did you?"

Alain grunted. "Nah, but Aimee probably would have had she been here."

Dev smiled as he thought about how cranky his sister could be when people were difficult. Aimee definitely had her moments. "Then it's a good thing you let her sleep."

"Absolutely." Alain looked down at the motorcycle helmet in Dev's hand. "You riding?"

"No. I'm standing."

Alain made a sound of supreme annoyance. "You know what I meant."

"Yeah." Dev put his helmet under his arm. "Feeling restless. Thought it might take the edge off."

Alain gave him a wicked grin. "I know something else that could take the edge off."

Dev snorted. "Yeah, well, I ain't had none of that in a while neither." He wasn't about to tell even his brother where he'd spent the morning. The less people knew about that, the better off he'd be.

"I noticed you haven't been mauling the babes who come in here like you used to. You feeling okay?"

"Not dead yet." But wishing he was, rather than to stand here longing for something he couldn't have.

Dev inclined his head to his brother. "See you in a little while." Without another word, he headed out the back door to where they kept their motorcycles stashed. His was a sleek 2007 black, silver, and red Suzuki GSX-R 600. Furiously fast, dangerous, and curvaceous . . .

Just like he preferred his women.

But the truth was, the gixxer wasn't what he really wanted to be riding. He'd much prefer something tall and blond who walked like she owned the world.

Don't go there, Bear.

If only he could stop his thoughts that easily. Damn, what was it with Sam that he couldn't stay focused on anything else? He started his bike, then pulled the helmet on while it warmed up. His adrenaline pumping, he gunned it out of the lot and headed into the street with no real destination in mind. He just needed to be away from people and animals for a while.

He went screaming down I-10 at over a hundred miles an hour—a suicide pace for a human. It wasn't really smart for a shapeshifter either. And in the end, it didn't do anything to settle his mood. He still felt like he was on edge.

After an hour, he found himself down on St. Charles Ave. Some of the most beautiful homes in New Orleans were located here, but it was one in particular that drew him to this street.

Sam would probably kill him if she knew he was outside her black wrought-iron gate like some lunatic stalker. He'd be the first one to admit it was creepy. He damn sure wouldn't like anyone doing it to him.

Yet here he sat like some lovesick teen hoping to catch a glimpse of his latest crush.

I seriously need help.

Maybe Grace Alexander would be able to fit him into her client list. She was a psychologist who catered to the preternatural crowd, surely she could help him.

Bear, there ain't no help for you. You're pathetic. Chasing after a woman who threw you out of her bed . . .

He wasn't going to argue that.

Dev shut the shield on his helmet, intending to head home. But as he reached for the throttle, a weird sensation went down his spine.

Daimons.

There was no mistaking the feeling. It was hot and stinging. Turning the bike off, he put down the stand and listened carefully. If he knew Sam better, he'd flash into her house to check on her. But she was as likely to stab him as she was to thank him for that.

You're being stupid. There's nothing here.

Just his pathetic subconscious looking for an excuse to get invited into her house again.

Yet he couldn't shake the feeling.

Sighing at his own idiocy, he started his bike and peeled off.

SAM WALKED THROUGH a haze of memories she wasn't familiar with. Dozens of blond children and adults. They were laughing, playing . . .

Dying. It was awful. Men and women in the height of their youth were decaying into dust. Screaming in pain as their bodies aged and then disintegrated.

She was dreaming, she knew that . . .

Why am I seeing Apollites and Daimons? Worse than that, she was afraid and angry at the entire world. Vengeance scorched her every bit as deeply as it did when she thought about her own family. She wanted blood so badly she could taste it. Rage suffused every part of her being.

Wake up! her subconscious screamed out as it realized she was channeling the emotions of someone close to her.

Real close.

Why can't I move? She opened her eyes to find herself in her bed, trapped underneath a shimmering gold web. *What the crud is this?*

There was a gorgeous blond man standing to the right of her bed, staring down at her with a snide grimace. "Don't fight, Dark-Hunter. There's nothing you can do."

Ah, now that was like telling a snake not to strike. She pushed with everything she had.

Nothing happened.

The Daimon male who'd spoken to her laughed. "I told you, you can't fight. Your powers won't work against the diktyon."

Sam cringed as he identified the net covering her. It was a weapon of Artemis's and he was right. It rendered her powerless. Only a god could fight or break its hold.

And even then it wouldn't be easy.

He looked over to a woman on the other side of her bed. "Sophie, open the portal."

Sam inched her hand out from under the net. If she could just get to the knife she always put beneath her pillow before she went to sleep . . .

And all the while, their memories and emotions poured into her with a ferocity that was disorienting and confusing. But at least it gave her some insight into them and how to attack with words.

Sam met the man's gaze. "You know, you're right, Karos. Sophie's been cheating on you with your best friend... what's his name? Jarret? She's not really going to her sister's like she says. She's snaking on you, hon, and enjoying every minute of it. She thinks you're a pathetic waste of a Daimon."

His head snapped to the woman. "What?"

Sophie's beautiful features paled. "It's not true. She's lying."

"Bullshit!"

"I swear, Karos. I haven't gone near him."

Sam snorted. "Not in the last six hours anyway. But last night... it was definitely on, or off if you're talking clothing."

He curled his lip at his wife. "I knew you two were up to something. You lying bitch." He rounded the bed and slapped her hard across the face.

She came back with an impressive haymaker.

While they fought, Sam freed her hand enough that she could use her telekinesis to bring the knife into her grasp. She tried to cut the net, but big surprise there, it didn't work.

Suddenly, the knife flew out of her hand.

Cursing, Sam looked to find another Daimon—a young woman—standing in the shadows.

The Daimon tsked at her as she fingered Sam's knife. "Nice try, but it won't work." She glanced at the combatants. "If you two don't stop, I'm going to rip out both of your spines. Open the portal and let's get this trash to Stryker before it causes any more conflict."

Stryker. Sam remembered him from the demon's memories. Oh gods, they were planning to take her into Daimon central.

They would kill her there. Why else would they want a Dark-Hunter in their domain unless it was to gut her?

I'm going to be their entertainment.

Panic set in as she fought against the net. A shimmering green mist appeared in the corner of her room. It grew larger until it was big enough for them to walk through.

Sophie went in first while the man came over to pull Sam off the bed.

Sam jerked and struggled as hard as possible, but it was useless. The net wouldn't let her move. He picked her up like she weighed nothing at all and cradled her in his arms.

I'm going to die.

She knew it with everything she possessed. No one would ever know what happened to her. The Daimons would take her into their realm and do who knew what with her before they ended her life.

So this is how my life ends. Not in battle with me taking as many of them as I can. Not in a heroic act of sacrifice.

She was going to be carried to her grave in the arms of her enemies.

Chapter 6

With no other weapon to rely on, Sam sank her fangs into the Daimon's arm an instant before he would have taken her through the portal.

Cursing, he dropped her.

She hit the floor hard, but luckily it freed her arm and part of her body from the net. She moved to roll out from under it. The Daimon recovered and caught her, then tossed the net over her again.

Ugh! She tried to fight, but that damned net made it impossible.

He rolled her onto her back, bared his own fangs at her, then plunged a dagger deep into the center of her chest—something only a Daimon with superhuman powers could do. Had she been human or a Daimon, it would have killed her instantly.

As it was, it just burned like madness. And if the idiot had possessed a brain, he'd have known that had he left it in her heart, that too could have killed her. But lucky for her, his education was stringently lacking and he pulled it free to let her bleed.

Something that wouldn't kill her. It'd just piss her off.

"Hurts, doesn't it?" he snarled. "How many my people you kill that way?"

"Apparently I missed one," she ground out between her clenched teeth as she struggled against the pain. "But I won't make that mistake again."

He laughed.

Then he went flying over her, head first into the wall.

Completely stunned, she watched as Dev whipped the net off her body and tossed it to cover the Daimon. Using the net, he spun the Daimon around, then let him fly into the wall on the other side of her bed. The Daimon hit it so hard, he went through the plaster and landed in a tangled heap half in her bedroom and half in the hallway.

The bear had strength. There was no denying that.

Sam pushed herself up only to slip on the blood that still poured out of her chest. She grabbed the dagger the Daimon had dropped and went for the bastard.

Unfortunately, his tumble through the wall had thrown the net off most of his body, allowing him to push himself to his feet. He stood to attack.

"Move, Bear," she growled.

Dev didn't have time to obey before a dagger went whizzing past his cheek so close he swore it trimmed his whiskers. It buried itself in the Daimon's chest.

With one last foul curse, the Daimon exploded into a shower of golden dust, leaving the net that had been wrapped around his feet to fall to the floor.

Turning, Dev narrowed his gaze on the portal the women had vanished into. As long as it was open, the Daimons could return and grab Sam, who now slumped against her bed. She was bleeding like crazy and panting from the agony of her injury. That sight made him want to reanimate the Daimon so that he could rip his heart out and feed it to him.

But first he had to get her out of here.

Without a second thought, he scooped her up in his arms, grabbed the net from the floor to keep the Daimons from reclaiming it, and used his powers to teleport her to Carson's examination room in Sanctuary where the doctor could hopefully help her stop bleeding.

Sam was completely disoriented as she found herself inside a windowless room that appeared to be a hospital. There was a stretcher for a bed and glass and metal cabinets that held surgical instruments and medicine. The bear must have used his powers to teleport her.

A little warning before he yanked her out of her house would have been nice. As it was, it made her feel like she was about to be sick. Literally. The bear was lucky he wasn't wearing her last meal.

Before she could think to protest, Dev laid her down on the bed while he called out for someone named Carson. The moment her skin touched the sheets, other people's emotions ripped through her. Someone had died on this bed ... recently. She could feel his panic as he desperately sought to stay alive and the tears of his mate when he'd lost that fight.

Someone else had been badly wounded while another had been sick ... one of the bear cubs. Dozens of images and emotions hit her and, being wounded, she had no defense against it. Her head felt like it was going to explode. She couldn't breathe. Couldn't think. Couldn't escape.

Help me!

Dev winced as Sam started screaming. She curled into a fetal ball where she trembled and shook. It was like she was being tortured.

What should I do?

Carson flashed into the room beside him, then took a step back, his eyes wide as he took in her hysterical condition. Dev had never seen anything rattle the Native American shapeshifter before, but Carson was definitely wary over this. "What's going on?"

Dev held his hands up. "She was wounded. . . . I-I don't know why she's screaming." For once he hadn't done anything to cause it.

Then he remembered her powers. . . .

Shit.

Dev picked her up and held her close, pulling her as far away from the bed as he could. "Shh, Sam," he whispered in her ear in an attempt to calm her. "I've got you. I'm so sorry I forgot."

Sam tensed as the emotions fell away so fast that it left her weak. One moment she'd been in absolute agony.

In the next . . .

Total peace. It was like being in a sensory dep cocoon where nothing intruded. There were no thoughts. No feelings. It was just her and her alone inside her head. Astonished, she looked up at Dev who watched her with concern creasing his handsome brow.

"You okay?"

She nodded slowly, still waiting for the assault on her senses to return. But it didn't. Whatever Dev had, it was still holding. Thank the gods. She laid her forehead against his right cheek and cupped his left one with her hand, so grateful for the silence that she could weep.

Carson approached her cautiously. His long black hair was pulled back into a braid that fell down his back. Extremely handsome, his features were sharp and something about them reminded her of a bird. He reached his hand out to touch her.

Sam cringed and wrapped herself tightly around Dev. "Don't."

His features offended, Carson pulled up short. "Beg pardon?"

"You can't touch me. It'll open a conduit between us and I'll see everything about you and I do mean *everything*. Any instrument you touch me with and I'll know things about everyone you've ever used it on. No offense, but I don't want to be that intimate with you."

Carson let out a low whistle as he held his hands up in surrender. "No offense taken. I don't want to be that intimate with you either. No wonder you went crazy a second ago."

He had no idea.

Dev scoffed as he shifted her weight. "Yeah, and I don't want to know what she's getting from me right now. I cringe at the mere thought."

Sam met his gaze. "We both know what a perv you are."

He actually blushed which made her wonder what *was* on his mind.

Deciding to alleviate his embarrassment, she wrinkled her nose. "Relax, Grizzly Adams. I'm still getting nothing from you."

Carson laughed. "Damn, Dev. Remi's right. There *is* nothing going on inside your head."

Dev cut him a vicious glare. "You better be glad I'm holding her, Birdman, else you and I'd be going round right about now."

Carson ignored him as he returned his attention to Sam. "How are you feeling right now?"

"Aside from the gaping hole in my heart and the pain it's causing, I'm strangely okay."

Dev looked less than convinced. "So what do we do about this, Doc? You have to have something to fix it."

Sam shook her head. "It won't kill me. Take me home and I—"

"No." Dev cut her off before she could finish her thought. "You can't go home. The Daimons could come back through the hole they made or be there waiting for you and you're in no shape to fight them. Why the hell did you invite them into your house to begin with? What were you thinking?"

His accusing tone seriously offended her. "You think I'm insane? I did not invite them in. I . . ."

They both fell silent as the reality of that thought went through them simultaneously. Daimons couldn't enter a private residence without an invitation—that had been part of Apollo's curse that was designed to protect humans from them. If a place was public domain, they could enter.

But her private residence should have been completely off-limits. . . .

"How did they get in?" she whispered, trying to think of something she might have done. But there was nothing. She'd been extremely careful about setting up her home and no one other than she had been in it.

Oh crap.

Dev shifted his weight before he spoke again. "You really didn't invite them in?"

She shook her head.

Carson stepped closer. "Maybe they came in as pizza delivery or something and you forgot."

That was a ludicrous thought. How could she forget something so intrinsic to her sanity? "No one comes inside my house. No one. Not for any reason. I know better. If they touch something, even briefly, it contaminates it and I have to throw it out." Another valuable lesson she'd learned from her one-night stand with Ethon.

Dev met her gaze. "Then how did they get in? You leave a window open with a note on it or something?"

She gave him an irritated smirk. "Yes, yes I did. I told them to come in and make themselves at home and while they were at it, to immobilize me and stab me straight through the heart 'cause I'm just that effing bored."

Carson laughed. "Wow, someone who has your knack for sarcasm."

Dev glared at him.

Sam sighed before she continued with only a tiny bit less venom. "I don't know how they got in. I happened to have been asleep at the time they entered. Maybe whatever's allowing them to walk in daylight is also allowing them to come into a house uninvited."

Carson's face paled as if the thought of that horrified him. "This can't be good."

"Oh, I don't know." Dev's voice was saturated with his own sarcasm this time. "I think it's great that they can come in and suck us dry. Remind me to leave my window unlatched tonight. Oh wait. It don't matter anymore. Day. Night. Whatever. Come steal my soul, you worthless bastards. I'm open like a twenty-four-hour blood diner donor."

Carson didn't respond to that in the least as he kept his attention on Sam. "If they can come into any home anytime they please and we can't stop them . . . We have skidded off the hell ramp into Shitsville." He indicated Sam's injury with a jerk of his chin. "We need to get that tended before you weaken any more."

"No. I'll be all right." She had no intention of anyone touching her if she could help it.

Dev notwithstanding. And she definitely didn't even want to think about Dev and the fact that he held her like she was petite—something she most certainly was not. Nor did she want to think about how feminine and dainty he made her feel.

Or how great it'd been to make love to him . . .

Forcing those thoughts away, she focused on the matter at hand. "What we have to do is tell Acheron they can get into homes and let the other Dark-Hunters know before they're attacked like I was."

Dev arched one brow. "I can't do anything if I'm holding you. Not that I mind. I'm just saying."

She looked down at the floor, wishing she could stand on her own two feet. "I need some of *my* shoes."

Carson frowned. "You can't even touch the ground?"

"No."

"Dang," Dev breathed. "Artemis got her jollies with you, didn't she?"

"Yeah. I definitely didn't get one of the better powers. Now could you please get my shoes for me?"

Carson stepped back to give them room. "I have a thought. If you're immune to Dev ... would his room work for you?"

Dev looked down at her. "Want to try?"

She wasn't so sure about that. The last thing she needed as bad as she currently felt was another assault on her senses. But she couldn't stay in his arms all day either and if she couldn't go home ...

"Let's try it."

Dev heard the reluctance in her voice. "Just because I'm a bear doesn't mean I live in a cave, you know?"

She frowned up at him. "Pardon?"

"My room's not gross. You don't have to have that I-am-so-disgusted-by-the-mere-thought tone."

"That wasn't what I meant. And do we have to argue this while I'm in pain and bleeding?"

Dev flashed her into his room, then cringed as he realized he was a bear in a cave. *Why didn't I make up my bed before I left?* And for that matter, pick up a few of the dozen car and motorcycle magazines on the floor. The bag of potato chips ... and the three pairs of dirty socks. Good thing he didn't wear underwear or there would probably be a pair or two on the floor to mortify him even more.

His mom had been right. He'd finally lived long enough to be embarrassed by his messy ways.

When he started to put her on the bed, she clamped around his neck so tight, it strangled him.

"Um, Sam . . . you're killing me. I'm not immortal. I really do need to breathe."

She loosened her hold. But only by a little bit. "Sorry. Reflexive habit." She swallowed. "Let me try this before you set me down completely."

"Try what?"

She reached out with one hand and gingerly touched his pillow.

Sam held her breath as she waited for the pain to start and his memories to surge through her.

But just like touching him, they didn't. There was nothing in her head but her own thoughts.

She wanted to shout in relief. "Set me down."

He hesitated. "You sure?"

"I think so."

"All right." Dev very carefully lowered her to the bed, then stepped back. He didn't go far though. He hovered near, just in case.

Sam didn't move for several minutes as she waited for the images to come. Not until she was sure she was safe. At least in a manner of speaking. The warm masculine scent of Dev was all around her. That conjured images, but they were fantasies of what she wanted to do to him and had nothing to do with his memories or thoughts.

She leaned back on the bed, still free of his emotions. It was so amazing. "I think I'm good."

Dev gave her a cocky grin. "Cool. Let me go get something to clean you up and—"

"No!" She rudely barked the word, then regretted the sharpness of her tone. "I mean . . . if anyone other than you has touched whatever you bring . . ."

He rubbed his jaw as he considered that. "Maybe it's not just me. I'm an identical quad. You think whatever immunity I have spreads to my brothers too?"

Oh, now that would be nice. But it was too much to hope for. Still, it was worth a shot. "We could test it."

Dev searched the room with his gaze until he spied Remi's book he'd borrowed a week ago. By now the stench of his brother should be off it. He picked it up from his nightstand and handed it to her.

She barely touched it before she withdrew her hand and hissed as if it'd burned her. "Did you know Remi listens to the Indigo Girls when he's alone in his room and that his favorite movie is *Just Like Heaven*?"

He burst out laughing at the idea of his surly brother watching such a chick flick. Gah, he'd rather have both eyes gouged out and force fed to him than watch that. "Really?"

She nodded. "Yeah. He'd die if you knew that. And whatever weirdness you have seems to be yours alone."

Good, 'cause he definitely didn't want her picking up on his embarrassing habits. Though to be honest, they weren't nearly as bad as Remi's. And he liked the idea that what he had with her was special and wasn't shared with other people. "We still need to tend that wound. If nothing else, it needs to be bandaged so that you're not leaking blood all over my sheets."

"No offense, I'd rather keep bleeding."

He gave her a sharp look before he headed to his chest of drawers and pulled out a T-shirt. "No lip from you,

Amazon. We're going to stop that bleeding. I know it won't kill you, but it does weaken you."

Sam watched as he tore up his shirt to make a bandage for her. She didn't know why, but it touched her that he'd do such a thing. It'd been a long time since anyone was so kind to her. He returned to the bed and carefully tended her wound. "You're not bad for a nurse, Bear."

Dev smiled. "I have my moments . . . few and far between, I will grant you, but on rare occasions I can almost pass for a human." He paused as he had another thought. "If you're this sensitive to everything, how do you wear clothes? I mean they'd have the same property as a bandage, right?"

"Acheron conjures them for me."

"Well, why didn't you say that before I tore up my favorite shirt?"

Before she could ask him what he meant, he'd conjured a bowl of water and a washcloth.

Sam backed away as he reached for her with that cloth. "Test. Test!" she shouted when he didn't get the hint. "Don't stick that on me until we know for a fact that you have the same power Acheron does to keep cooties off that stuff."

"Cooties? You did not go there. Now who's being the big baby, huh?" He put one corner of the cloth on her arm. "There. You hallucinating yet?"

She took a minute to make sure before she answered. "No and you're lucky I'm not or I'd skin you and turn you into a rug."

Smirking at her, he wrung out the excess water and gently cleaned her injury while she lay on his bed.

Sam didn't speak as she let the heat of his skin soothe her. His hands were large and calloused, his knuckles scarred from centuries of fighting, yet at the same time his touch was gentle, soothing as he pushed up her shirt, baring her completely to his gaze. She didn't know why it made her feel vulnerable, but it did. He traced the cloth over her breasts, removing the blood before he bandaged her.

It seemed incongruous that a man so tough could be like this. That he'd been so tender earlier when he made love to her.

She'd been sure she was dead when the Daimon had picked her up to carry her through his portal. But for Dev, she'd be in Kalosis right now at their mercy. No doubt being tortured and killed. She owed him.

Big time.

"Thank you, Devon, for rescuing me."

He paused to look at her. "Dev is short for Devereaux, not Devon."

Wow, she'd never been wrong before. It was a weird sensation after all these centuries to not be able to pull out information like that when she needed it. "Devereaux Peltier." She savored the syllables of his name that flowed and rolled from her tongue. "It's very soft sounding."

He made a sound of disgust in the back of his throat. "Oh thank you so much. That's what every man wants to hear about his name. You might as well call me 'Little Pecker' while you're at it and tell me you'd love to have me go shopping with you for feminine hygiene products. Oh and by all means, carry a big, sparkling pink bag with flowers on it and make me hold it."

She laughed at the images he described, then winced as it sent a wave of pain through her chest. "I didn't mean it that way. It's a beautiful name and I doubt even an oversized pink purse could erode your tough machismo."

"Mmm-hmm. Too late. You've emasculated me. There's no coming back from it now."

"None at all?"

"No. I've been relegated to gay friend status. It's all right though. They have a cool bar down on Canal and I have a lot of friends there. I'm sure they'd let me watch the door for them. Probably pay me more than my family does, too, so you've actually done me a favor. Thanks."

Dev got up and went back to his chest of drawers. He pulled out another T-shirt and brought it to her. "I'll leave you alone to change 'cause you might share your cooties with me and I haven't had a recent vaccine against them." He vanished before she could say a single word.

"You are so weird, Dev Peltier." He was an absolute nut and yet she found him strangely entertaining.

What is wrong with me? She was never really attracted to a man, not even when she'd been human. Ioel had been the lone exception. As a Dark-Hunter, she'd taught herself that the only male companionship she needed came with batteries.

But Dev made her rethink that lifestyle. He made her remember what it was like to laugh with someone she cared about.

Don't go there. She didn't really care about Dev. She barely knew him.

Still . . .

Herding her wayward thoughts, Sam changed her torn, blood-soaked gown for the shirt he'd given her, then leaned back wishing she'd thought to grab her cell phone on her way out. It actually angered her that she hadn't thought about it at the time.

You are insane. Getting out alive definitely trumped getting more injured trying to grab her iPhone.

True, but she needed to warn the others and to do that, she needed *her* phone.

Dev came back a few minutes later with a laptop. "Out of curiosity. How do you eat?"

She paused as she remembered that she'd been able to eat the food he'd given her . . . strange. But why didn't that extend to the other things?

With no answer, she moved to his question with what the truth had been prior to this morning. "There's a reason I'm thin. I live on a lot of salads that I grow in a garden behind my house. You ever try gardening at night? Really sucks."

"Man . . . I'm sorry."

She appreciated his sympathy, but there was no need for it. It was what it was. "You get used to it."

"I don't know, Sam. I can't imagine life without steak. I think I'd rather be dead. Why didn't you tell me this at your house?"

"Because it was my stuff in my house and I don't have anything there that will cause me pain. Here, I'm not so lucky."

He pulled his phone from his pocket and held it out to her. "No one's touched it but me so it should be safe for you."

If only it were that simple. "Thanks, but someone put it together. It too is kryptonite."

"All right then. I'll get started notifying Acheron and crew." He called Ash while she leaned back to listen and

103

mull over everything that'd happened since last night. It was almost more than she could even follow. How could so many things be crammed into so little time?

But what amazed her most was that she couldn't even overhear Dev's phone conversation as he talked to Acheron. For the first time in five thousand years, she felt normal. It was so peculiar.

At least that was her thought until she saw the look on Dev's face.

"You sure?" he asked Acheron.

She frowned at his tone. There was a hint of anger in it. What had happened to trigger it? Had a Dark-Hunter already been killed by the Daimons?

Or something worse?

She bit her lip in trepidation as she listened.

After a few minutes he spoke again. "I'll tell her.... Yeah, you too." He hung up the phone and stared at the wall for several heartbeats as if trying to come up with the right words.

A sick, cold knot formed in her stomach. "What?"

"Two demons were found drained this morning and left out on the Moonwalk for the humans to see. Apparently there's been a rash on demon slayings lately and Ash thinks it's a harbinger for us, saying we're screwed."

Chapter 7

Sam grimaced at Dev. "What do you mean two demons were found drained?"

He slid his phone into his pocket. "The police found their remains this morning right out in the open for the world to see. Luckily, the demons were in a human form so we don't have to do cleanup with the mundanes. But that makes Ash think it was done as a warning to us and not to scare the humans. Why else leave them exposed for the police when they'd assume the killings were just a bunch of unlucky humans who were mugged?"

That made sense to her, but she did have one question. "If they're in human form, how does Acheron know they're demons?"

"Their remains were sent to the deputy medical examiner for Orleans parish. Simone's a half demon married to a half demon demigod and they live with two ghosts. If that's not enough, her boss is a Squire with a long history of covering up preternatural blips on the human radar. Believe me, she knows demons when she sees them—both before and after she autopsies them."

Sam gave a short, dark laugh. "This is an interesting town."

"Ain't it though? And you have to figure Acheron can tell the difference between a demon and a human too. Not like he'd mistake one for another."

That was a very valid point. But it still concerned her. "Any idea who killed them and why?"

"Not a bit. You got any ideas? Ash said they'd been completely drained of blood. Other than that, they looked normal. Simone thinks it's some kind of demon ritual where another group must have needed their blood for something. Why else would they drain it out of them? Not the usual modus operandi for demon deaths."

Sam fell silent as she remembered what she'd seen last night through the slug demon's eyes. . . .

The demon on the floor as the Daimons fed on him. *Oh my God.* In that one moment she knew exactly what'd happened.

"Daimons did it."

He frowned. "What?"

She ignored his question as a wicked premonition went through her. There was no doubt in her mind what had happened and who this message was meant for.

Her.

"Can Acheron get me a photo of the demons they found?"

Dev scowled. "Why?"

"I have a bad feeling. I saw the Daimons kill a demon in their hall and I'm wondering if it was one of the two the police found on the street."

He frowned. "What are the odds of that? I think it's a long shot."

"What if it's not?" What if they really did want her to know what was going on? It could be some kind of head game or something else entirely.

Either way, she had to know.

Dev pulled out his phone and started texting. Less than a minute later, he received a text back. He checked it, then held the phone up for her to see. "Look familiar?"

The pictures expanded until she could clearly see the two vics on the ground. Their pale features were contorted by the last few horrific moments of their lives. Their faces were a permanent mask of their torture. The worst part was that she recognized one of them.

Oh yeah, this was really not good for them.

Sam met Dev's gaze. "The one on the right. I saw the Daimons killing him."

The color drained from Dev's face as he looked at the picture. "You sure?"

She nodded. "The slug demon was his servant. There were several Daimons feeding on him until he died. I saw the whole thing. . . . Well, not his actual death, but that I felt as the slug demon so there's no doubt that the Daimons feeding on him are what killed him. They did this."

Dev cursed. "They're taking demon powers the way they take a Were-Hunter's."

"That has to be what allows them to walk in daylight. It has to be. Nothing else makes sense."

Still there was doubt in his eyes. "But they don't get that ability when they take down one of us, and we walk in daylight."

"Why else do it then? The Daimons basically have the same powers as most demons. More so most of the time . . . except for daylight. There's no other reason for them to target the demon population. Not when humans are such easy prey for them. You know a demon doesn't just lie down and let them feast. Not without a brutal fight, hence the bruising on the bodies."

Dev considered that. She might be right. Why else would the Daimons feed on a demon? "You think that's why they were trying to get to you? See if they could pull some powers out of you?"

"No. Dark-Hunter blood's poisonous to them."

Oh yeah, he'd forgotten that. "Then why come after *you*?"

"I have no idea. Maybe because I saw them?"

"How would they know that?"

Sam shrugged.

Dev tucked his phone in his pocket as he tried to think of what the Daimons could want from Sam. But he kept hitting a wall. "Did they say anything to you when they showed up in your house? Did you pick up on anything from them?"

"What I picked up was useless. Friggin' pansy Daimons. More worried about their love life than me. The only thing they said was that they were taking me to Stryker."

"The Spathi commander?"

"Yeah. Or it was someone else sitting on his throne surrounded by Daimons in their command center."

Dev let out a low whistle. "You're in trouble. That is one seriously messed-up man with a hard-on for Acheron and Apollo in the worst way. There's nothing he wouldn't do to kill either one."

"Why?"

"I assume he hates Ash for being the Dark-Hunter leader. Apollo because he's Stryker's father."

Sam gaped at the last thing she expected to hear. "What?"

Dev nodded. "Apollo created the Apollite race intending to use them to take over the Atlantean empire, then Greece and finally the Olympian pantheon. He wanted to rule the world and displace Zeus as the king of the gods. But when the Apollites killed Apollo's mistress and child, he went postal on them and in his madness forgot he was cursing his own half Apollite child and grandchildren too. Stryker never got over it and he's been looking for a way to kill his father ever since. Damn that whole vengeance quest. Not that I blame him. I'd be looking for blood too if I had to watch my children die because my dad was a flaming moron who couldn't keep his dick in his pants."

Sam held her hand up as she tried to digest everything he was telling her. But it wasn't making any sense. If what Dev was saying was true, Stryker would be ...

Acheron's age. Which would be over eleven *thousand* years old.

No. It wasn't possible. "Wait. There aren't any Daimons that old. Most of them drop after a few decades. Some lucky ones every once in a blue moon might make it to a hundred or better. But they never—"

"Stryker has a whole army of people who are thousands of years old."

Sam refused to believe it. "Bullshit." How would *that* have failed to make the go-round in the Dark-Hunter gossip mill?

Dev shook his head, his gaze burning into hers with his sincerity. "No, for real. I know this for a fact. The Spathi Daimons are all thousands of years old."

She still found that hard to believe. She was five thousand years old and in all that time she'd never seen a Daimon more than a few decades old. The Dark-Hunters were too proficient at hunting them. They always found their prey. "How?"

"They're real good at what they do. Killing humans and surviving."

"No, not that. How do you know they're out there? It could all be a lie or like the Dread Pirate Roberts where it's one guy saying he's this Stryker while the real Stryker has been dead for centuries."

Dev grinned as if he appreciated her *Princess Bride* reference. "One of Ash's servants happens to be Stryker's son and is over eleven thousand years old himself. I've had many a talk with Urian about his father and their history."

That hit her like a punch in the gut. "And Acheron has never seen fit to tell us about this?"

"And risk you freaking out? Why would he?"

Because Daimons with that kind of training had to be brutal to fight. "Don't you think we need to know this?"

"You've lived how many centuries without it?"

Yes, but knowledge was power and they had a right to know who and what they were fighting. "You're just like Acheron."

"I'll take that as a compliment."

"It wasn't intended as one."

"I know. But it irritates you that you're not irritating me." His grin widened. "I can live with that."

She rolled her eyes at him. "Whatever."

"Give me 'tude, woman. I live for it. And none of this is germane to why the Daimons are now after *you*."

No kidding. "That is *the* question."

Dev sobered as he gave her a look that chilled her all the way to her missing soul. "No. The real question is ... how many more of them are going to come after you?"

Chapter 8

Stryker stood over the smoldering remains of the Daimons who'd failed him. He *really* couldn't stand incompetence.

Zephyra beat a staccato rhythm on the arm of her chair with her long red nails as she watched him with an amused light in her eyes. "Feeling better, love?"

"Not really. Thinking I should reanimate them just so I can kill them again."

She wrinkled her nose in amusement. "I do so love you, bunny." Only she could get away with calling him that. Anyone else would be ...

Another stain on the floor.

Stryker let out a frustrated breath. "Our little Huntress knows we're coming for her and that we have Aunt Artie's nets. . . . You know the problem with sending out morons who have no vested interest in accomplishing your goals?"

"They don't care," she answered. "But I would think breaking their eternal curse would make any Daimon have a vested interest in succeeding."

"You would think." He gestured to the steaming remains on the floor. "But obviously you're wrong. They were more concerned about who was cheating on whom than saving our race. Pathetic imbeciles."

Zephyra didn't comment on that. "Do you want me to go after her then?"

He would say yes, but to get Samia now would require they go into Sanctuary and drag the bitch out. That place was teeming with preternatural predators who enjoyed bloodletting as much as he did. He'd just gotten his wife back. He wasn't about to risk her to such a venture.

He would go himself, but that would violate a treaty he had in place. . . .

Alliances sucked. One day he'd learn better than to make them.

"No. I think I have a better idea."

Zephyra stopped tapping her fingernails. "Which is?"

"Someone who wants the Huntress more than I do. He will bring her to us. Of that I have no doubt."

Stryker only hoped his messenger didn't dismember her first.

SAM FASTENED HER jeans, then froze at a peculiar sound she hadn't heard in a long time.

A little girl giggling.

She turned fast to see the door open a quarter inch then slam shut. The giggling got louder.

What in the world?

Using her powers, she opened the door gently so as not to hurt her Peeping Tom. The girl stumbled into the room in a flurry of blond curls and bright blue eyes and dimples. Around four years old in human years and dressed in a cute pink dress with some cartoon character on it that Sam didn't know, she was absolutely beautiful.

"You weren't supposed to see me," she said in a whispered shout. "Uncle Dev said he'd have my entire tail section if I bothered you. I'm not bothering you, am I?"

Yes. The sight of her tore through Sam viciously. It made her ache for her own daughter and was strong enough to form a lump in her throat and to cause her eyes to water slightly. It was so harshly wrong how even after all these centuries her arms felt empty and itched to pick up and hold a baby close. To have one of those precious moments back when she used to bury her face in her daughter's curls and inhale that sweet baby scent . . .

I sold my soul for the wrong thing.

And that hurt most of all.

Sam offered the little girl a smile. "No, sweetie. You're not bothering me at all."

That thrilled the little girl as she slammed the door shut and ran into the room, closer to Sam. She grinned wide as she held her hands behind her back. "Uncle Dev said that when people touch you, you can tell things about them. Can you?"

"I can."

She jumped up and down in her excitement as she clapped her small hands. "That's so neat. I don't have my powers yet. I keep hoping they'll come in . . . along with my breasts, but so far nothing. How long did it take you to get big breasts?"

Sam hesitated before she answered a question that strangely made her laugh. "When I was about twelve."

"Hmmm, I wonder what that makes in Were-Hunter years? I can't ever keep that straight." She looked down at her flat chest. "Obviously I'm not there yet. At least that's what I hope. Otherwise I'll have to stuff my bra like my cousin does. Her breasts look really, really lumpy. Like oatmeal lumpy. But I think it's 'cause what she uses to stuff them with. Kara says toilet paper isn't as good as socks. It's really gross and it makes her papa really angry."

"Yessy! What are you doing in there?"

The little girl jumped as the door swung wider to show an older version of herself. It was like looking into a time warp to see Yessy around the age of twenty. Tall, slender, and yes, big boobed. Dressed in baggy jeans and a green pullover, the older girl was stunningly beautiful.

Yessy backed into the wall. "I'm not doing anything wrong, Josie. You're just being mean."

Josie let out a long-suffering breath as she met Sam's confused frown. "First thing this morning she tries to bake Remi's Baskin-Robbins ice cream cake in the oven 'cause she thinks that's what a Baked Alaska is, now she's defying orders and disturbing you. I am so sorry." She looked back at her sister. "I swear, Yessy, you're trying so hard not to live. I keep telling you, Papa eats the dumb ones."

Dev snorted as he came up behind her. "Well, that can't be true, Jo-Jo. You're still here."

She rolled her eyes at him in a way only someone close to Dev could do and live. "You have no idea how trying she is."

Dev scoffed. "Of course I do. I was here when you were her age."

Josie stiffened in indignation. "I *never* acted that way."

"No," he said in a dry, flat tone. "You never behaved like that ever. You were a perfect angel. Always. Why is there still a hole in the north stovepipe again?"

If looks could kill, Dev would be seriously wounded. "That was different. Alex was bothering me and he was the one who bought the firecrackers."

"Uh-huh. God help us and our customers when your dad decides you're old enough to wait tables. Now get out of here, both of you, before I feed you to Remi."

Josie grabbed Yessy's hand. "See, I told you they eat the dumb ones."

As Dev moved to shut the door, Yessy came running back in to hug Dev on the leg. "Love you, Uncle."

He pulled her up into his arms and gave her a tight hug and kiss on the cheek before he set her down again. "Love you too. Now you better run, muff, before Josie goes grizzly on you."

Yessy cocked her hip and held up two small fists in a fighting stance. "I can take her."

"Yessy!" Josie called from out in the hall.

Dropping her arms straight down her body, Yessy made a small O with her mouth before she darted out of the room.

Dev laughed as he closed the door behind her. He smiled at Sam. "Sorry about that. Didn't know Yessy had gotten off the chain. You gotta watch that one like a hawk. I swear she moves so fast she leaves a vapor trail most days."

Sam used to feel the same way about hers. God, to have one day back where she had to chase after Agaria . . .

She forced herself not to think about it. "She's adorable. Who does she belong to?"

"My brother Zar."

"And who's Alex?"

"Josie's older brother. Zar is a breeding machine. Don't ask. He's been turning out cubs for so long that we're dizzy from it. Luckily they're all cute enough that we tolerate most of their crap."

Sam shook her head at his joke. "Where do you keep them? All the times I've been here, I never seen any children."

"They're not allowed in the restaurant during operating hours. The cubs are kept here in the house and guarded until they hit puberty and can change into humans. The human children are watched and some sent to school when they're old enough—if they want to be. Otherwise we homeschool."

That explained it. She could well understand being highly protective of them. "Why don't you let Josie wait tables? She seems old enough to me."

His expression turned grim. "Everyone thinks we're all Kattagaria. A Were-Hunter sees Josie or one of the other human kids at those ages and they'll know immediately that we're not . . . at least not all of us."

She didn't see the problem with that. "Is that a bad thing?"

By the feral look in his eyes, she could tell it was. "When my mother was alive, it would have cost her the seat on the Omegrion. She was the Kattagaria bear rep.

Can't have the seat unless you're loyal to our species. The other Kattagaria bear clans would have viewed her being mated to an Arcadian as a conflict of interest—which, believe me, it wasn't. My mother was loyal to her species to the bitter end. Then there's the lovely fact that many of our kind don't like half-breeds. They think of us as mongrels—barely one step up from a cockroach and some not even that. I'd have to kill anyone who made one of my nieces or nephews hang their head in shame. And you don't want to know what Remi would do to them."

That was one of the things she really liked about Dev. He reminded her a lot of herself. Family first and death to anyone dumb enough to tread on it.

He inclined his head to her chest. "How are you feeling? The wound still bothering you?"

"I slept and healed. A little sore, but almost as good as new." Not entirely true. It burned like crazy. If she was anything other than an Amazon she'd probably complain.

However, that wasn't in their code. Amazons carried on no matter what.

"Good." He tucked his hands into his back pockets in a pose so sexy it actually quickened her heartbeat. "Now do you want the bad news?"

Her stomach shrank. There was a major buzz kill. It put an instant kibosh on her hormones as her brain started coughing up all kinds of things that could have gone wrong while she took a short nap. "You have rabies, don't you? And somehow it's contagious to Dark-Hunters. Body parts are going to start falling off, but first the hair will go. Right?"

"Ha, ha. No. You should be so lucky."

Great. Just great. Why did she bother getting up? "Do I need to sit down for this?"

"I probably would. But I'm lazy that way."

Sighing, Sam leaned back against his dresser and crossed her arms over her chest. "What?"

"Ash, in his infinite concern for you, has called in a couple of the Dogs to help us guard you until we find out why Stryker wants you so desperately."

Oh, this was bad. Maybe she should sit before asking the rhetorical question she didn't want answered. "Who did he send over?"

"Ethon Stark and—"

"No." She refused to have him near her. It hurt on so many levels that at this point it was cruel and unusual punishment to even have him in the same town.

"You'll have to take that up with the big guy. I got no control over his personnel assignments. I get enough shit dealing with mine down in the bar."

She didn't comment on that as she steered him back to the main point. "Dare I ask who the other is?"

"Your buddy Chi."

Well, at least there was that. If only she could can Ethon . . . in more ways than one. "I can't believe Ash would send over Ethon to protect me." Ash didn't know the extent of their history—she hoped—but he did know that she didn't care for her fellow Greek solider. "I'm in hell." She ground her teeth as she bit back a curse. Then she sighed as she realized she had one small break. "At least I don't have to tolerate him until the sun—"

"He's actually downstairs, waiting for you."

Of course he was. 'Cause that was just her luck and Ash's sick sense of humor. "How? It's still daylight."

"Tate. The coroner I was talking about earlier? He has body bags he can transport Dark-Hunters around in."

Sam scowled at his explanation. "Why don't I know about this?"

"Probably because with your powers, putting you in a body bag would be a really bad thing since you'd pick up all kinds of traces from its previous occupants."

She growled low in her throat. "Can I put Ethon in one permanently?"

"I wouldn't care, but again, you'd have to take it up with the big guy, who might."

She hated whenever Dev made sense. "Is Chi here?"

"Yes. She's in the bar playing a mean game of Ms. Pac-Man on one of the machines in back." He moved closer.

Sam tensed out of habit.

He cupped her cheek in his hand and that comfortable feeling washed over her. His eyes darkened as he studied her face while his breath fell gently against her skin. "Are you really all right?"

No, not when he stood this close to her and made her feel normal. She both loved and hated it. The scent of his skin teased her as she felt an overwhelming need to nip his chin. How could any man be so good-looking?

So sweet and fierce? It was an unbelievable and sexy combination.

He reminded her of all the things she'd given up for this life. All the things that had once meant more to her than anything else.

An image of him holding his own child went through her. *Damn, I should never have seen him with his niece.* Now that image would haunt her forever. She'd always loved the sight of a man holding a baby or child. It was what had made her fall in love with Ioel. They'd been walking through town when a small peasant child had tripped and fallen into the mud.

Without thinking about his noble station or the expense of his clothes, he'd picked the boy up and quieted him, then carried him home to his mother. Ioel's chiton had been covered with little muddy handprints.

He'd laughed at the sight of them. *"It'll wash. Better I be a little dirty than a child be hurt. Clothes can be replaced. Children should always be cherished."*

That memory stabbed her hard through her heart. *Why did you have to die?*

Even after all these centuries she was angry at him for having died on her and leaving her alone in the world. But she knew wherever he was, he was watching over their daughter for her.

Just like he'd promised.

Focus, Sam. She had much more important things to think about than a past she couldn't change. Like why she was suddenly a Daimon magnet.

Were they planning on singling out each Dark-Hunter and taking them to Kalosis one on one to torture and kill them?

Or something worse?

Dev cocked his head as if he was listening to a sound only he could hear. When he looked back at her, he was scowling. "Nick Gautier is downstairs too."

"Nick?" He was the one she'd been moved into New Orleans to guard. Even though he was a Dark-Hunter, he was transitioning into something Acheron wouldn't elaborate on. All they'd been told was that Nick had to be guarded until he learned how to corral his powers. If they allowed the darker elements to get near him, it would corrupt him and they'd have something a lot more dangerous than the Daimons to worry about.

And no way to stop it.

Sam shook her head. "What's he doing here?"

"Don't know. He just head-popped me"—a Were-Hunter slang term that meant Nick had contacted him telepathically—"and said he needs to see you. You want him to come up here or you want to go down?"

Nick's telepathic power made her raise an eyebrow. When Acheron had briefed her on Nick's abilities, that one had been missing. Made her wonder if Acheron knew everything about him or if Nick's powers were growing even faster than their fearless leader knew. Or if it was another case of Acheron withholding pertinent information. "Gautier has telepathy?"

"Either that or I'm hallucinating. I'd hate to think I'm wasting a perfectly good hallucination on Nick Gautier, especially where you're involved."

Sam gave a short laugh at Dev's inability to take any-thing seriously. "Send him up."

The words had barely left her lips before Nick appeared in front of her. Sam didn't know why but something about the Cajun set her nerves on edge. Even though he'd never been anything but cordial to her, it was like he had a core of evil. Something about him made her nervous. Wary.

Not scared, just tense.

He's not right. . . .

Tall and sinfully gorgeous, Nick was dressed all in black. The one thing that differentiated him from the rest of the Dark-Hunter crew was that where they usually had their bow-and-arrow marks hidden, his was right on his cheek and neck in a way that suggested Artemis had bitch-slapped him when she'd brought him over.

For the merest nanosecond, Sam could swear she saw his eyes flash red before he let out a short, sinister laugh.

"You're so screwed."

Sam glanced to Dev before she gave Nick a flat, emotionless stare. "How so?"

"You can't stay here," Nick said darkly. "The Daimons know where you are and they're gearing up for total war."

Dev scoffed. "Tell us something we don't know."

Nick shot a look at Dev that said he thought the bear was an idiot. "You really have no idea. You have kids here and Savitar isn't on your side right now. Stryker knows that and he's planning to take advantage of it."

Dev was less than convinced. "And how do you know what Stryker has planned?"

Nick didn't answer. "Look, you two can stay here and argue, or you can trust me."

Dev hesitated. Part of him still thought of Nick as the same snarky little kid who grew up downstairs hustling pool in their back room and watching over his mom when she'd worked as a waitress for his family.

But that Nick had vanished the night his mom had been murdered by a Daimon and Nick had killed himself in order to become a Dark-Hunter to get revenge on her killer. The boy hadn't been the same since.

More than that, Nick had powers that the average Dark-Hunter didn't. Freaky powers. Every animal instinct in him could feel it resonate. Those powers were extreme and intense. Even worse, they were malevolent and cold.

Corruptive. They came from something a lot darker than the goddess Artemis.

And today . . .

Dev picked up on something else inside him. Something about Nick was even more wrong than it'd been. . . .

A shiver went down his spine.

Because of that, Dev gave him no quarter. Until he knew whose side Nick was on, he assumed him an enemy regardless of where he'd stood with them in the past. One thing he'd learned the hard way, people turned on each other. "We've shown we can handle anything thrown at us. I think she'll be all right here."

Nick scoffed. "You evaced your children last time. Got them out of the line of fire. They're back. You ready to put them in harm's way?"

Now that went over him like an acid wash. "Are you threatening our cubs?"

Nick's entire expression and stance was unreadable. "I'm trying to save all of you."

Dev wanted to believe him. He did. But something wasn't right and he couldn't put his finger on it. "Look—"

Nick's look turned thunderous and dark. "Why don't you take the hint, Bear, and leave?"

Dev stiffened. "You don't talk to me like that, boy. Not ever."

Sam pulled Dev away from Nick as something weird flashed through her mind. She saw Nick surrounded by Daimons. Saw . . .

It was gone before she could really get a fix on it. Crap. She hated whenever her powers did that.

Nick narrowed his gaze on her. "We should leave before anyone here gets hurt."

Suddenly, Sam realized what was wrong. Nick was here by himself. Alone. "Who's watching you right now?"

"Excuse me?"

"You heard me, Nick. Who has watch duty on you?"

He scoffed. "No one has watch duty over me. I told Acheron that. All of you are wasting your time. But whatever." He looked past her to where Dev watched them with a stern grimace. "If you don't want to leave. That's fine." His expression turned cold. "Stay. Get killed. No sweat off my balls. I was only doing this as a favor to Acheron anyway."

Sam screwed her face up in distaste. While the attitude was vintage Gautier, he wasn't normally quite so crass.

He dragged his thumb down the side of his face before he sneered, "They're all yours. τρώω το περίδρομο!"

She scowled at his Greek that meant to eat until you were stuffed.

No sooner had Nick spoken those words than a bolthole opened in the center of the room and a dozen Daimons came out of it.

Chapter 9

Sam cursed as she used her telekinetic powers to open the bedroom door and shove Dev through it so that she could face the Daimons.

With a bellow of rage, Dev kicked the door open and charged back to the fight.

Throwing her hand up to get more punch behind her mental powers, she tossed him out again and this time put the bed in front of the door to keep him out.

Dev stood in the empty hallway, gaping. What the hell? He tried to go back into his room, but couldn't. He heard things breaking and people cursing, but he was effectively locked out.

Anger ripped through him. "Ah no you di'in't."

His powers surging, he used them to teleport into the room where Sam was surrounded by Daimons. He manifested two KA-BARs and went after the Daimons with everything he had.

Sam turned as she felt a new presence in the room. Expecting it to be another Daimon, she froze at the sight of Dev taking out two Daimons with one powerful blow. Her heart hammered and in that one instant she felt her Dark-Hunter powers wane as old memories ripped through her and left her brutalized.

It wasn't Dev she saw now. It was Ioel.

The firelight had flickered against his dark skin and hair as Ioel had gently pushed her toward their daughter's room. "Take Ree and get to safety."

She'd stubbornly refused. "Not without you."

He'd placed his hand on her stomach where their baby was kicking and kissed her on the lips while the attacking Daimons broke into their home. "Go, Samia. Now. Think of our children, not the battle."

Amazons never retreat. They don't fall back.

They fight.

The sound of splintering wood echoed through the house as the Daimons broke in, shouting in victory.

"Mommy!"

Her daughter's terrified scream had pulled her away from her husband and she'd run to her daughter's room with everything she had. But her advanced pregnancy had left her winded and unstable on her feet. Trembling, she'd pulled her frightened daughter into her arms and held her close as her anger sizzled inside her. She wanted blood for this.

The sound of furniture breaking and clashing steel rang in her ears as she looked about for an escape.

There wasn't one.

She had to get her baby to safety. . . .

Sam started for the hall, but was stopped by a flash in the fire-lit room.

And then she'd seen it. That one sword stroke that had pierced Ioel's chest and left him staggering back. Blood poured over him as the Daimons moved to take his soul.

Her own scream had lodged in her throat while she clung to her daughter and felt the life of her unborn baby in her stomach. In this condition, she wasn't strong enough to carry her daughter through the hall—not if she was to outrun the Daimons.

She rushed back into her daughter's room. "Under the bed, Ree. Now." She'd set her daughter down on the floor and watched her scamper to hide. "Not a sound, baby, whatever you do."

Sam had barely grabbed the lamp from the table before the Daimons stormed the room. She'd flung the oil and fire at the first one who reached her. Lunging at him, she'd grabbed his sword and whirled, stabbing the one right behind him. But her distended belly had unbalanced a move she'd made a thousand times in battle.

She'd stumbled back and they'd fallen on her in such a number that she'd been unable to fight them off.

The last thing she'd seen before she died had been her own sister's face at the back of the Daimons.

"There's one more brat to kill. Whatever you do, don't let her live. She has to be here somewhere. Find her and make sure she can't inherit anything except a burial."

Brutal, impotent rage and betrayal had ripped her asunder. Even now Sam could hear the scream of it as it radiated inside her. So fierce. So terrible, it had summoned the goddess Artemis to her side. And before the Daimons had had a chance to capture her soul, Sam had sold it.

But it'd come too late to save her daughter. . . .

The piercing agony of that ripped her apart now and it left her dizzy as she watched Dev fighting to protect her.

No! Never again!

Throwing her head back, she let loose with a fierce battle cry before she laid into the Daimons.

Dev paused as he heard the sound a banshee made when it buried a loved one. Haunting and piercing, that baleful screech went down his spine like a shredder. In the blink of an eye, Sam sprung forward, slashing and tearing through the Daimons with a power and skill that was unrivaled. Never in his life had he seen anything like it.

Never.

Damn, woman . . .

And he'd pissed her off? What the hell had he been thinking?

More Daimons came through the bolt-hole to attack. Dev caught the one going for Sam's back and expired him where he stood. Still they kept coming.

Just when he was sure both he and Sam would go down, the bed against the door went skittering sideways. He grabbed Sam and leapt over it an instant before the door was splintered.

Ethon and Chi, along with Fang, came running in to help with the fight.

With his arm around Sam, Dev tried to guide her into the hallway where she wouldn't be in the thick of it. But she was having none of that.

She turned around to fight.

He tightened his grip on her and forced her to move through the door.

"What are you doing?" She looked up at him.

Dev gasped as he saw her green eyes. By that, he knew she'd lost her Dark-Hunter powers. They could kill her. "Getting you out of harm's way."

"I run from no one."

"We're not running," he said as one of the Daimons broke the window and spilled daylight all over his room. "We're regrouping to fight another day."

Sam wanted to choke him as he tossed her over his shoulder and headed for the stairs. If she still had her powers, she would have, but without them she was relegated to holding on like some pathetic little girl—something that set her temper on fire even more.

One second they were in Peltier House, the next they were inside a strange warehouse-looking place that she'd never seen before. Unlit neon signs that formed an intricate pattern were hung all over the walls. To her left was an industrial bar that was well stocked with alcohol. A large mirror, also wrapped in unlit neon, was behind it. It appeared to be another club, only it wasn't open. And there was no one here. Not even a whisper of a sound.

Dev set her down.

Sam immediately slapped at his hands. "Get away from me! I'm so mad at you I could claw out your eyes!"

He stepped back to give her a peeved glare. "You're welcome."

"For what? Pissing me off?"

"I saved your life."

She scoffed at that. "No. You didn't. You pulled me out of a fight I needed to finish. Gah! I can't believe you left Chi and Ethon there while carrying me off like some helpless child. How dare you!"

Dev took a deep breath to calm himself before he escalated this fight to nuclear proportions. One of them needed to have a calm head until he figured out what was going on. Something during the fight had triggered a profound and unexpected consequence for Sam. The one thing he knew about Dark-Hunters was that they only lost their powers whenever they confronted a memory from the event that had caused them to sell their souls.

Sam was hurting and all he wanted was to help her. Her uncharacteristic screech had told him that. No one made that sound unless they were torn completely up.

"I saw them going for the windows and knew I had to pull you out of daylight before they shattered them. Which they did. Had I not grabbed you when I did, you'd have been killed or at least severely burned." Even with her Dark-Hunter powers drained, she still wouldn't have been able to stand in daylight.

She made a sound of profound aggravation as she surveyed the concrete floor and light blue, riveted metal walls around them. "Where are we anyway? Hell?"

He flashed a charming grin at her. "It's much cooler than that. Club Charonte."

"Which is what?"

He didn't answer. Instead he pulled his phone out and made a call.

Crossing her arms over her chest, Sam glared at him.

Dev recklessly ignored her seething fury at him as Ethon picked up the phone. He wanted to make sure his family was all right before they carried this conversation any further. At least Ethon answered—that in and of itself was a good sign that Sanctuary was still standing. "Hey, what happened when we left?"

"The cowardly bastards vacated right after you did. Chi and I tried to take as many down as we could, but we had to exit the range of that seriously annoying yellow ball in the sky that was dancing all over your room. You know, Bear, you should have smaller windows. Fang went after them, but they vanished back into their hole and he withdrew to protect the family in case they returned to another area for vengeance's sake. Anyway, the fanged brigade is probably tracking you guys right now, so watch your back."

Like Dev cared? "Bring it if they dare, which I doubt." Either way, his family was clear and that made him deliriously happy. His evil plan had worked and the Daimons had withdrawn—at least for the moment.

"Don't be so cocky, Bear. They were open for business." The humor vanished out of his tone. "Is Samia all right? They didn't hurt her, did they?" There was a note of concern in Ethon's voice that seemed deeper than just one Dark-Hunter worried about another one.

Dev couldn't put his finger on it, but it made the bear in him sit up with suspicion as to why Ethon would feel so deeply about a colleague. "She's fine. I got her out of there before they toasted her any. What about you guys? Any of my family get hurt?"

"Fang's fine. As for us, nothing that won't heal." Then Ethon changed the subject. "So where are you now?"

"Club Charonte."

Ethon gave a short laugh. "Nice. Very nice. I highly commend your choice." The Charontes were the mortal enemies of the Daimons and the Daimons wouldn't dare come near this place. At least not right away. The one thing about a Charonte, they were perpetually hungry and lived to eat things that wouldn't get them arrested.

Daimons were one of the things they could lavishly feast on with immunity.

Ethon sobered before he spoke again. "Are you sure Sam's safe there?"

"Oh yeah. But I might not be in a few minutes. She looks like she's about to gouge out my eyes and beat my ass until I'm a quivering bear mat."

"Poor you."

"Tell me about it. I don't envy me right now."

Ethon spoke to Fang in a muffled tone that suggested he had his hand cupped over the receiver. "It's not important. I'll be all right." Then he returned to Dev. "We'll get over there to you as soon as we can."

"Sounds good. By the way ... what happened with Gautier?"

"Nick? What's he got to do with anything?"

What's he got to do with it? The little bastard would be lucky to live next time Dev ran into him. "He's the one who summoned the Daimons."

"Nick?" Ethon repeated.

"Nick." Dev snapped the syllable. He was getting tired of the Spartan's obtuseness.

"Nick?"

"Ethon. Stop."

"Sorry, man. I just can't wrap my mind around that. He hates the Daimons with a passion to rival your Charonte buds. Trust me. You say that word and the man flips. I had to pull him off the ceiling just a few days ago when the subject came up. I can't imagine him summoning them unless it's to kill one."

"Yeah, well, I know what I saw. Nick was in league with them."

Ethon let out a low whistle. "I'll notify Acheron then and we'll get to you immediately. Just in case."

Dev glanced to Sam, who was still eyeballing him like she wanted to carve off some vital piece of his anatomy. The weird thing was, she was strangely attractive with that fire in her eyes and it turned him on.

I am so messed up.

"You guys be careful moving in daylight. See you soon." Dev hung up his phone.

Sam gestured around the room. "You brought me to an empty club? Why?"

Dev turned her stiff body to the left and pointed up toward the steel rafters where two dozen demons were hanging like vampire bats. The rest would be sleeping in contorted positions in the upstairs rooms. He had no idea why the Charonte slept like that, but they did.

Sam's jaw went slack as she saw the demons, whose flesh was a bicolor swirl of reds, oranges, and blues. Their yellow, white, and red eyes glowed from the ceiling as they silently watched them as if trying to decide if they were friend or foe. She knew they were demons, but had no idea what classification or pantheon they belonged to. "What are those?"

"Charontes," Dev said in her ear. "Ever been around them?"

"No."

His breath tickled her ear and even though she couldn't see him, she had the distinct impression he was grinning at her. "They're not exactly sociable and not particularly fond of me."

That made her curious about his choosing this place. "Then why are we here?"

" 'Cause I'm betting Dev has some shit he wants to drag me into and you can friggin' forget it, Bear." There was no missing the venom in that deep masculine tone. "I'm done with you *and* your sister and don't even mention that worthless Wolf's name to me 'cause I'm not your bitch and I ain't leaving here. Stick a fork in me, Bear, 'cause I repeat, I am done. D to the O and you know the rest so get the hell out of my club before I feed you to my boys."

Dev laughed as he turned to face the demon who'd flashed in behind them. "Nice seeing you too, Xedrix. Always a pleasure."

"Yeah, for *you*. Never for me."

Sam had to force herself not to gape at the spectacle in front of her.

With swirling blue skin and black hair, Xedrix dwarfed Dev's height. Something that wasn't easy to do. Dressed in a T-shirt and jeans, Xedrix had a pair of oversized wings that twitched behind him. Whether it was from a need to attack or fly or strictly from irritation, she wasn't sure. But there was no missing the malice in his glowing eyes.

The strangest thing, though, was that even with a small pair of horns jutting out of his head and his short black hair that was tousled from sleep, the demon was incredibly beautiful and very masculine. There was just something about him that made you want to reach out and touch him.

Weird.

Xedrix narrowed his stare on her. "Why you bring a Dark-Hunter here, Bear? You know how we feel about them and they're not even on the menu, which double sucks for us."

"We have Daimons after us."

That got Xedrix to widen his eyes. Several of the demons dropped from the ceiling. They twisted in midair so that they landed gracefully on their feet around Xedrix.

Their happy expressions were almost comical. "Dinner!" The tallest one started licking his lips in eager expectation as he high-fived one of the other demons.

The shortest one shook his head. "No. Snack time. Unless there's a bunch of them. Let's hope there is."

"Need some sauce," the orange demon said to the other two. He shoved at the short red one. "Ceres, grab a bottle. Extra hot."

Xedrix held his hand up to silence them. "We're not lucky enough for home delivery, guys. Trust me. They won't come here."

The demons around him actually pouted.

Ceres didn't seem to buy his argument. "One of them might be stupid. Daimons not real bright. They *could* come here. Maybe we could lure them in with a tourist or two?"

The tall one brightened. "We could tie some Dark-Hunters outside as bait."

They all seemed to like that thought.

Except Xedrix, who rolled his eyes. "They're not that dumb. Believe me and you tie a Dark-Hunter outside, Acheron will go Atlantean on us and the last thing we want is to be sent home to mama. Or do you guys really want to go back into slavery under the Destroyer's not-so-delicate fist?"

"Fine," Ceres said petulantly, his wings drooping. "Should have known it was too good to be true." He sighed.

The demons shot back to their places in the rafters, but not before they muttered a few choice insults for Dev getting their hopes up.

Sam looked at them as they wrapped their wings around themselves and seemed to cocoon into the ceiling. That was interesting . . . Odd, but intriguing.

Xedrix stood with his hands on his hips. "Why you here, Bear?"

"The Daimons want Sam. I don't know why—"

"Duh." Xedrix gestured at her. "She's their mortal enemy. Of course they want her. In pieces, I'm sure."

Dev shook his head. "That's just it. They don't want her dead. They've tried twice now to kidnap—"

"You both realize that I'm right here and I don't need either of you talking about me like I'm mentally defective, right? I can speak for myself."

At least Dev had the decency to look sheepish. "Sorry, Sam. We know. I'm just trying to get Xedrix on our side." He looked back at the demon. "They want her alive. Do you have any idea why?"

" 'Cause she'd be tastier that way?"

Sam ignored the demon and scowled at Dev. "Why are you asking *him* that? He's not a Daimon."

Dev gave her a droll stare. "He used to live with Stryker and serve Stryker's mistress in hell so he might have some indication why they're after you."

Xedrix made a rude sound. "They're not exactly my favorite people and I have no idea why they'd be after her. Bad luck?"

"Xed . . ."

"Don't growl at me, Bear. It's early and I haven't eaten yet." He passed a pointed look at both of them as if sizing them for his pot.

Dev let out a deep sigh. "Whatever they want her for, you have to figure it's not good. For *any* of us. I need someplace safe to keep her until night."

Xedrix pointed over his shoulder with his thumb. "The door's that way."

"Show her to a guest room."

Xedrix flashed his fangs at the soft, gentle voice.

Sam looked past him to see a tiny, ethereal woman. Her features were pale and absolutely stunning. Her blond hair seemed to glow and her eyes . . . white and vibrant, they were truly eerie.

Xedrix didn't appear all that happy to see her either. "Kerryna . . . you should still be asleep."

She approached him slowly and placed a gentle hand on his shoulder before she rose on her tiptoes to lovingly kiss his cheek. "My fierce protector. Don't worry. I'm fine." She held her hand out to Sam. "I'm Xedrix's mate, Kerryna."

"Sam." She looked down at Kerryna's peace offering and cringed. Even though her powers were down, she still didn't want to chance pulling something out of the demon's past. "Sorry I can't touch you. Not to be offensive. My powers won't allow that."

Kerryna dropped her arm. "Understood and no offense taken."

Xedrix pulled Kerryna's hand in his and held it against his heart as he glared at Sam and Dev. "You bring war to my family and I will eat both your hearts ... without sauce."

The way he said that, Sam had a feeling it meant something.

Dev inclined his head to Xedrix. "Got it."

Sam hesitated as she had a memory flash in her mind from the night Dev's parents had died. It was brief, gone in an instant, but clear. She frowned at Xedrix. "You fought with us when the wolves attacked Sanctuary. But you were human then." Which was why she hadn't recognized him. His features had been similar, but the differences without the marbled blue skin were marked.

In one heartbeat, Xedrix turned from a demon into a handsome human with black hair and no wings that she remembered from the battle. "Not human. I just looked like one. Kind of hard to walk around the streets in my real form. Halloween notwithstanding. It tends to freak out the humans and I don't want to deal with their crap."

"Unless you barbecue them," Ceres called down from the ceiling. "Then humans are quite tasty."

Xedrix looked up at him. "So are Charontes who don't mind their own business."

Ceres covered himself completely with his wings.

Xedrix returned his attention to Sam and Dev. "And if I kill the humans, I violate the treaty that allows us to stay here and we all get sent back to Daimon hell to serve the biggest bitch-goddess you ever met." He started for the stairs that were set off in the far corner of the bar. "Now follow me."

As they moved across the floor, Sam realized something. She was walking barefoot and not picking up anything from the floor.

How odd.

Her head was still completely quiet. Was it from Dev or something the Charonte did? She had no idea, but she was grateful for it. It was really nice to live as a normal human again.

Even for a few minutes. For that alone, it was worth being a Daimon magnet. But the madness did need to cease soon—she was tired of them popping in without an invitation.

Rude, insensitive bastards.

Xedrix took them to a small room halfway down the upstairs hall where there was a bed, a chest of drawers, and a small nightstand with an old-style electric lamp. One that was decorated in pinks and Victorian frills— very feminine and sweet—a complete dichotomy to the testy, overtly masculine demon.

Pausing in the door frame, Kerryna gestured toward the door over her shoulder. "Our room is just across the hall if you need anything."

Xedrix made a noise of protest, but Kerryna ignored him.

Sam tensed as she heard the sudden cry of a toddler wanting its mother coming from the room next to theirs.

Kerryna vanished immediately while Xedrix's look turned even more fierce. "Like I said, Bear, you bring war to my family and I will make sure it's the last mistake you make."

Dev held his hands up. "Peace, brother. I would never hurt anyone's family. You know that."

His features stern, Xedrix closed their door and vanished.

Sam pushed away the pain inside her as the toddler stopped crying. Bittersweet memories washed through her, making her wish again for one more second of time with her daughter. Gods, how aggravating those cries had seemed at the time, especially when Agaria had colic. Sam had feared she'd lose her mind as she dreamed of a time when she wouldn't hear that sound ever again.

Now she'd give anything to hear it one more time. To be able to carry her screaming infant and rock her through the night even with frazzled nerves and sleep deprivation.

If only she'd known at the time just how precious it was, she'd have savored every heartbeat and headache. Every messy diaper . . .

She flinched, wishing mistakes had a do-over. It was the cruelest act of Fate that there was no rewind at all.

And thinking of the past achieved nothing. So she made herself focus on the present and what was important now. "Kerryna's not a Charonte, is she?"

Dev shook his head as he made sure there was no window under the faux curtains that opened onto a brick wall. "No. The Charonte are Atlantean. Kerryna's a Sumerian dimme demon."

Now that was a combination you didn't find often and there had to be a story in how the two of them had met and ended up mated with a child. "How did she get to New Orleans?" It was a long way here from ancient Sumeria.

Dev turned to face her. "Like you, she was being chased by her enemies and wound up here. Actually that's an oversimplification. Kerryna and her sisters are fierce killing machines and they were cursed and bound."

Ah, now that didn't sound good. "Where are her sisters?"

"They're still trapped. She alone escaped."

"And she's okay with that?"

Dev laughed. "Yeah, freaky, huh? Apparently family togetherness wasn't her forte. I'm not sure what drew her to New Orleans, but once here, she met the Charonte and more to the point, Xedrix. Somehow they settled in and decided to protect her. Makes me glad I'm not a demon. 'Cause I don't want to know what kind of funky monkey stuff went down that they let her in . . . if you know what I mean and I know that you do."

Sam let out a "heh" at his semi-humorous words. "And her enemies? Are they still after her?"

"Probably, but only a fool would try to pull her out of a home filled with Charontes ready to lay down their lives for her."

That made the least amount of sense to her. "Where did they come from? Why are the Charonte here in the middle of the city?"

He laughed. "Mardi Gras, baby. Mardi Gras. Time when all manner of weird shit cuts loose and parties down."

"Dev . . ."

He sobered before he gave her the real answer. "A few years back, one of the gods opened the portal between

142

their realm and this one, wanting to unleash destruction on the world. They escaped and Acheron sealed it, then allowed them to stay. They've been living here happily ever since."

"Even though they were going to destroy us?"

"Well, not them per se. Their mistress was. They were just following orders and now that they're here, they obey Acheron, who set up the rules they have to follow—such as no eating humans—or he'll send them back to their realm. They've been here for a while so the arrangement seems to be working." He gave her a cute grin.

Shaking her head, Sam was still trying to get a handle on all of this. "And how do *you* know them?"

"They tried to eat my kid brother, Kyle, who talked them out of it. He showed them how to start a club and function in the human world as normal citizens—the hanging from the ceiling thing notwithstanding. They've been friendly with us ever since ... at least most of the time."

Sam sighed. "This town is so strange."

Dev laughed as he pulled her to him. "Yes, but ... there's no place else quite as exciting."

True. Very true.

He traced the line of her lips with his finger. "We've got to find out what the Daimons want from you."

"Well, we both know it's not world peace."

"Definitely not." Dev traced the line from her mouth up to the corner of her eyes. "Are you aware of the fact that your eyes are green?"

Sam gasped. "What?"

"Your eyes are green."

She pulled away from him to run to the mirror. Sure enough he was right. No wonder she'd been unable to pull anything from the floor. She had no Dark-Hunter powers left. The very fact that she could see herself in the mirror was testament to that. To help them retain their stealth while they hunted, no Dark-Hunter could cast a reflection unless they used their powers to do it.

And right now, she was human. At least temporarily. "Is that why you pulled me from the fight?"

He nodded.

Because he knew the one truth she did. In this form, she could be killed.

ETHON STARK HAD cut his teeth on battle. It was what had succored him as a human being. As a Dark-Hunter, that need for blood always simmered just below his surface. Nothing gave him more pleasure than stomping his enemies into the ground and watching them bleed all over his expensive shoes. It was what the warrior in him lived for.

All it lived for.

His friends were counted on the fingers of one hand and right now one of them was in serious trouble.

Sam.

She hated him, he knew that. But he didn't blame her. He was a monster and she'd glimpsed the darkness that lived inside him. The darkness that made him insane on his best day.

Even so, he still counted her as a friend. He always would no matter what her feelings might be for him. So he would give his life to keep her safe—even if it meant eternal damnation and an existence so foul that he would spend the rest of time screaming in utter misery.

She was worth that to him.

With that thought foremost in his mind, he teleported from Sanctuary to Nick's house on Bourbon Street. It was a power he didn't use often since he didn't like for anyone to know what he was capable of. Knowledge was power and the less anyone knew about his powers, the fewer people he'd have to kill to keep his secrets.

He materialized at the foot of a hand-carved staircase. "Nick!" he shouted, stalking up the stairs and through the house in search of the one who'd betrayed them and jeopardized Samia's life.

No one answered.

"Nick!"

Again it was silent.

Closing his eyes, Ethon used his powers to crawl through the house.

There wasn't anyone here.

Nick must still be with the Daimons, plotting who knew what against them. Rage over that ripped through him as it opened wounds that Ethon struggled every day to keep closed.

"Fine, you little bastard. You better stay in hiding."

Sooner or later, Nick would be back and Ethon would kill him.

DEV STARED DOWN as Sam finally slept. Even though she was tall and a fierce fighter, something about her looked incredibly vulnerable while she slept.

Why am I so attracted to you?

All he wanted was to keep her safe and that made no sense whatsoever. It was like she was under his skin and just being near her made him feel more alive than he ever had before. In fact it was taking all of his willpower not to strip his clothes off, lie down beside her, and wrap her in his arms.

This was so not him. He was normally more than content to have his one-night stands and then send them on their way as soon as he could.

He heard a light knock on the door.

Stepping away from the bed, he opened it to find Ethon on the other side. "Chi and I are downstairs. The Charonte are beginning to stir so that they can get the club ready to open. Do you guys need anything?"

"No. Thanks."

Ethon inclined his head to him. "Acheron said to keep her here even if she protests."

"And she will."

Ethon laughed. "Yeah, probably." He moved to close the door.

Dev stopped him before he withdrew completely. "You and Sam seem a little tight. Do you know how she became a Dark-Hunter?"

Ethon's expression was as dry as his tone. "She sold her soul to Artemis."

Dev let out an irritated breath at his smart-ass comment. "I'm being serious, Ethon."

He glanced to the bed as indecision marked his dark gaze. Finally he looked back at Dev and answered. "Her sister betrayed her. Sam had just been voted in as queen and her sister wanted the crown. So she made a pact with

a group of Daimons for them to kill Sam and her immediate family to remove them from the line of succession."

That news hit him like a blow to his gut. The cruelty
of it was unfathomable. What kind of bitch would do
such a thing? "You've got to be kidding me."

"I would never kid about this. I think it's why Sam has
the power of psychometry."

Dev frowned. "I don't follow."

Ethon swallowed hard before he lowered his voice.
"Had she known what her sister was thinking and planning, she'd have been able to save her family."

In a weird way, that did make sense. "So who all did her
sister kill? Sam and her other sisters?"

"Sam only had the one sister." Ethon's features turned
sharp. Deadly. "They killed her husband, Dev, and her
three-year-old daughter, right in front of her eyes as she
lay dying."

Pain slammed into him with those words. For an entire
minute, he couldn't breathe. How had she stood it? He
wanted her sister's blood for her. What kind of bitch could
do that to her own family?

Her own sister? Her niece.

And he hoped with every part of him that Sam had
gone for her sister's throat and ripped it out.

"No wonder she fights like she does."

Ethon nodded. "It's why she can't stand to feel powerless. Had she not been pregnant, about to deliver her next
kid, they would never have—"

"What?" Dev's heart stopped beating.

Ethon's expression told him that the Spartan was every
bit as sickened by what had happened to her as Dev was.

"She was pregnant when they killed her. I thought you knew."

"How would I know that?" He scowled at Ethon. "How do *you* know that?"

There was no mistaking the agony in Ethon's dark eyes. The grief and guilt. "Her husband was my little brother."

Just when he thought nothing else could shock him . . . that sent him to the floor. "What?"

A tic started in Ethon's jaw. "Ioel, her husband, was my brother."

Dev gaped. No wonder Ethon protected her the way he did. It made complete sense now.

Ethon fell silent as his emotions churned. He'd been so jealous of Ioel's happiness with his Amazon bride. The two of them had had the most incredible relationship. And while he was happy for his brother, he'd been bitter. Ioel had been raised by their mother away from the Spartan culture. While Ioel was a fierce warrior, he'd lived a pampered life of luxury and kind doting.

Unlike Ethon.

Everything Ioel had ever wanted had come to him. And Ethon had been forced to claw and fight for every table scrap he could find in the gutter. And to this day, he could still remember the first time he'd met Sam.

In full armor, she'd been breathtaking. Her zest for life was infectious as she joked with her friends and his brother.

But she'd only had eyes for Ioel.

So he'd buried his feelings for her and stood back to watch as they married and started their family. Anything they'd needed, he'd given them to make their life easier and happier. His brother didn't need to know the harsh lessons that had been rammed down his throat.

And when Agaria had been born, he'd loved his niece so much. . . . She'd looked just like her mother. There was nothing he wouldn't have done for any of them.

Nothing.

Until the night they'd died. He'd been in battle when the news of their deaths had arrived. Wounded and bleeding, he'd headed straight for his horse instead of the physician. Stupidly, he'd thought that if he could just reach them that he might be able to change it.

To save them. That maybe it was a lie and they weren't really dead.

By the time he'd reached them, Ioel and Ree had been cremated and Sam's body had been missing.

They'd found her sister's slaughtered remains the next day. The viciousness of that kill had told him well that Sam had had her vengeance. However the truth was, her sister had gotten off easy. What Sam had done to her had been a mercy killing compared to what Ethon would have done had he found her first.

He'd hunted for Sam after that, but he'd never found her. Not until centuries after his own death when they'd both been stationed in Athens.

They'd met in battle against the Daimons and then, with the dawn coming, she'd taken him into her house.

The bloodlust and their past ties had overwhelmed them. He looked enough like his brother that Sam had welcomed him to her bed.

For one single instant, he'd almost had a moment of peace.

Until she'd come to her senses.

And him.

By then it'd been too late. The guilt and pain had been more than either of them could bear. So they'd gone their own ways, crossing paths every now and again.

Still Ethon loved her. Even though she couldn't stand him. Even though he had no right to. He loved her.

He always would. But that was the past. And right now, Sam needed him.

Ethon would not fail her again.

He met Dev's stare. "I'll be downstairs if you need me."

Dev didn't speak as Ethon withdrew. His head was still reeling from what he'd learned about Sam. Gods, how painful it must have been for her to see the bond he shared with his family while knowing her sister had taken everything from her.

Even her life.

His gut knotting, he sat down on the bed beside her and brushed his hand through her curls. His poor Amazon. So fierce and proud.

Unable to protect the things she loved most.

Now he understood why she'd freaked out in the fight and locked him out in the hallway. It'd probably reminded her of the night she'd died and she'd reacted on instinct. But he wasn't a human.

He was a bear.

And it would take more than a Daimon to kill him. A lot more.

"I won't let them hurt you, Sam," he whispered as her curls tugged at his fingers. The silken strands wrapped

150

around his skin the same way foreign emotions for her wrapped around his heart.

If the Daimons wanted her, they were about to get the fight of their lives. And yet as that thought went through him, it was followed by another.

An image of her dying in front of him the way his mother had while he was powerless to stop it. Pain lacerated him.

This wasn't a fear, he knew it.

It was a premonition.

Chapter 10

Dev stalked through Nick's Bourbon Street mansion searching for a sign of the little prick. He had to have gone somewhere. It wasn't like Nick had simply vanished into nothing. And this was still the most likely place to find him. No matter what, Nick would always return to his home. The fact he was here as a Dark-Hunter after only having died a couple of years ago said it all. Artemis normally required a minimum of a hundred years to pass before a Dark-Hunter returned to the city he'd been killed in—the idea was that after that amount of time any immediate friends and family would be dead and the memories wouldn't be quite so harsh. But Nick needed his touchstone—this house and this city. He couldn't function without them. It was like New Orleans fed his soul, which Dev could understand. And right now he was grateful for that because it would bring Nick back into his circle.

Yeah, Ethon had told him he'd stopped by earlier looking for him and he wasn't here, but it wasn't the same.

Ethon wasn't out to kill him. He only wanted to hurt the Cajun.

Dev intended to use Nick's entrails as shoelaces, but first he needed Nick's fresh scent. *No one betrays me. No one.* There was too much history between him and Nick for Dev to let this one go. The fact that the little Cajun guttersnipe had brought Daimons into his home—no, *his room*—was a declaration of war. Nick had offered all of them up to the Daimons and Dev wanted a piece of him so bad he could already savor it. Not to mention the small fact that Nick had hurt Sam.

Yeah, the bastard was going to pay with his life.

But Nick wasn't here and from the looks and faint smell of things, he hadn't been in here in a couple of days. The house appeared to have been abandoned. The bed wasn't slept in. There were no dirty towels or even a wet sink to say he'd brushed his teeth or bathed. His Jaguar XK-R was still parked in the garage. None of his clothes or shoes seemed to be missing.

Weird. Where could he have gone? Nick had told his guard Dogs that he was going to bed. No one had seen him since and that had been four days ago.

Leaving the immaculate bedroom, Dev paused in the upstairs hallway as he spied one of the pictures on the wall that made up a huge montage of Nick's early life— something his mom must have placed here. While Nick could be an arrogant ass, he usually wasn't conceited.

The photo that drew his attention was one of him, Nick's mom, Aimee, and Nick, who'd been around the age of fifteen at the time. The women had been try-ing to get a good photo with him, but Nick had been

Nick—goofing off and cutting up. So Dev had come up behind him and wrapped him in a headlock. Dev's mom had snapped the photo that had Nick laughing while Dev pretended to choke him and Aimee and Nick's mother had feigned shock. It was a really cute photo.

And that one moment made him take a step back from what was going on. How could that boy have grown into a man who'd threaten Dev's family? Nick had fought on their side against the wolf pack just a few months back. Sanctuary was as much his home as this house was and while Nick wasn't quite right anymore, he wasn't *that* different.

Was he? Could he really have betrayed them all?

What if he didn't and you're wrong about him? What if he had a reason for what he'd done?

Something strange was going on. In his gut, he knew it.

Now that he thought more about it, Nick wouldn't have breached Sanctuary without a damn good reason. The Cajun might be a lot of things, but he'd never been a turncoat.

"Boy, what have you gotten yourself into?"

"WE HAVE A problem."

Acheron froze as Urian materialized directly in front of him. Thank the gods he'd pulled on a pair of pajama bottoms before he came into the kitchen to get his wife the bowl of Chunky Monkey ice cream she'd been craving. Otherwise Urian would now be blind and he'd be even more pissed at the interruption. "Were you raised in a barn?"

A loud knock sounded on the back door.

Acheron rolled his eyes at Urian's sarcasm when it was obvious Urian had thrown the sound as a "screw you" to him. *Lucky for you, I just had great sex with my wife that put me in such a happy place not even your assholishness can disturb it.* Otherwise Urian would have been a flaming stain on the wall. "What's up?"

"Dev's not on crack."

Acheron licked the back of the spoon before he set it in the sink. "Never thought he was. . . . Ketamine maybe, but never crack. Why did you?"

Urian watched Ash return the ice cream carton to the freezer. "I just came away from a chat with one of my old friends." A term Urian reserved to describe one of the Daimons who still served his father. At one time, Urian had been Stryker's right hand. But that had been before Stryker had cold-bloodedly murdered Urian's wife and cut Urian's throat, then left him for dead. And to think, Urian was such a rotten bastard that he carried a grudge against his father for that.

Yeah . . .

Stryker was seriously lacking a screw in his drawer.

"He told me that the Daimons are able to take gallu demon souls into their bodies and that Stryker is converting his army with their blood."

Acheron froze at those words. The Sumerian gallu powers were intense. The ultimate in evil, one of them in a Daimon's body would make one hell of a weapon. More than that, gallu bites turned the victims into mindless drones. One could make thousands.

Crap. A Daimon would now be able to make more of their kind.

155

Ash could take one down without breaking a sweat, but a normal Dark-Hunter ...

That would be bloody indeed. If not fatal.

"What's Stryker planning?" he asked Urian.

He gave Ash a stare that doubted his mental functionality. "What he's always wanted. To kill my grandfather and subjugate the humans."

Ash returned the "duh" expression. "I didn't ask for the goal, Urian. I've known that. What I need is the game plan. Why is he converting his people?" Ash's phone rang. He started to ignore it until he saw it was from Ethon.

What now?

Sighing, he looked at the bowl of melting ice cream on the counter. Tory hated ice cream soup. He refroze it then flashed it upstairs to where she waited in bed for him while he answered his call. Good thing his wife was used to his weirdness and would understand why he didn't deliver it himself.

However that didn't stop the fact that he felt like whimpering over the interruption of what *he'd* planned on doing with the ice cream and his wife. . . .

Some days his job seriously sucked. Why couldn't humanity clean up after themselves?

Ungrateful bastards.

He flipped open his phone.

"Nick is working with the Daimons," Ethon said without preamble.

"Nice hearing from you too, Spartan. Care to tell me why you think this?"

"'Cause the little shit tried to kidnap Sam out of Sanctuary. He was there in all his glory, offering her up to our enemies." Ethon continued speaking after that, but Acheron didn't hear a single word of it.

Instead he saw images in his head that he couldn't quite place. Something was profoundly wrong with this entire scenario. He knew that Nick was tied by blood to Stryker, but Nick had been fighting that bond. . . .

Had something happened to put him back under Stryker's command?

No. No way. Nick was too stubborn for that. Not even Ash could control him.

He hung up the phone and met Urian's curious gaze. "Get over to the Charonte Club and ride herd on Dev and Sam. Anything comes at her, I don't care who or what, you protect her."

"Okay. What's going on?"

"Just do it." Ash didn't explain himself to others. Ever. He honestly had no idea why Stryker would want Sam, but whatever the reason it had to be diabolical. Stryker didn't move without purpose and precision. And because Stryker's actions directly affected Ash, he couldn't use his powers to see what the hell the bastard was doing.

Urian vanished.

Ash summoned his Charonte protector, who currently resided on his biceps in the form of a dragon tattoo. Simi peeled herself off to take human form in front of him. Appearing around the age of nineteen, she was only slightly shorter than his six-foot-eight stance even though she could pick any height she wanted. Her long black hair with a red stripe in the front matched his and she was dressed in a short plaid skirt, tall biker boots, and a black leather corset.

She flashed a set of happy fangs at him. "Hola, akri. We going to the movie now with Akra-Tory and Marissa and N.J.? The Simi wanna see that tall green ogre man 'cause he reminds her of her uncle—"

"Not quite yet." He hated to interrupt her word flow, but Simi had a tendency to babble on forever at times. Which he loved, and it was usually humorous as hell, but right now they had to stay focused. "I need a favor, Sim."

Her eyes lit up as she rubbed her hands together in excitement. "I get to eat something you don't like? Can I eat the bitch-goddess finally? She be tasty with the right sauce! Take the bitter right out of her meat." She grinned widely.

Ash laughed before he kissed her on the forehead. "Not quite. I want you to go upstairs and guard Tory for me."

Simi gasped. "Akra-Tory okay? Our baby not hurt, is it?"

When he'd first told Simi Tory was pregnant, he'd been terrified Simi would be jealous since she was technically his baby and had been for eleven thousand years. Instead, she'd been as thrilled about it as they were and now she claimed part ownership.

"She's fine, Sim. I just don't want to leave her alone while I do something." And if anyone was dumb enough to come at his wife and powerful enough to break the shield he'd put around his house, he wanted Simi here to tear them to pieces.

Simi was the only person he trusted with his wife.

"Tell Tory I had an emergency and that I'll be back real quick."

Simi cocked her head suspiciously. "Where akri going the Simi can't go with him?"

"Out, Sim. Now please protect her and remember, any-one tries to hurt her, don your mitt, baby, and feast on their entrails."

She saluted him before she vanished.

Ash summoned his street clothes—a long black leather coat, black jeans, and a T-shirt—before he flashed himself from their small modest house in New Orleans to Artemis's temple on Mount Olympus. From the outside the temple was beautiful. Made of gold with forest and nature scenes emblazoned all over it. But it, like Artemis, was definitely a case of skin deep.

His gut twisted in anger as he was forced to go to the place where the bitch-goddess had once tortured him. He hated this temple with a passion that burned as deep as a thousand suns. Now that he was free of Artemis and had discovered what being with someone who really loved him was like, it was hard to go back even for a visit.

He forced eleven thousand years of bitter resentment down as he walked through the gilded doors then pulled up short.

The temple was completely devoid of people. Not even Artemis's handmaidens were in attendance. *Oh, this ain't good.* He felt sick as he recognized what that meant.

Nick, you poor sonofabitch. What are you doing?

That boy had always possessed a suicidal streak in him and it made Acheron sick to see how badly he and Artemis had screwed up Nick's happy-go-lucky life. Guilt gnawed at him, but there was nothing he could do about the past.

This was about the future.

"Artemis?" Ash called. His deep voice echoed through the marbled room.

She instantly appeared in front of him. Perfect in a way only a goddess could be, she was dressed in her customary white sheath dress that hugged her voluptuous body. Long red hair framed a face so perfect it was hard to even look at it. Yet his centuries of being under her thumb robbed him of the ability to appreciate anything other than her absence, and that he was truly grateful for when it came.

She chewed her long, red thumbnail as she shifted from foot to foot. Ash let out a long-suffering sigh. By the nervous way she was twitching, he knew it was going to be bad.

"What's going on?"

She bit her lip before she answered, and tried to look innocent. She failed miserably. "What do you mean?"

"Dammit, Artemis, don't play this shit with me. I'm done. Where's Nick?"

"Nick who?"

Growling, he grabbed her arm and pulled her toward him. Yes, it was rougher than it should have been, but she'd brutally beaten him for centuries and then tried to kill his wife. She was lucky he was a forgiving god, otherwise . . .

"I know he's here. I traced his powers. You seem to forget I'm one of the handful of gods who can do that."

She swallowed before she gestured to her bedroom.

More nausea consumed him as he realized what that meant. "You tied him to you?"

She shrugged his hand off her arm. "What business is it of yours? You left *me*, remember?"

It amazed him that she made it sound like he was the one in the wrong given what she'd put him through. But she was right about one thing. It wasn't his business. Nick was a grown . . . whatever the hell he was.

Still, this was beyond the pale. She'd now aligned herself to one of the beings who wanted him dead.

Great. Just great. He saw this train wreck coming and unfortunately, his foot was caught in the rails.

"You are such a piece of work," he snarled. Stepping past her, he used his powers to sling open her bedroom doors. They made a resounding crash as they hit the walls.

The moment he entered her room, he froze.

As expected, Nick was naked on her bed. However, he was in the throes of some kind of fever. Completely unconscious, his entire body glistened with sweat. But what concerned Ash most was that Nick whispered in a language Ash didn't know. As a god, there wasn't supposed to be a language he couldn't speak or comprehend.

He had no idea what Nick was saying. Was it gibberish? And yet it sounded too precise and formed to be random. The hairs on the back of his neck stood tall.

Ash glared at Artemis. "What have you done to him?"

Artemis shrugged as she moved to stand a few feet from the white ivory bed that was shrouded by sheer gold drapes. "Nothing. He's been cooling down for over a day now."

"Burning up, Artie. The words are 'burning up.'" Why couldn't she ever get her colloquialisms straight?

"Oh, whatever." That lackadaisical attitude made him want to choke her. Nick could have died and her only care would be how to dump his body without the other gods seeing her.

Trying not to think about that, Ash lifted Nick's eyelid to see that his eyes were demon red. His skin burned like the fires of hell. Nick's fangs were longer than normal. Serrated.

What was going on? Was he mutating into something else?

Most of all, who or what had control of him?

"How long has he been like this?" He made a sound of disgust before she could answer. What a stupid question. Time had no meaning to Artemis. "Did he say anything before he fell ill?"

"No."

Aggravated, Ash used his powers to delve into what had happened between them. All he saw was them having sex and then Nick falling back in pain.

He hadn't moved since. But as Ash delved deeper, he went from this Nick to other Nick incarnations. And there he saw . . .

"Oh, shit."

Artemis jumped. "What?"

Ash ignored her as he jolted Nick with a vicious god bolt straight to his heart.

Nick came out of his coma swinging. Especially once he saw it was Ash who'd hit him. He moved to grab Ash, but Ash spun away, out of his reach. Nick let out a furious grunt. "What the hell are you doing here, asshole?"

Ash put a little more distance between them. Not out of fear of Nick hurting him, but out of fear he might hurt Nick. "I would ask the same thing about you." He glanced to Artemis. "I would have thought you knew better."

Nick lunged at him.

Ash shielded his body so that Nick couldn't come near him—again for Nick's protection. The Cajun had a way and a mouth on him that eroded all of Acheron's patience and motivated him to violence faster than Artemis stalking him.

"Do you remember what happens when a demon masquerades as someone?" Ash asked.

Oblivious to the fact he was completely naked, Nick sneered at him. "What kind of stupid question is that? Of course I do."

The victim being duplicated was left comatose . . .

Or dead.

Ash narrowed his gaze on Nick. "What was the last day you remember?"

"Today. Tuesday."

Ash shook his head. "It's Saturday, Nick. You've been in a coma for three and a half days." He used his powers to pick up Nick's hand and rub it against the whiskers on his cheeks that confirmed what Ash was telling him.

That finally took away some of his bluster. "What?" Then he stiffened. "Quit playing with my hand, you friggin' perv."

Ash released him and manifested a blanket over him. "Dude, I'm not the one standing with my schlong hanging out. Have some dignity."

Nick flipped him off before he wrapped the blanket around his waist.

Ash ignored his hatred. "Just so you know, Gautier, I have a couple of Dark-Hunters and Were-Hunters who want a piece of your ass because they think you attacked Sanctuary."

Nick gaped. "I haven't been near it since the wolves attacked."

"I know. I'm just updating you on what's going on since you were kind enough to loan your body to someone who's been masquerading as you and turning your protectors against you."

Nick cursed, then glanced at Artemis as if remembering her presence. He actually blushed before he returned to glaring at Ash. "I'm going to kill Stryker."

"Stay away from him. You haven't mastered enough of your powers yet to even think about taking him on. Trust me. All you'd do right now is make him a nice mincemeat pie."

Nick fell silent before he said something to betray himself. He had more abilities than Acheron knew about and for some reason they seemed to be growing exponentially. He wasn't the weak-kneed neophyte. But Ash didn't need to know that.

Not yet.

Nick flinched as a peculiar surge went through him. He'd been getting them a lot lately and he didn't know why. Sharp and intense, they took his breath. Another one shot up his spine, driving him to his knees.

"Nicky?" Artemis ran to his side.

Nick held her back as weird images danced in his head. He saw things from his past rearrange. . . . People he didn't know and others who'd died . . .

What the . . . ?

"You all right?" Ash asked.

No, but he wasn't about to admit that to Ash. No one would ever again know his weaknesses. What was going on was his business. Ash had already betrayed him once. He wasn't about to give him another chance to damage his life, such as it was.

And in his head, he heard the voices that had been getting louder lately. Voices that wanted him to hurt the people around him. They were so seductive and with them came a power so fierce it was hard to resist.

He felt his eyes turning red.

There was a raw, primordial power coming and it was out for blood. The only question was, whose?

Chapter 11

"Mama?"

Sam jerked awake at the sound of a very small voice that was just learning to speak. She lay in bed, wondering if she'd dreamed it.

She hadn't.

"Shh, munchkin, not so loud. We have guests." Kerryna kept talking in that sweet octave mothers reserved for their children as she walked out of hearing range.

Sam cursed under her breath. If she heard or saw one more child . . .

It seemed like the gods were taking pleasure in punishing her lately. And she wanted to weep as her grief choked her. Why couldn't she have raised her own children? Seen them grow and held them all the days of her life? That had been the plan. She and Ioel, growing old together . . .

Damn you, gods.

No. She had her sister to blame for their loss and it changed nothing. The pain was still there and it was raw and bleeding.

Suck it up, Amazon. You're a Dark-Hunter. Mother to the entire human race she protected. She saved their lives even while she'd been unable to save the lives of her own family. The irony of that had haunted her for centuries. And it was what had given her the strength to tear out her sister's throat even while the petty bitch had begged her for mercy.

Mercy, my ass . . .

That wasn't in her. Not anymore. It hadn't been since the day she'd crossed over and seen the real horrors life had heaped on not just her, but countless others. Images of the past burned her while she lay there and they left her aching. Wanting.

Please help me. . . .

A light snore behind her drew her attention away from the past to realize that a heavy, muscular arm was draped protectively over her. To the fact that a warm body was pressed up against hers.

Dev.

The bear held her like she was unspeakably precious. Like her husband had once done . . .

Tenderness swept through her. How she'd missed waking up like this. That feel of a man's body entwined with hers. Of his prickly hairs rough against her legs. His hard cock resting against her hip. She didn't know why she liked being with Dev. He drove her straight up the walls with no stop sign in sight. He manhandled her, which she hated with a passion, and was the epitome of a male horn dog at times.

He was arrogant. Hard-headed . . .

And he risked his life to keep her safe. Even now he didn't have to be here and yet there he lay.

Like a teddy bear. She silently laughed at the thought. There was nothing cuddly about Dev. He was all sinewy muscle and he was huge.

Her gaze went to the bow-and-arrow tattoo on his arm. He hadn't made the sacrifice she had, but he understood the call. Sam swallowed. *I don't want to be dead anymore. . . .*

She'd been alone for so long. Had hurt and sucked up her tears for centuries. Nothing had ever eased it.

Until now. For whatever reason, Dev took away the pain she felt. He somehow made things better with his screwed-up humor and peculiar outlook.

It was so wrong. She was a Dark-Hunter and he a Were-Hunter. They were supposed to be enemies.

Yet it didn't feel that way. And right now with his breath falling on her skin and his arms wrapped around her, she wanted him. She wanted to bathe in the warmth he gave her. Breathe him in until she was drunk on his scent . . .

Dev came awake to the sweetest kiss he'd ever been given. Tender and hot, it set fire to him as Sam draped her naked body over his. Her breasts were pressed against his chest, reminding him of why he was so glad he was a man.

She nipped his lips with her fangs before she pulled back to look down at him. Her nightgown was gone, she'd thrown it on the floor before she woke him, and her curls spilled around her creamy shoulders. Her eyes were once again dark brown. She was the Dark-Hunter and right now, he was her willing victim.

He smiled at her. "Now *that's* the way to wake a guy up."

She shook her head, causing those curls to bounce beautifully. "No . . . *this* is the way to wake him up."

Before he could ask her what she meant, she slid down his body and dipped her head to take him into her mouth. His mind spun as pleasure ripped through his entire being.

Yeah, she was definitely right on that account. This was a much better way to wake a guy up. Ah, hell, he'd gladly wake up in a good mood every day if it started out like this. He sucked his breath in sharply as her tongue darted down the length of him before she took him completely into her mouth. His eyes rolled back in his skull as he shook all over.

He sank his hand in her soft, honey curls as he watched her savor him. Damn if she wasn't the most incredible woman he'd ever known. He loved the fact that she wasn't shy or inhibited in any way. She loved him like it would be the last time she'd ever touch a man. Like they would be dead in a minute and this was her last chance to live.

Her intensity and skills were incredible. He laid his hand against her cheek as his powers surged. What was it about her that she could feed his abilities the way she did? More than that, she touched him in a place no woman ever had before.

His heart.

All his life, he'd been alone. Yeah, he'd been around people, but no one had ever seen him. He'd never allowed people, not even his brothers, to get that close to him. Not after he'd lost Bastien and Gilbert. As a young cub, he'd worshiped his older brothers and when they'd died protecting Aimee . . .

He'd never gotten over their loss. Not really. It was why he'd always been so protective of his sister and mother. He'd wanted to make his brothers proud. To let them know that even though they were gone, the snot-nose cub left behind could hold his own.

Life was shit. He knew that as well as anyone else and he hated just how much it had crapped all over Sam. He wanted to take her away from the pain that had been thrown at her. Take her away from the hostile world they both lived in.

But right now, she was the one taking him away from the hurt and the misery.

Sam growled as she nibbled on Dev. She'd always loved the way a man tasted. The way he smelled and felt. And Dev . . . He was sweeter than anything.

Hungry for more, she gave one last lick before she crawled up his body and impaled herself on him. He gave a deep, manly growl. She lifted his hand from her breast so that she could nip and tease the pads of his fingers while she rode him soft and easy. Oh, how she wanted to stay with him like this forever.

But they had lions tearing at the doors. Enemies after both of them and a world that depended on them to fight for it. She understood her calling. She believed in her cause. Yet right now, she wanted something for herself. A moment of peace and connection.

Was that too much to ask?

"You are so beautiful," Dev said as he slid his hand between her legs so that he could heighten her pleasure.

Sam hissed. "Are all bearswain so gentle?"

He laughed at her question. "I don't make a habit of sleeping with male bears, so how would I know?"

She joined his laughter. Then her laughter died under a wave of supreme pleasure. She let it flow through her, making her shiver and tremble.

Until her gaze accidentally fell to the door and reality interrupted her mood. It would be dark soon. She could sense it. Then she'd have to leave him and hunt the Daimons who were after her. For his sake as well as for hers. She couldn't afford for the Daimons to return to Sanctuary. Not when it endangered his family.

She wasn't worth it.

Why can't I have one moment of peace?

Because she'd sold her soul for the sake of the world. . . .

Dev sensed that something about Sam had changed. A wall had come up between them even though they were naked in each other's arms. He pulled his hand back. "Did I hurt you?"

"No, baby. You definitely didn't hurt me."

But there was a shadow in her eyes. One of pain. How he wished he could take that from her.

Dev sat up so that he could hold her while she continued to grind against him. He buried his face in her neck and tasted her as he continued to stroke her in time to her thrusts. The scent of her made the bear in him feral.

Sam reveled in the sensation of Dev holding her. She ran her hands through his long hair, letting them tangle with his curls. Gods, he was gorgeous. It wasn't every day a woman was lucky enough to find a man like him.

With a sharp growl, Dev pulled back from her and gave her a look so hot, it made her blood sizzle. Before she could ask him what was wrong, he shifted their weight and had her on her side in the bed. He used his thigh to separate her legs and entered her from behind. Completely wrapped around her, he drove himself in deep.

She felt exposed and at the same time powerful. "What are you doing?"

He cupped her breast in his hand before he breathed in her ear. "This is how a bear takes his woman."

She couldn't think as he quickened his strokes and her pleasure mounted. She didn't know if it was his powers or what, but she'd never in her life experienced anything like this. Every thrust was a study in ultimate ecstasy.

And when she came, it was the most intense orgasm she'd ever had.

Dev laughed softly in her ear until he joined her. Then, still hard, he stayed inside her, holding her close as he breathed raggedly. His warmth enveloped her and made her feel blissfully safe and strangely sane.

Sam could feel his heart thumping against her shoulder blade as she savored this moment and his heat. "No wonder you're a horn dog. You're really good at what you do."

He brushed her hair back from her cheek before he placed a tender kiss there. "Don't cheapen this moment, Samia. I've never done that with any woman. It's something we reserve for our mates."

"Then why did you do it with me?"

"Because, as stupid as it sounds, I care about you in a way I've never cared about anyone else. As a rule, I don't really like people much. I tolerate my family, but at the end of the day I much prefer to be left alone. You're the only woman I've ever sought out."

Did she dare believe that? It seemed impossible and yet . . .

She wanted it to be true because she understood it too. She felt the same way about him. "Why?"

He kissed her nose. "I have no idea. Aside from my little sister and nieces, you're the most infuriating woman I've ever met. All I can figure is that I'm either sick in the head or a total masochist."

She elbowed him in the stomach.

"Ow!" he groused at the same time his phone started ringing. "See what I mean? I have to be addicted to abuse to put up with you." He reached over her to the nightstand to grab his phone so that he could answer it. His hair fell over her as he gave her a look that managed to be both adorable and vicious. "Be nice to me, Amazon, or I'll touch you with my phone and give you visions."

"You probably would, too."

Smiling, he rolled away before he answered it.

Sam wrapped the sheet around herself as she realized that her powers were back and that the sheets weren't contaminating her. . . .

What was going on? Why wasn't she picking up on other people?

"Are you sure about that?" Dev brushed his hair back and scratched his head as he listened to whomever was on the other end of the line. "Yeah, okay. I trust you. We'll be watching and I'll let you know if something happens." He hung up the phone and looked at her. "According to Ash, that wasn't Nick who let the Daimons in."

"What?"

"He swears it was someone pretending to be him."

She wrinkled her nose as she flashed back to her conversation with the Gautier lookalike. "I don't know. The Nick we saw was pretty convincing."

"True, but Ash wouldn't lie to us. He might withhold things, but he wouldn't lie, especially about something like this."

That much was true. And as she sat there, she remembered the twinge she had that something about Nick hadn't been right. Had she picked up on the imposter? "So if it wasn't Nick, who was it?"

"That's the question no one has an answer to."

Sam leaned back against the brass headboard as she tumbled the thought around her head. "Why come to us as Nick? Were they trying to turn us against him?"

"It would make sense. Drive a wedge between him and the people who are on his protection detail."

"But why?" No matter how she sliced it, she couldn't come up with a reason for framing Gautier.

"Maybe it's as simple as they wanted to get close to you and Gautier was the only one they could impersonate."

That might work, and Dev was right. As suspicious as they were right now, it would be hard to get close to them. "But why not just attack?"

"It could be that they didn't want to take on my family. As Nick, our guy was able to get right into the room with you and open the portal. Less bloodshed than coming in the front door and battling their way to you."

Another valid point.

A knock sounded on the door.

Dev used his powers to manifest clothes on his body at the same time he tossed a thicker cover over her. "Come in."

Sam was impressed with his reaction time. The man was definitely skilled in many ways.

The door opened to show them a Charonte carrying a large tray of food. "Xedrix thought you might be hungry."

Sam smiled up at Dev. "I don't know about you, but I worked up quite an appetite."

Grinning, Dev got out of bed to take the tray. Just as he reached it, the Charonte flung the tray at him and used it to drive him back into the wall. Dev head-butted him, but it didn't faze the demon. He grabbed Dev by the hair and took a bite out of his neck so deep, it literally ripped him open.

Dev staggered back as blood poured down his shirt so fast, he knew he wouldn't have long before he bled out. Stumbling away, he manifested a towel and tried to seal the wound.

Even though she was still naked, Sam came off the bed and scissor-kicked the demon while Dev struggled to stay conscious. She wasn't about to let him get hurt any worse. Not if she could help it.

Dev used his powers to quickly dress her in a pair of jeans, boots, and a T-shirt. While he appreciated her being naked, he knew she wouldn't prefer it. Though he definitely appreciated her putting his life before her modesty.

Why the hell can't I get this wound to stop bleeding? It was like there was a spell on it to guarantee he wasn't going to survive it.

The Charonte lunged for her.

Sam caught it by the chin and drove her fist into its windpipe three times in fast succession. Coughing, the demon staggered away. Sam pursued it, punching and avoiding its bites with everything she had as she whaled on it like a pro.

Dev was impressed by her abilities, but it was time to stop this while he could. He went to rejoin the fight and tear the head off its shoulders.

No damn demon kills me and lives. If he was going to go down, he was taking the Charonte to hell with him.

Laughing, the Charonte lifted Dev up with one hand and flung him into the wall, five feet off the floor, then it turned on Sam and wrapped itself around her body. One moment she was fighting. The next, she and the demon were gone.

Dev lay in a bloody heap on the floor, horrified and stunned by what had happened.

The demon had ripped her right out of their existence.

Chapter 12

At Dev's call, Ethon came running into the room with Chi and two more Dogs one step behind him. Dev was still trying to stave off his bleeding and failing miserably at it. Unlike the Dark-Hunters, he wasn't immortal, and if he didn't get control of this soon, he would die.

The first one to reach him was El Escorpión, so named for the black daggers he'd been using since the Middle Ages when he'd become a Dark-Hunter that had scorpions engraved down the blades and on the hilts. No one knew what his real name was and most referred to him simply as Scorpio. The only thing about his past that he'd cop to was that he'd been a knight in medieval Spain—he wouldn't even verify what century. That was if and when you could get him to speak—something that happened about as often as a Mac product going on sale.

Scorpio knelt beside Dev so that he could examine the wound.

Realizing there was no immediate threat, Kalidas retracted the spike on his arm into his black leather armband. At six foot five, Kali was taller than the average Indian male and rumored to have once been an ancient prince during the Classical Period of India. It was something Kali would neither confirm nor deny. But the way the two of them fought, it was hard to believe anyone had been able to kill them.

Ethon turned around in the room, looking for Sam. "What happened?"

Kali's tone was as dry as his expression. "Obviously, something was hungry and bit the bear."

Ethon flipped him off.

Dev ignored their animosity toward each other. "A demon grabbed Sam and took off with her. They were here one second and gone the next."

Chi joined Scorpio on the floor next to Dev. She cringed as she saw his bite. "Oh, that's nasty."

Scorpio didn't comment. Covering the wound with his hand, he locked gazes with Dev. "Take a deep breath, Bear."

The moment he tried, Dev let out a foul curse. Scorpio's touch singed his skin like nobody's business. It felt like the Dark-Hunter was shooting electricity through him—something impossible since Dev was still in human form and not out of control changing back and forth between human and bear. But that was the only thing he could liken it to. The good news, though, was that it stopped the bleeding and sealed the wound better than if Scorpio had cauterized it.

Dev created a damp towel to clean up the mess. "Thanks."

Scorpio inclined his head to him.

Ethon was busy looking over the remains of the food and where they'd fought as if trying to re-create the fight in his head. "What kind of demon was it?"

Dev grimaced as he pulled the towel back and saw how much blood he'd lost. "A Charonte. But I'm thinking it must have been the same person who was pretending to be Nick earlier."

That got Kali's attention. "A shapeshifter?"

"Yeah, but not a Were-Hunter. Maybe a demon of some kind? Demigod? I have no idea. All I know is he knew how to fight and he snatched her out of here with an ease that pisses me off."

Ethon growled. "I'll notify Acheron."

Scorpio held his hand out to Dev and helped him to his feet, then mumbled in Spanish. He wasn't sure, but it sounded vaguely like bad mojo.

Dev changed his clothes into something a little less bloody as Chi seemed to fall into some kind of odd trance. He started to ask about it, but the Dogs acted like it was normal for her and since Dev didn't really know her well enough to judge, he ignored it too.

Kali pulled out his phone and after a few seconds, he cursed. "I can't track her."

A tic worked in Ethon's jaw. "Whatever has her will be blocking us. Damn shame none of us has a power that can track."

Dev gave him a droll stare. Didn't the Spartan know anything about Were-Hunters? "I do."

The skepticism on his face was irritating. "How?"

"I'm part animal." Dumbass—For the sake of peace and the fact that getting to Sam was more important than

179

fighting with Ethon, Dev only said that word silently in his head. Though to be fair, Ethon probably hadn't been around enough Were-Hunters to know what they were capable of. "I can track like a bloodhound."

But as he tried, he realized that his powers didn't work after all.

How could that be? Were-Hunters could track across five dimensions and there was no way she'd be in the sixth....

And it wasn't like her scent wasn't embedded in his senses. Yet there was no trace whatsoever that she was anywhere at all.

"Well?" Ethon asked in a less than impressed tone. "What's your super smeller telling you, Gus?"

He gave the Dark-Hunter an evil glower. "Stop with the *Psych* reference, asshole. Remember, I am one of the few species who can rip you limb from limb."

Ethon scoffed. "Do I look intimidated by you, rug?"

"You two stop!" Chi snapped as she came out of her weirdness. "We have a major problem here. Sam wasn't taken by a Daimon or a Charonte. It was one of the empusae who took her."

"Ah now, that's just wrong." Kali shook his head.

Ethon and Dev cursed simultaneously. The empusae were a rare breed of shapeshifting Greek demons capable of all manner of cruelty. But the one they were most known for was draining the blood from their victims, victims they could enslave and control. They were the original Greek demons who'd started the vampire legends.

And they were often mistaken for Daimons by those who didn't know the difference. The main things that set

180

them apart were that the empusae could walk in daylight and they weren't cursed to die at twenty-seven. Most of all, Dark-Hunter blood wasn't poisonous to them.

If one of them had Sam . . .

It could get ugly fast. The empusae were demigods and far more powerful than either the Dark-Hunters or the Daimons. No wonder Dev hadn't been able to track it. It *would* be in the sixth dimension.

Shit.

Chi jerked her chin toward Dev. "Call Fang and see if he can use his Hellchaser powers to track our demon." She looked at Ethon, Scorpio, and Kali. "You guys, go downstairs and sharpen your knives and look intimidating."

Ethon scowled. "Any particular reason for that?"

"It'll keep you out of my hair and off my nerves until we can catch her trail. Now go. We have to find Sam before this thing kills her."

SAM WANTED TO fight the beast that held her as he carried her down a dark alley in the Art District. But she couldn't. The moment he'd taken her into his arms, he'd locked gazes with her and something inside her had snapped and broken. She'd gone completely numb. Every muscle in her body was limp and worthless. It was a struggle just to breathe. In her mind, she saw the people he'd killed. Heard them screaming and begging for their lives while he'd laughed at their pain.

He was insane. He didn't care who he hurt or why. All he wanted was to feel the power he had over them as he made them suffer.

The demon laughed. "That's right, bitch. I own you and I'm going to torture you in so many ways you will know ultimate suffering for the rest of eternity."

The Amazon inside her screamed out, wanting to fight. But her body absolutely refused to cooperate. She was at his mercy and he hated her with an unfathomable depth.

What had she done to make him feel that way? She tried to sort through his memories to find the answer, but if there was one, he had it buried deep. So deep that trying to get to it was giving her a vicious headache.

"Lazaros!"

The demon turned to the right at the call. Deep in the shadows was what appeared to be a man's outline.

"Let her go." Not a shout, but a quiet, powerful demand that carried an undercurrent that said if Lazaros didn't obey, he would regret it.

Lazaros sneered at the shadow he deemed nothing more worrisome than a pebble in his shoe. "You don't give me orders, *imisysmorfi*."

Sam sucked her breath in at the ancient insult that meant the man was malformed or half-witted. Though the literal translation wasn't as foul as the meaning behind the word. In her time, men had killed each other over it. For the demon's sake, she hoped the man wasn't an ancient Greek. Otherwise there would be bloodletting aplenty.

The shadow vanished, then reappeared right behind them. "Boo."

Lazaros dropped her straight down and turned to fight. Ow! Big ow! She hit the ground so hard, it knocked the breath out of her. She would definitely feel that tomorrow.

If she didn't die tonight.

And it was yet another reason why she wanted to kill the bastard scum. If only she could move. Meanwhile the shadow and the demon tore into each other with a venom the Furies would envy. But at least they weren't stepping on her.

Yet.

Sam was still under his control, and honestly, she was getting tired of it. She wanted to fight, not lie in the street like a worthless lump. With every piece of iron will she had, she tried to inch away from them as they went at each other like Titans after Zeus. It was impressive and made her really want to take them down. The shadow cut and dodged, and hit the demon with enough power that it lifted him almost ten feet off the ground.

Don't pay attention to them. If she could just crawl into the alley next to her, she might be able to get free while the demon was distracted.

Come on, body, don't fail me now. You can do it.

But that was easier said than done. What had the demon done to her that she was so helpless? Worse, that feeling of being powerless was eking away at her Dark-Hunter powers as memories of her death surged.

Stay calm, Sam. Focus.

If only she could . . .

Another shadow fell over her.

Sam cringed as someone rolled her over, onto her back. She looked up and met the face of a perfect blond angel. Skinny as a rail and yet muscular, the woman should have been an Amazon. But the eeriest part was her eyes—dark brown with ribbons of bright yellow twisting through the iris.

Was she another demon?

She angled Sam's head until their gazes locked. Something inside Sam snapped like a pane of glass. One moment she was basically paralyzed. The next, she was free of whatever the demon had done to her.

Her blood rushing through her, Sam flipped up onto her feet and started for the demon only to have the woman grab her by the waist and stop her. "Cael has him."

Yeah, right. Like she was going to let this go after what he'd done to her? "Oh, like hell. This is a grudge match."

"More than you know, Sam. Stay back."

How did she know her name? That shock kept her still as Amaranda's past went through her. She saw Amaranda as a little girl in Seattle growing up in her family's business, playing with her sister. But what floored Sam wasn't Amaranda's family.

It was the fact that the woman was a Daimon. . . .

And something more.

Something . . .

Sam tried to delve deeper into that, but Amaranda released her before she could get any more details from her. Lazaros turned toward them and realized she was on her feet. He ran for her then, but Cael grabbed him from behind and tackled him straight to the ground.

Lazaros tried to bite Cael, who quickly dodged him. "Don't need a DNA sample. Thanks for the offer though." He punched Lazaros hard in the side.

Howling, Lazaros hissed at Cael, then vanished into a foul-smelling cloud of sulphur.

"Gah! What did you eat?" Cael snarled. He fanned the cloud as he jumped back trying to escape it. "Coward!

Get your ass back here and fight like a demon, you sniveling waste of a scary monster. C'mon, who trained you? Casper?"

The woman next to Sam laughed. "Quit taunting the weak, love. It's pointless."

Cael flashed a grin at her. "Yeah, but did I impress you with my fighting prowess?"

"You always impress me with your fighting prowess, baby. Ain't nobody better." Those words were said in an almost mocking tone.

Cael walked toward them with the deadly lope of a predator. His hair was a riot of loose black curls that framed a face chiseled out of stone. He was stunningly handsome. And one arm was covered with an intricate tribal tattoo.

Ignoring Sam, he slid up to the woman and pulled her into his arms to give her a kiss that was so hot, Sam felt awkward watching it. The two of them kissed like they hadn't seen each other for years and one of them had a terminal disease that would claim them in less than a minute. Any second she expected clothes to go flying.

Okay . . .

Sam stepped away from them. "Tell you what. You two get a room. I'm going back to—"

"No!" Cael pulled back from his kiss and grabbed her arm to keep her from leaving. "You can't go back there."

She shrugged his touch away but not before she saw a glimpse of him with Acheron. . . . a glimpse that told her he was a Dark-Hunter.

With those demonic eyes?

Something was wrong. None of this made sense. None of it.

And she wasn't going to stick around to sort it out. "Stop me, asshole."

That cockiness died as she took a step away from them and something hit her hard in the chest.

With a gasp, she crumpled to the street.

SAM WOKE UP with her head splitting sideways. Front ways. All ways. Never in her life had she hurt so badly. She actually felt nauseated from the pain.

What had caused . . .

Suddenly, she remembered the demon taking her and then the weird couple who had "rescued" her. Anger and panic mixed as she opened her eyes to find herself alone in a small room. It strangely reminded her of something out of the Victorian era. What? Did all demons like that time period? The beige walls were stenciled with a dark brown scroll print and the bed she lay upon was Gothic black wrought iron. The headboard and footboard reminded her of spiraled cathedral windows.

Ah gah, I'm trapped in the Victorian Trading Company catalog. Not that their stuff wasn't beautiful, it just wasn't her cup of tea. And right now, she really wanted to know what was going on.

Danger didn't seem imminent, but then she'd been kidnapped, which tended to make her think she wasn't as safe as she appeared. She moved from the bed and realized someone had put her in a short pink gown.

Yeah, this was getting creepy and it was made creepier by the fact that she wasn't getting any vibes from the clothes or anything else. For that matter, she hadn't dreamed of other people.

It was like being with Dev, only without the warm comfort of his touch.

She went to the door and quickly learned it didn't have a doorknob. There was no way to open it.

Sam turned around slowly, looking for a window or some other means to leave, but there wasn't one. She was trapped here. Alone. There wasn't even a cockroach sending thoughts to her.

"Hello?"

Big surprise, no one answered. Oh, how she didn't like this.

Okay, girl. Don't panic. Not that she was particularly prone to panic, but . . . She wasn't used to being locked in rooms that looked like they'd been taken off a Hammer movie set either.

Great. I've been captured by Boris Karloff.

A low sinister laugh whispered in her ears. "I'm not exactly Boris and he's not the actor you're thinking about anyway. That would be Peter Cushing. Never dawned on me before that they favored, but I'll give you that. However I do have one thing in common with both—"

"You abduct women?"

"Not as a rule, but I do tend to creep people out. At least those who have common sense."

She turned around trying to locate a source for the voice. It seemed to be all around her and again, she picked up nothing from him. How could this keep happening?

Be careful what you wish for, you just might get it.

Because right now, she wanted that power back in the worst sort of way. It was only now that she understood just what a blessing it'd always been. She always knew where she stood with other people. Always knew what they were thinking and what kind of person they were.

Now . . . nada.

Yeah, bring me back my weirdness.

"Who are you?" she tried again.

He tsked at her in that deep, provocative tone that sent a shiver over her. "You don't really care about my name, sugar. You want to know why you're here."

"Yes, yes I do." She moved around the room and his voice followed her. Was he a ghost?

Or a figment of her imagination?

"I'm here to keep you safe."

Why didn't she believe that? Oh wait, because she was a prisoner being held by a man who didn't even have the guts to show his face. She pulled a finial off the bed—that should serve to put a pack in her punch if she had to fight her way out of here. And yet again, nothing came to her from the cold metal.

"Then let me go."

He laughed. "Are we really going to have this conversation? If I were going to let you go, you wouldn't be here. That would suck for both of us. So just make yourself comfortable, Dark-Hunter. You're going to be here for a while."

She felt the presence leave. *Oh, this is great.* She was trapped in a fluffy, frothy hell and there was no exit in sight. *At least you're not pulling images or emotions from the stuff in here.*

Yeah, but for once, she needed to. She had to know what she was dealing with.

188

Closing her eyes, she summoned her powers from deep within and tried to find out who and what held her hostage.

At first there was nothing. Not even a trace. Then a thick fog swirled until she began to see images through it.

In the back of her mind, she saw a gorgeous man with dark blond hair and perfect features. Dressed in medieval armor, he led an army that appeared to have been forged from hell itself. At full speed, with his bloodred pennant rippling in the wind, he raced down a hill and straight into the heart of his enemy to battle them.

Only his enemy wasn't human. It was a legion of demons who were bent on his total annihilation. They tore at him and pulled him off his demon horse, which reared, slashing at them with its black hooves that sent their blood spurting like in a Quentin Tarantino film. Still, even wounded and on foot, he fought them with a rage that would have made him a Dog of War had he been a Dark-Hunter.

He let loose a fierce battle cry as he cut his way through their number, slashing and hacking with his sword. He was a warrior without rival. . . .

Sam pulled back. Why was she seeing that demon knight? Was he the voice she'd heard?

If he *was* her captor, she was thoroughly screwed. Defeating a man like that would not be easy. If even possible.

Then suddenly the image was gone. She tried to call it back to further understand who and what she'd seen, but it didn't work.

Instead her vision turned to another blond. . . .

Dev. She saw him as a young man with two older men who could have almost passed for his twins. By their clothes, she knew it had to be the late Georgian period. There were the three men and one bear cub hunkered down in the stall of some barn. It was pitch-black and the horses around them were going wild as they tried to escape.

Dev's long hair had begun to come loose from his queue and hung in unruly curls around his teenaged face. His black vest was missing two buttons and there was red blood smeared on his white shirt. "I can fight the Arcadians."

The older bear shook his head. "You're too young, Devereaux. We need you to get Aimee to Papa and Maman. She is our only female. You know she has to survive. We can't let anything happen to her."

"But—"

Gilbert grabbed him by the scruff of his neck and shook him hard. "Don't argue with me. We're depending on you, *mon frère*. Don't let us down."

Dev scooped up the cub, who whined in protest. She was too young to be teleported with their powers. They couldn't use them on her without the risk of killing her. Solid black, she was huge in Dev's arms as he cradled her to his chest.

Gilbert buried his face in the cub's fur. "Stay safe, *ma petite*." He kissed her on the ear.

Bastien stood up and it was then Sam realized he was the twin brother of Zar . . . the father to Yessy and Josie. Poor Dev, to have stared into the face of the brother he'd lost. . . .

And poor Nicolette.

"I'll draw their fire." Bastien glanced down to Aimee and Dev. *"Bonne chance. Je t'aime."* Good luck. I love you.

Then he was gone so fast Dev couldn't even say good-bye. A heartbeat later, Dev heard the sound of gunfire. He clutched Aimee harder as fear ate at his insides.

Please don't be dead. . . .

"Go!" Gilbert snapped.

Dev didn't want to. He knew the human-Arcadian bears would kill both of his brothers. That he'd never see them again. His heart shattered as he was torn between the loyalty he had for his sister and that he had for his brothers.

How could he choose between them?

They'd only come here this afternoon to pick black-berries and let Aimee roam away from humans while his brothers had helped him train and hone his magick. It was supposed to be a perfect, happy afternoon. And it had ended when the Arcadians had come for Gilbert.

Not because he'd done them wrong.

Because he'd been mated by the Fates to the Arcadian bears' sister. They wanted Gilbert killed before he completed the ceremony so that their sister wouldn't be forced to lie down with an animal Kattagari.

For that, Bastien and Gilbert would die. And the worst part was that Bastien was an Arcadian too. Those bastards were about to commit murder even in the eyes of the Omegrion.

And they didn't even care. So long as they took out Gilbert, the rest of them were simply collateral damage. Animals to be slaughtered.

191

If Dev told them he was an Arcadian, they would spare him because he was one of them. But not his sister. The Arcadians would kill Aimee too and use her fur for boots. Gods, it was so unfair.

He heard Bastien cry out—a cry that was cut short to a silence so foul it tore through him. An instant later, the Arcadians cheered. "Is it the right animal?"

"No. It must still be inside."

Gilbert gripped Dev's shoulder. "You must go now. Protect Aimee for us."

Dev nodded as his brother stood up and slipped from the stall to turn into a bear—Gilbert's weakest fighting form, but it would distract the Arcadians and give Dev more time to escape. The Arcadians knew there were four of them. Once they killed Gilbert, they'd seek out him and Aimee.

I have to go.

Tears flowed down his cheeks as he buried his face in Aimee's fur. Holding her close, he slipped out the back while Gilbert fought their enemies. It was so cold outside.

He heard more gunshots and then a loud shout of jubilation from the Arcadians.

Gilbert was dead. . . .

The Arcadians cursed as they realized Gilbert was human and that they had just committed a murder that would cost them their lives. "Find the other two. We have to kill them before they tell what we've done."

Aimee let out a baleful cry.

Dev held her close as he covered her mouth with his hand to muffle her wail. "I've got you, Aimee. I'm not going to let anyone hurt you. I swear. I'll never let anyone hurt you." And with that vow, he slipped out the back and into the trees that surrounded the farm where they'd taken temporary refuge.

It took him an entire night to make it back to the small house in London his family called home. He was completely exhausted. Weak. His wounds were bleeding profusely.

But Aimee was unharmed.

The moment he opened the door, his mother was there in her gown and bathrobe. Beautiful and blond, she was a study of grace as she looked past his shoulder, into the dawning sky. "*Mon Dieu,* Devereaux! Where have you been? Have you any idea of the hour? We've been trying to track you and . . ." She paused as he came in and locked the door. The panic in her eyes tore through him. "Where's Gilbert and Bastien?"

Dev choked on the words he didn't want to utter. He'd used his powers to mask his scent so that the Arcadians wouldn't be able to track him. He'd never thought about the fact that his parents wouldn't have been able to do so either.

His mother moved past him to look out the door. "Are they in tending horses? What keeps them?"

Dev laid his sister's sleeping body down before he turned to face her. "They're dead, Maman."

The look on her face emblazoned itself on his heart. It was a look of pure agony . . . a look Sam knew far better than she'd ever wanted to.

All the color drained from Nicolette's cheeks. "What?"

"We were attacked and—"

She slapped him hard across his face. "You left them to die?"

Dev wiped his hand across his mouth, smearing the blood that ran from his busted lip and nose. "I protected Aimee."

Nicolette screamed out, waking up the rest of the house. Aimee went running to hide under the table while their mother seized Dev by his shirt and shoved him back against the wall. "You're the one who wanted to go. You lured them there."

"No, Maman. I would never have gone had I known."

Still she screamed at him, accusing him of leaving them to die while he ran like a coward.

"Nicolette!" his father snapped as he pulled her away from Dev. "What's happened?"

"My sons are dead." She gestured to Dev. "That mongrel bastard ran and left them there to die." She sneered at Dev. "You worthless human! I wish it'd been you who'd died!"

Dev sucked his breath in and held it as his father picked her up and carried her out of the room. The rest of his siblings followed, wanting to comfort their mother. They left Dev there shattered as her words echoed in his ears.

"I wish it'd been you who'd died."

It should have been me. It should have been me. . . . Guilt and agony ripped him apart as his tears flowed. Why had he bothered coming home? It would have been so much easier had he died with them.

Aimee came out from under the table. She licked his hand before she crawled into his lap and licked his chin. Dev held her then and let out all the pain inside him.

But it was a pain that he still carried with him and it broke Sam's heart. His mother had never really forgiven him for that night. Yes, she'd been grieving and hurting. But for the rest of her life, he'd seen the darkness in her eyes when she'd looked at him. Had heard the sharp tone in her voice that hadn't been there before.

It was why he'd tried so hard to please her and why he'd never left Sanctuary.

Aimee had been his tie that kept him there, and for his sister, he would do anything.

Sam wanted to weep for her bear. Dev was such a good man. Not that she'd doubted it, but now she knew his scars were every bit as harsh as hers. He blamed himself for their deaths and for tearing out his mother's heart. Every time he'd overheard her crying over her children had been like a knife through his soul. He believed that he'd caused it all.

It was why he'd never tried to mate. He didn't want a woman to turn on him, or worse, have her family come for his. So he'd avoided sleeping with his own kind, knowing that it was rare for a Were-Hunter to be mated to a human. Yes, it happened, but it wasn't a common occurrence and even if it did, a human would never be able to hurt them. So he'd played those odds, even though the one thing he really wanted was a family of his own. . . .

Sam swallowed the lump in her throat as she wished Dev was here for her to hug. She wanted to take his pain away from him and to tell him the one thing no one in his family had ever said. Not even the sister he'd risked his life for. The sister he'd hand carried through the darkness to make sure she was safe.

I'm so glad you survived.

She blinked back her tears, angered over the fact that she felt them. Tears were weakness.

They accomplished nothing.

"Why am I channeling his memories?" She couldn't sense them at all when she was around him. So why were they here now?

And as she contemplated that, she swore she could feel Dev with her. Feel his panic that she'd been ripped out of his arms and that he hadn't been able to stop it. Right now, he was in turmoil. Every part of him was desperate to get her back.

For that, he was willing to bust hell itself wide open if that was what it took.

Tenderness spread through her in a way it never had before. And with that warmth came an awful realization. . . .

She was falling in love with him.

I can't be.

But there was no denying the emotions inside her. It was a feeling she knew well and one that had filled her every day she'd been with Ioel.

There was no doubt in her mind. Because right now, when her life was in danger, she wasn't thinking about herself. She didn't care what they did to her. Whatever it was, she'd go down swinging. What was on her mind was the fear of what her death would do to Dev.

She didn't want to die because she had a reason to live. She didn't want to die because it would destroy her bear. . . .

"And that's why you're here."

She tensed as that disembodied male voice was back. "Excuse me?"

"You have to let Dev go."

"Why?"

"Because if you don't, it *will* get him killed."

Chapter 13

Dev paused in the doorway of Sanctuary's office. His stomach clenched as it always did whenever he walked in and saw his mother's empty desk. No one had moved anything on it. They hadn't had the heart. Even the last pen his mother had used was right where she'd laid it by the phone. It was so eerie and as long as it stayed that way, he kept expecting to see her there, looking at him over the rim of her glasses as she waited for him to say something.

He had such mixed emotions where she was concerned. He'd loved her more than anything and yet . . .

She hadn't been all that lovable. A true mother bear in every sense of the word, she'd been fierce and stern. While she could show affection—especially toward those she favored, such as Griffe, Bastien, Kyle, and Aimee—it hadn't been easy for her. She'd expected only the best out of them and she'd been real quick to let them know when they failed her. Most of all, she'd never refrained from severely punishing any of them, including her favorites, when she thought they'd screwed up or jeopardized the family.

But that wasn't why he was here and he was in a hurry. The only thing that needed to be on his mind right now was Sam.

He'd come here seeking Aimee. She sat at her desk along the wall just like she did every day when she did the paperwork. Like their mother, she could be pretty nasty when crossed or interrupted, but there was an innate kindness to her that took the edge off even her worst moods.

"Hey, babe," she said with a smile as she looked up and saw him. Somehow she'd always been able to tell him apart from his identical brothers. "How are you guys doing over at Club Charonte?"

"We were doing great until a demon broke in and snatched Sam out."

She gasped.

"Have you seen Fang? I tried to call, but it keeps going straight to voice mail." Which was what had brought him back to Sanctuary. They needed to get Fang on the demon's trail as quickly as possible.

"He's with Remi helping to unload a shipment into the freezer. You need me to help look for her?"

That explained the crappy phone reception. The steel of the freezer was so thick, not even a nuke would be able to penetrate it. "Thanks, but I'd rather you sit on the sidelines with this one. I don't want to be pulling you out of another demon realm anytime soon and I'm pretty sure Fang feels the same way."

She made a sound of petty annoyance.

As he started to leave, she stopped him. "Dev?"

"Yeah?"

"You okay?" He saw the concern on her face as she studied him. "You look . . . strange."

Strange? He felt awful. He didn't know why but he kept reliving the night his brothers had died. He was eaten up with that same helpless feeling and he hated it. He couldn't stand the thought of someone he cared about being in harm's way.

Sam's nothing to you. Not really. They were barely more than strangers.

It didn't feel that way. There was a part of her that lived inside of him even though he knew they could never be anything more than friends.

Maybe the occasional booty call.

Don't go there. Especially not with his sister looking at him. That was just creepy as hell.

"I'm fine." He'd never let Aimee know the truth. Then again, he never let anyone know his emotions. He hid them behind wisecracks and sarcasm.

It was safer that way.

Closing the door, he flashed himself to the freezer where Remi and Fang were stocking meat.

Hefting a box onto a shelf, Remi curled his lip at Dev's unexpected appearance. "It figures you'd show up after all the hard work's done. You always had an uncanny knack for that."

Dev ignored him as he walked over to where Fang was standing on a stepladder. "Fang. I need your demon expertise."

Fang pulled back from the steak boxes he was rearranging to look down at him. "For what?"

Dev gave him a "duh" stare. "Demons, obviously."

Fang flipped him off as he came down the ladder. "Why do I live here with you people again?"

Remi snorted. "'Cause you love our sister and she won't leave. Believe me, I know. I've been trying to run her off for years."

Fang shook his head at him as he turned back to Dev. "What's going on?"

"One of the empusae took Sam and we can't find her. I need you to tell me where to look."

Fang let out a low whistle. "An empusa isn't an easy thing to track. Are you sure that's what got her?"

"That's what Chi said."

"She would know." Fang scratched his chin. "Damn. This isn't good. Give me a minute to consult with my people and I'll get back to you."

"Could you kind of rush it? I have a bad feeling that the empusa who took her is the same one who came here disguised as Nick. If I'm right, then he's working with Stryker, and if he is, you can bet Sam's not being treated well at Hotel Daimon Central."

LAZAROS ROARED THROUGH Kalosis in his dragon form. Fury burned deep inside him as he used his powers to find Stryker, who was alone in his study in the main hall. He flew at the building's wall without slowing. Right as he would have slammed into it, he used his powers to go through it.

The Daimon lord arched a brow as Lazaros manifested in his true demon form in front of his ornately carved desk. But other than that, he had no real reaction.

Because Lazaros, like all of the empusae who were descended from the goddess Empusa, Lazaros only had one leg in his demon form. But one leg was all he needed to kick the ass of his enemies.

And right now he wanted to drive his foot straight up Stryker's sphincter. "Why didn't you tell me Nick Gautier was the Malachai?"

Stryker let out a long-suffering sigh as he cupped his head in his hands and leaned back in his padded black leather chair. "What is it with all of you pansies that *that* one word sends you to me with your tail tucked between your legs whining about how you pissed your pants because you saw him? Yes, he's the Malachai, so la di fucking da what?"

Lazaros moved to blast him.

Stryker caught the blast and sent it back to him tenfold with a counterblast so powerful it pinned the demon to the wall above his marble fireplace. He squeezed the power down, letting the demon squirm in agony. "Gautier isn't the only one with talents. You'd do well to remember that I, too, have the powers of a god. And I'm really not afraid to use them."

Lazaros bellowed in rage.

"Oh shut up." Stryker used his powers to muzzle him.

At least as much as he could. The demon still grunted and growled like a caged animal.

Stryker let out a frustrated breath as he lowered the demon to the floor. "I sent you to Gautier because I knew he'd be easy to manipulate right now. His powers are growing, but still nothing compared to ours. If you weren't such an idiot, you'd have been able to possess him like I wanted and turn the others against him."

He needed Nick on the run.

But that was the backup plan in case his primary one failed. Which it better not do.

And right now, he wanted Samia.

He glared at Lazaros. "If I release you, can you be an adult demon for five seconds?"

Lazaros returned the glare with an angry scowl.

"Didn't think so, but I'm going to remove your gag anyway, 'cause that's just the kind of guy I am. Don't make me regret it. If you do, I won't gag you next time. I'll decapitate you."

Lazaros took a step forward, then wisely checked his stupidity. "You're such an asshole!"

"Goes with the whole King of the Badasses. Kind of hard to lead an army of the damned if I'm the King of Nice."

Lazaros glowered at him.

"Oh, stop wasting my time with those pathetic looks. And speaking of, what cheesy excuse do I get for why Samia isn't with you this time?"

"I was attacked on the street by something I've never seen before."

Stryker scoffed. "They're called mosquitoes. I know they're rather large in New Orleans but—"

"Stop with the sarcasm. It was a demon mixed with the powers of a Dark-Hunter and a Daimon. What kind of Frankenmonster have you created?"

Stryker froze as that rang a very unfond bell. A bell that had managed to fall off the grid for quite a few years. Nice to know it'd finally resurfaced. "Cael?"

"Yeah. That's what the other woman called him."

"Sonofa ..." Stryker paced his office as his mind whirled with the new information. Cael's wife, Amaranda, had been an Apollite in Seattle. He still wasn't sure how a clan of Apollites had come to not only house, but protect a Dark-Hunter, yet they had. A few years ago an attack on them had left Cael and his bride being converted to Daimons.

No one had heard anything from them since.

Why were they here? Why now? Had they discovered his trick with the demon blood? Or was something else keeping them alive? He couldn't imagine a Dark-Hunter taking a human life even for pure survival reasons....

Perhaps the demon essence Lazaros had sensed inside them was the same trick he and his army were now using to empower their Daimon existence. What would that blood do to a Dark-Hunter?

It was a most intriguing possibility.

"Did he say anything to you?" Stryker asked him.

"Basically he told me to die quietly. Kind of like *you*."

Stryker grimaced at the fear he heard in Lazaros's tone. This couldn't be good. Not for them. He refused to believe it was a coincidence. He didn't believe in those.

Everything happened for a reason. Everything. Which made him wonder if Cael had known Stryker would send Lazaros for Samia. Or was Cael one of her protectors too?

He narrowed his speculative gaze on the demon. "Did you tell them anything?"

By the look on Lazaros's face it was obvious the demon wanted to leave his guts on the floor. Too bad he lacked the skills or the courage to try. Stryker was always up for a good fight. "Of course not."

"Good." He didn't have to kill the bastard after all. "Now be an obedient little demon. Go away and let me think."

Lazaros stepped toward the door, then stopped. "I'm not done with her, Stryker. She killed my family and now that you've freed me, I won't rest until I hold her heart in my fist."

That was why Stryker had descended into his grunduncle Hades's domain. Once he'd investigated Samia's past, he'd uncovered the origins of her sister's pact and the demon she'd made it with. Stupid Samia had assumed it was Daimons who'd killed her husband and child.

It wasn't.

Daimons couldn't make deals of that nature. Only the gods and demigods could, and Samia was lucky Artemis had covered for her after Sam had slaughtered Lazaros's brother. But for that one rare act of altruism on Artemis's part, Samia would have been killed immediately. Instead, Artemis had locked Lazaros in Tartarus to keep him away from her pet Amazon warrior.

Now Stryker held the key to the demon demigod's existence.

"Fine. Just make sure you pull her to me before you kill her. My needs take precedence over yours and if you fail me in this, I swear what I do to you will make Prometheus's punishment look like a joyride at the beach."

Samia was his key to killing his father and owning the world. Nothing was going to stop him this time.

FANG FLASHED THEM into a wickedly dark corridor. But for Dev's honed vision, he'd be blind. He put his hand on Dev's shoulder to keep him from walking on. "Remember, Bear, let me do the talking. You don't speak unless Thorn asks you something."

Dev shrugged his touch away. He didn't know who Thorn was—Fang had refused to elaborate. Honestly, he didn't care. All that mattered was the fact that this ... person had pulled Sam into custody and that alone warranted his death. "I don't play this cryptic shit, Wolf."

"And I don't want to clean up your entrails. Nor do I want to tell Aimee her beloved older brother was splintered on the floor. Comprende?"

"Got it."

"I don't think you do. Thorn is evil incarnate. Think Savitar on steroids."

That managed to give Dev pause. Savitar oversaw the Omegrion council that all Were-Hunters answered to. No one knew who or what he was. Only that he was about as close to omnipotent as a being could get and anyone who crossed him didn't live long enough to regret it.

In fact, Savitar had extinguished one entire Were-Hunter species when they'd dabbled in something that irritated him. Since then, everyone tried to give him a wide berth.

"Got it. Thorn rules here. Keep my mouth shut."

Inclining his head to him, Fang stepped away to lead him down that dark, eerie hallway that seemed to stretch on forever. There was no light at all. Yet Fang navigated the hall like a pro. It wasn't until they approached a door that Dev could see the firelight dancing through the crack at the bottom.

Dev still wasn't sure where *here* was. One minute they'd been in the freezer while Fang "talked" to his people, and the next Fang had teleported him into some lightless void that reminded him of the Nether Realm.

Or a bad *Night Gallery* episode.

Yet it wasn't that either. This was almost like a vacuum . . . like space without stars.

Pulling him to a stop, Fang knocked on the door. The sound echoed around them. A heartbeat later, a light came out of the ceiling to illuminate the door so that Dev could see the medieval construction that even had rivets around the outer side of the door. The steel at eye level swirled and formed the face of a demon woman complete with fangs and blazing red eyes.

She scanned them before she spoke. "The master is busy."

Fang didn't hesitate. "I need to see him."

She hissed, baring her fangs.

"Let me pass, Shara. I wouldn't be here if it wasn't important."

She tsked at him. "You're brave, Wolf. Very brave. Or perhaps stupid is a better term. Of all beings who serve here, you should know better." She melted back into the door.

"Who is she?" Dev asked Fang.

Before he could answer, the door opened slowly on a well-oiled hinge that made not even a whisper of a sound.

Light spilled into the hall, hurting his eyes until they adjusted.

The demon was now a beautiful, slender woman around the age of twenty-two. With pointed ears and short black hair, she was dressed in a sheer red sheath that left every part of her body exposed to them.

Licking her lips, she gave Dev a hot once-over that left him strangely cold. He wasn't interested in any woman right now, except a certain Amazon.

She closed the door and led them from the small spartan antechamber into a dark room where ancient weapons hung as decoration on the walls. Swords, axes, spears . . . Some others that Dev couldn't identify. There was a huge, ornately carved desk in one corner with an overstuffed chair. The carvings were so intricate that it looked like the gargoyles on it would come to life any second and attack.

Fang led him to a single chair . . . or throne would be a more appropriate term. Like the desk, it was huge and carved with the heads of dragons. As they drew nearer, the carvings opened their eyes to show yellow and red pupils that focused on them with interest.

One of the dragons let loose a belch of fire, stopping Fang from getting any closer.

Dev frowned at the man who sat there. Impeccably dressed in a black silk and wool suit, he'd left the top button of his black shirt open. Dev saw a hint of a scar that ran across his collarbone where it appeared someone had once tried to cut his throat.

His features were so perfect, he would have looked feminine but for the lethal aura of I'm-planning-on-picking-my-teeth-with-your-spine. He narrowed a cold dark stare on Fang, then shifted it to Dev. "You can't have her."

"Excuse me?" Dev asked in an offended tone.

He swept a dismissive gaze over Dev. "If I let you have Samia, Lazaros will kill her. Painfully. Believe me, I'm doing both of you a favor by keeping her here."

Dev shook his head. "I can protect her."

"And you're doing such an admirable job of it too. If I were Samia, I'd be tickled pink by your care." That tone was so patronizing that it took all of Dev's control not to go for his throat.

Thorn ignored Dev's anger as he continued speaking. "Arrogance . . . how I love the sound of rampant stupidity after a long, dreary day." He held his goblet up and the female demon came forward to fill it with something that looked more like blood than wine. "Tell your bear, Wolf, that he's not equipped to deal with our enemies."

"I tried, Thorn. He won't listen."

"Pity they never do. At least not until it's too late to do anything more than scrape up their remains." Thorn sipped his drink as his eyes changed from a freakish luminescent green to a bright yellow which matched some of the dragon eyes that continued to stare at them. "You know the problem with seeing the future?"

"You run out of enough banks to hold all your lottery winnings?"

Thorn gave a short, dry laugh at Dev's sarcasm even as Fang sucked his breath in sharply and gave him a warning glare. "You can't circumvent free will. *That* is the curse of your existence."

Dev put his hands on his hips. "Funny, I always thought of free will as a gift."

"*You* would. Just goes to show exactly how naive you are."

Naive maybe, but right now this asshole was really starting to piss him off with his B-grade movie theatrics and warnings. It was all he could do not to leap at his throat.

As if sensing his intent, Fang put a hand on his shoulder to remind him that reserve was the key to getting what he wanted out of Thorn. If he was like Savitar, overt aggression might get Sam killed.

For her and her alone, he'd corral his temper.

Fang cleared his throat. "You once told me that there's more than one kind of death."

Thorn savored a deep draught before he answered. "There is indeed."

"Then what kind of death will they have?"

One corner of Thorn's mouth quirked up. "You know I can't answer that, Wolf. Well . . . I could, but it might change things and that might suck. Might not, but who am I to tamper with such odds?" He looked over his shoulder. "Shara? Be a dear and fetch our latest two guests here at the Hotel California."

"You can check out anytime you like, but you can never leave. . . ." The reference to the old seventies Eagles song wasn't lost on Dev.

What is his deal? Dev mouthed to Fang.

Fang's eyes widened in warning for him to behave— something that was virtually impossible for someone who lived to irritate others.

Thorn rose to his feet.

Dev stepped back, not out of fear, but awe. There was a solid aura about him that was ancient and lethal. Something that said, in spite of his impeccable manners and speech, he was much more at home slashing throats than chatting. And for some reason, Dev had an image of him engulfed by flames.

Thorn glanced to Dev. "Forgive my rudeness. I'd offer you both something to drink, but trust me, you don't want any of what I have. Ever."

Okay . . . Nice boss, Fang. This guy was not Acheron. He was spooky as shit and definitely out to lunch. Dev had never thought he'd ever meet someone who could make Savitar or Ash appear normal, but Thorn . . .

Gods help them if the two of them ever combined forces.

And it made him wonder what Thorn might have done with Sam. Was she safe?

I haven't harmed her. Scout's honor.

He tensed at the sound of Thorn's voice in his head. He locked gazes to find a knowing look on Thorn's face.

Yes, Bear, I hear all, and Sam is quite safe.

Dev ground his teeth, reminding himself to keep his thoughts on the weather and not the freaky power of Thorn.

A few seconds later, Shara returned with . . . Dev wasn't sure what the two of them were. On first impression, they appeared to be Daimons, but he was picking up on something else. Another layer of powers that made no sense whatsoever.

Thorn indicated them with his goblet. "Amaranda. Cael. Meet Fang, who is one of your colleagues, and his brother-in-law Dev."

Amaranda was a stunning creature. In a pale pink summer dress, her tawny skin belied her nocturnal race. And with a feral aura that would give Thorn's a run for his money, Cael was dressed in a black vest with no shirt underneath and a pair of ragged jeans.

Dev's gaze went straight to the bow-and-arrow mark on Cael's exposed hip. "You're a Dark-Hunter?"

Cael flashed him a fanged grin. "Sort of."

Uh-huh ... Dev narrowed his gaze on him as all of his defenses ran into high gear. "What's *sort of* a Dark-Hunter?"

Thorn gave an evil laugh before he explained. "A Dark-Hunter who foolishly falls in love with an Apollite who turns him into a Daimon to save his life." He turned to Fang. "See why I tried to tell you love is far more sinister than anything I could ever do? I'm convinced it's why Acheron's wedding ring is black with skulls and crossbones on it." He paused to give Fang a pointed stare. "But you didn't listen to me either." He indicated Amaranda and Cael with a jerk of his chin. "I couldn't stand to see such warriors wasted so I took them under my wing."

Dev had a feeling that being taken under Thorn's wing was only slightly better than being run down by a Mack truck. And then backed up over just for good measure. "How so?"

"He saved us," Amaranda said. "We were on the run from my people and Cael's."

Dev gave her a droll stare. "Ya think? You live on human souls and people tend to get a little pissed off about it. Damn rotten bastards. Can't imagine why that would be a bad thing."

Cael tensed as if he wanted to slug Dev for daring to use sarcasm against his woman. "Actually we don't touch humans and never have. We feed on corrupt demons. They're much more palatable to all involved. Less calories. More filling."

Oh . . . now he felt stupid. Cael was right. No one could fault him for that meal.

"So they're Hellchasers like me?" Fang asked Thorn.

Thorn saluted him with his goblet before he handed it over to Shara to dispose of.

Fang exchanged a puzzled frown with Dev. "But why are they here?"

Thorn tsked. "You're asking things that are above your pay grade, Wolf. Stand down and don't worry about it. All you need to know is that they're your playmates. Share the sandbox or get spanked for it."

Yeah, there was an image Dev could have done without. Where was a gallon of eye bleach when you needed it?

But that still left Dev completely confused. "How can Cael serve both Artemis *and* you?"

Thorn scoffed. "Artemis doesn't care one way or another, especially now."

Dev was surprised by his cavalier attitude. The goddess could be extremely ruthless when crossed. "What do you mean?"

Thorn patted him on the shoulder. "Do you want to continue discussing them or would you rather talk about *your* girlfriend and her future well-being?"

"Sam's not my girlfriend."

"My mistake then." Thorn stepped back. "I will release her into your custody since it's what the two of you want.

I think you're effing idiots. But it's your choice. God forbid *I* ever interfere with your free will."

Instead of relief, a tremor of apprehension went through Dev. "It's that easy?"

Thorn laughed. "Nothing is ever *that* easy, Bear. Stryker wants your honey so he can destroy the world as we know it. You arrogantly claim that you can protect her better than *I* can even though I command an army and live in a place they can't reach. I say we should put it to the test. Best beast wins and all that."

Dev's hackles rose as his suspicions mounted. This had to be a trick. He didn't trust Thorn enough to even blink with him in the same room—the weasel was that crafty.

Wait for it. . . . There was definitely a trick coming.

"What do you have in mind?" Dev asked.

Thorn snapped his fingers and a portal opened in the wall. "I have a task for you, Bear. Have you ever heard of Hippolyte's Girdle?"

"The one Hercules had to fight the Amazons to get?"

Thorn inclined his head to him almost respectfully. "An expected oversimplification, but yes. It's the one Hercules had to fight to claim. And I don't know if you realize this or not, but Samia just so happens to be Stryker's cousin."

Now there was an intriguing off-topic tidbit Dev really wasn't expecting to hear, and it was one he wasn't sure he hadn't misunderstood. "What's that?"

Thorn spoke more slowly, again in that patronizing tone that made Dev want to bury his fist straight in the man's jaw. "Hippolyte—Samia's grandmother—the fabled Amazon queen? Her father was the god of war, Ares.

214

Since Ares is Samia's great-grandfather, it makes her and Stryker cousins, as it were."

That explained a whole lot about Sam's fighting skills. "Does Sam know this?"

"I should hope she knows who her great-grandfather is. Not like *that* was ever a secret. Hippolyte was quite proud of the fact she was a demigod."

Dev couldn't blame her for that. He'd spread it around too if he could claim such, but none of that was pertinent to what was going on right now. "What has this to do with me?"

"Nothing really, except that after Hercules stole the girdle, it fell into human hands for a time because they believed it would imbue the wearer with certain powers."

"Does it?"

Thorn's eyes turned a deep red. "Yes and no. It seems a vital piece of the tale was never recounted."

"And that would be?"

"That the wearer must be a descendant of Hippolyte for it to work." Thorn's tone changed from the refined gentleman to a deep demon baritone. "You want Sam back . . . get her that girdle so that it can protect her and I'll let her go with you."

Oh yeah, this mission was going to be a doozie to rival the one his sister had asked him for when she'd wanted to pull Fang out of demon hell. "And where *is* this girdle?" No doubt someplace that stank, was hot, and more lethal than a cobra venom farm.

Thorn let out a sound of profound aggravation. "What? You want me to draw a map for you? Take you there and point it out like a bird dog?" He snapped his fingers. The

215

wall to his left shimmered before a giant black resin clock appeared. Its face was that of a dragon with vibrant red eyes that oddly matched Thorn's. Its hands were the dragon's wings.

Dev's prickly host pointed to it. "You have one day, Bear. Twenty-four hours from this very second. Return with the girdle or Sam stays here . . . and so do you." He paused before he added the last condition. "Forever."

That was a long time to stay anywhere and Dev had a feeling that Thorn was not going to make his stay here a day at Disney World—unless one counted the torture part of the Pirates of the Caribbean. "If I refuse to play this game?"

His expression was stone-cold evil. "You're already playing it. You stop now and I throw you out and Sam stays here until hell freezes over. Maybe even a day or two after that."

Dev didn't like the proposed terms and he wanted to take Thorn down a notch. He knew he didn't scare the demon lord, but he knew one person who might. "Acheron will most likely have something to say about that."

Thorn arched one regal brow. "Are you going to cry to him like a baby with a broken toy and ask him to fix it?"

Dev took a step forward and would have attacked him for that comment had Fang not caught him and stopped his suicidal charge.

"Don't," Fang whispered.

Don't, my ass. . . .

But it did click his common sense back into play. Dead, he couldn't help her at all. Couldn't do much for himself either.

And that common sense begged him to tell Thorn to shove it up a part of his body he was sure Thorn kept clenched tight enough to form a diamond.

His mind flashed on an image of Sam's beautiful face. She didn't like being around unfamiliar things. Most of all, she wouldn't want to be locked in a cage no matter how gilded the bars were, any more than he would.

"So what's it to be, Bear?"

Dev lifted his leg and gave a sarcastic slap to his thigh. "By golly, I'll take Door Number Two, Bob. You know the one that calls for straight suicide with a side of mutilation and pain? Sign my hairy ass up for that and don't be late."

Fang cursed while Cael laughed.

Cael attempted to sober, but couldn't. "Damn shame you're going to die, Bear. I really think we could have been friends."

There was amusement in Thorn's eyes, but the rest of him didn't so much as quirk a muscle. "You have four clues to find the location and—" He glanced to the clock. "—the hands are ticking."

"You going to give the clues, hoss? Or do I have to guess?"

Thorn patted him on the cheek like a teacher with an errant child. "In plain sight on the banks of the Champs-Élysées, the girdle lies hidden away. At the brink of the darkest night, the location fills your sight. To see what can never be found, look for the circle round. To reclaim that which the gods rescind, you must face mightiest Whirlwind."

Dev had a sudden urge to punch that smugness right out of him. "You know, the migraine from all of that really isn't going to help me locate it."

"You have your clues, Bear. Good luck."

Chapter 14

Sam watched as Dev was pulled out of Thorn's domain and returned to Peltier House so that he could prepare for his journey. A sob lodged in her throat. She couldn't believe what he was willing to do for her. The risk he was taking.

Just don't die. Please.

Not because of her. Especially not when she couldn't help him. What kind of torture was this?

Damn you, Thorn.

"Sam?"

She jerked around at the soft sound of Amaranda's voice. "What are you doing here?"

"Risking a lot more than we should. But we know the terror you feel and we can't let you suffer."

"We?"

"Me, Cael, and Fang." She gestured toward the bed. "If you lie down, Fang and I can pull your essence out and you'll be able to go with Dev."

"You can do that?"

"We think so."

"Think" was not a power word, especially the hesitant way Amaranda had said it. A chill washed over her. "What aren't you telling me?"

"There's a chance that you might not be able to come back . . . intact."

Oh yeah, that was bad. "Care to elaborate?"

Amaranda's eyes echoed her uncertainty. "I'm going to have to take you into a deep unconscious state—not something I've ever tried to do before. I might screw this up and it could leave you outside your body forever. Or you could be left in a perpetual coma."

Sam glanced back to the wall where Dev was writing down Thorn's riddle so that he could decipher it. He was risking his own freedom and his life for her.

Could she do anything less for him?

"I'll do it."

Amaranda bit her lip. "Do you understand the risks?"

Sam nodded. "Thank you for at least trying. I really appreciate what you're doing, and if you screw this up, I promise I won't hold much of a grudge."

She made a sound that basically said she thought Sam was an idiot for agreeing to do this. "I hope you still feel that way in the event I can't put you back together again."

"Believe me, I will."

Amaranda gestured toward the bed. "All right, then, lie down and let's attempt the impossible."

Sam obeyed her. Flat on her back, she met Amaranda's nervous gaze and smiled before she repeated the Amazon battle motto. "Who wants to live forever?"

Especially if she couldn't live it with Dev.

DEV SAT AT his desk with his head in his hands. He let out a long frustrated breath as he studied words that made no sense to him whatsoever. "In plain sight on the banks of the Champs-Élysées, the girdle lies hidden away. At the brink of the darkest night, the location fills your sight. To see what can never be found, look for the circle round. To reclaim that which the gods rescind, you must face mightiest Whirlwind."

The Champs-Élysées was a road in Paris and there was a circle at the end of it. While it was near the water, it wasn't *on* the water. So how could it have a bank?

And never mind that whole whirlwind nonsense. He'd never known something like that to strike Paris.

"This is hopeless," he muttered as he reached for his iPhone to Google info on Paris. Even with all of this being a long, long shot, he wasn't going to give up.

Not on Sam.

A knock sounded on his door. "I'm busy," he called, assuming it was Aimee wanting to annoy him with something petty like he forgot to put the seat down on the toilet or left a sock in the bathroom. She was forever yelling at him over bullshit.

"Dev?"

He paused at Fang's muffled voice. "Yeah?"

Fang pushed the door open. "We know where you need to go."

"The mental ward?"

Fang laughed. "Yeah, but I was talking about your current matter, not your long-standing reservation." He slid a meaningful glare at the paper Dev was studying.

A whisper of hope ignited inside him. "You know where the girdle is?"

"I don't. But I think I know someone who does." Fang opened the door wider to show him a flickering image of Sam.

A dagger of relief plunged so deep into him that it actually made his eyes water. Before he could think better of it, he was on his feet and across the room. His heart hammering, he went to pull Sam into his arms only to learn that his hands passed right through her body.

What the hell?

She smiled at him. "I'm not exactly corporeal."

Fear exploded inside him. "Are you dead?"

"No," she and Fang said simultaneously.

Sam indicated Fang with her thumb. "Amaranda and Fang combined their powers so that I could help you do this."

Dev scowled. "Help how?"

"You're French. You know nothing about Greece. Meanwhile, I'm a walking encyclopedia on the subject."

"Fang's Greek."

Fang shook his head in denial. "My last name's Greek, but I was born in medieval England. Believe me, I know very little about Greece."

"As I said," Sam's tone was firm, "I can help you both."

Yeah, *if* he was willing to risk it. But he wasn't. "I have to do this alone."

Fang stepped forward. "No, you don't."

Dev cut him off. "Look, dude, the only thing that scares me more than Thorn is my sister. Trust me, anything happens to you and she's going to sugarcoat my boys and eat them for breakfast." He locked gazes with Sam. "And I can't risk you."

"Why?"

"Because you're not the only one who has issues with people dying around them."

She let out an aggravated sigh. "Well, it's kind of hard to die when things go right through me. Unlike you."

She had a point. But he still wasn't ready to give in. "Thorn's clue wasn't about Greece. It was about Paris. That's where I was born and it's my territory."

She scoffed. "Don't be silly, Dev. There's more to the clue than what Thorn said. Nothing is ever that overt. Not when dealing with beings like him."

"How about this? I refuse to let you go."

She gave him no quarter. "What you say against this doesn't matter. The die is cast. I'm here and as Thorn said, the clock's ticking. So you either deal with me or you're going to waste so much time that we're both sunk."

Fang scratched the back of his neck as if their argument made him uneasy. "Damn, Dev, don't you know anything about women? You leave her behind and she'll only find another way to follow you and probably get hurt doing it. She goes with us, at least you have a chance to protect her and you can definitely watch over her."

He clenched his teeth, wanting to choke both of them, but Fang was correct. Sam's obstinacy knew no boundaries. "All right. You said you know where we're supposed to go?"

"Yes. Hades."

Dev lifted one brow. "The Greek god of the Underworld?"

She nodded. "In plain sight on the banks of the Champs-Élysées—that's French for the Elysian Fields"— Duh, he knew that. He'd just temporarily forgotten it.— "which is in the Underworld, also known as Hades. The Underworld has five rivers running through it. I assume one of them has the banks where the girdle is kept."

That did make more sense than what he'd been thinking and if it was in the Underworld, there would most likely be a freak whirlwind and other hazards. "What about the rest of the riddle?"

"They must be clues we'll find once we're there. But you'll need me to translate them."

Dev snorted. Yeah, 'cause he was too illiterate to figure it out.

And he still wasn't sold on taking her with him. Her safety would be a big distraction for him . . . as would the fact that right now all he could really think about was kissing her—once he choked her.

Hard to think straight when her mere presence, even noncorporeal, gave him a flaming hard-on.

"Couldn't we have taken Ethon and used him to decipher it?" he mumbled under his breath.

Sam grinned. "Ethon's not as cute."

Yeah, but if Ethon died, Dev really wouldn't care. Hell, he might even offer him up as a sacrifice if they needed one.

Which begged the next question he asked her and Fang. "So how do we get to Hades, anyway?"

They exchanged a confused stare.

Dev cursed as a wave of nausea went through him over that look. So much for all their bravado. "You don't know.

Miss I'm-Greek-and-know-my-legends, you don't have a clue, do you?"

She made a face at him. "I have a clue. The Underworld is located beyond the western horizon. Odysseus reached it by sailing from Circe's Island."

Dev was impressed. Maybe they stood a chance after all. "Which is where?"

She bit her lip before she answered in a low tone. "It kind of sank and was lost. No one's sure where it was anymore."

So much for being useful. Dev let out a short "heh" sound. "That's what I thought. We're in the deep end with cinder-block shoes chained on our feet and no bolt cutter." He went to the desk and picked up his phone.

Sam moved to stand right behind him. "What are you doing?"

"I'm using my help line to call in the one real expert on this subject."

Sam widened her eyes. "Artemis?"

Dev would have laughed, but he knew better. It would only offend her and if she ever made it back into her body, she'd exact revenge on him for it—and she wouldn't be naked when she did it. "I don't think she'd take my call." He paused as his expert picked up. "Hey Ash . . . I have a situation here."

AFTER DEV HAD explained what was going on, Ash manifested into the room between him and Fang. He leveled a killing glare at Sam before he swept them with the same chilling look. "Are you people out of your ever-lovin' minds?"

Dev gave the collective answer. "Yes." He glanced over to Sam. "But at least me and Fang are still in our bodies." He jerked his head toward Sam. "Unlike some people I can name."

Ash growled deep in his throat as he held his finger up and kept a silent beat with it that made Dev think he was counting to ten before he spoke again. The look on his face said he was trying not to break Atlantean all over them. "At least the Daimons won't get you *there*. Other demons and gods might eat all your entrails, but your souls are safe." His attention went to Sam. "You I expected better of." He turned his swirling silver gaze to Dev and Fang. "You two not so much."

Dev shrugged his anger aside. Not like Ash hadn't ever done something stupid. Hell, he'd even witnessed a few of Ash's more award-winning moments of dumb. "You want to play tour guide with us?"

Ash sighed. "Not that easy. I can't enter there without negotiating with Hades, who isn't exactly keen on letting me into his space."

"Why not?"

"Politics, and right now with Persephone not around, only an idiot would try to negotiate anything with him. He's not in the best of moods." His gaze went back to Sam. "And as a Dark-Hunter you're not supposed to be around any god, you know that. They will destroy you on sight and that includes your semi-real state that you're currently in."

Before she could respond, Dev broke in. "Can't we avoid them? How many gods are there in the Underworld anyway?"

"Oh . . . tons." Ash's tone was as dry as his stare. "Hades isn't the only one with a grim Goth fixation. He has an entire court of gods and demigods who hang out with him. Many for the sole reason they get to torture the damned, which means they possess a total lack of empathy or regard for anyone else and they're constantly on the move in the Underworld. Chances of running into one are pretty stellar and that's without Murphy's Law coming into play."

Dev scratched the back of his neck as that unwanted news put a crimp in their plans. "That settles it then. Sam stays behind."

Heat suffused her cheeks. "Like hell."

But he was in no mood to back down. "Like nothing."

Her eyes blazing with fury, she stood toe to toe with him. "You're not going without me. I won't allow it."

Dev growled, knowing she wouldn't give even an inch. So he turned to a reinforcement she had to listen to. "Ash, tell her to stay put."

"Can't." Ash had drifted to the desk to look over the riddle Dev had written down.

"What do you mean?" Dev asked.

Ignoring the question, Ash picked up the paper. "Are these your clues?"

"Yeah."

Ash rolled his eyes and let out a short, bitter laugh. "Of course they are . . ." He locked stares with Dev. "Thorn set your ass up, Bear. You guys don't have to search Hades for the girdle. I can tell you right now exactly where it is."

"And that would be?"

"Down the street."

That news hit Dev like a punch. "Excuse me?"

Ash read the clues out loud. "In plain sight on the banks of the Champs-Élysées, the girdle lies hidden away. At the brink of the darkest night, the location fills your sight. To see what can never be found, look for the circle round. To reclaim that which the gods rescind, you must face mightiest Whirlwind." He turned his gaze to Sam. "You should know who the mightiest Whirlwind is. At one time, she was the guardian of the girdle."

"Aello?"

He inclined his head to her.

Dev was more confused than ever. "Who's Aello?"

"My grandmother's right hand and bodyguard. She was the first one to fight Herakles when he came for the girdle and she was the first one he killed."

Dev gestured for her to elaborate. "And that's important to this how?"

Ash returned the paper to the table. "She's basically invincible."

"Apparently not if Hercules handed her her lunch."

Ash followed the line of his eyebrow with his middle finger. "That's because he was wearing the skin of the Nemean Lion at the time. Anyone care to venture where they think that trophy currently is?"

Dev didn't need to guess. He already knew. "Somewhere not good or handy and I'm sure retrieving it would be a death-defying act of courage."

Ash sarcastically rang an invisible bell with his hand. "Ding, ding, ding. Give that boy a trophy." He crossed his arms over his chest. "And without it, you won't be wearing a cloak of invincibility when you face her like old Herc was, and I should probably add that you won't be fighting her while she's human. . . . She's now a man-hating, angry spirit who craves blood and can't be killed."

Dev rolled his eyes. "Well, thank you Mr. Cranky Pants, but right now, I think a more optimistic outlook would be more productive. Unless you know some way to schmooze Thorn into freeing Sam and letting me off the hook, we have to try something and as bad as this is, it's all we got."

Ash rubbed his head like he was contracting Dev's earlier migraine. "Yeah, that's not going to happen. Thorn's not real fond of me. . . . Fine. There's nothing to be done until sunset."

Dev didn't understand that. "You said it's just down the street. Why do we have to wait?"

"In another dimension, Sparky. One you can't access until sunset, hence the darkness line on your page."

Oh, that made sense . . . now. Funny how riddles seemed easy when you knew the answers. And since Ash was being so chatty . . . "Anything else we need to know?"

"Yeah. The circle round part?"

"What about it?"

"It refers both to the location you'll need to travel to and to the shifting cycle."

Dev's gut clenched at something he was sure wasn't going to be pleasant for them. "Shifting wha—?"

Ash glanced at each one of them before he came back to Dev. "You guys are going to head into a trap maze that will constantly shift and you'll have to navigate it to the center where Aello will be waiting to battle. Think of it like a bad video game. Just when you think you're all right, the floor will drop out from under you and the walls will shift and leave you dizzy . . . or dead . . . and all without the extra life points."

Fang rubbed his hands together. "And will you be joining us on this fun suicide run?"

"Love to, but can't."

"Why not?" Sam asked.

"If I go, Thorn will cry foul and refuse to honor his part of the bargain by saying you cheated with me."

Dev frowned. "Won't he do that with Fang?"

"No. Fang's not omnipotent. There's a good chance Fang could get killed. With me, not so much."

Sam screwed her face up. "That's just sick."

Ash shrugged. "No one's going to argue anything else. Thorn doesn't exactly have many friends."

"I've noticed," Fang said under his breath.

Ash inclined his head to Dev. "Remember, you have to get to the center and defeat the guardian."

"How do we get back?"

"No idea. I've never been inside the maze."

Dev sighed. "This would be funny if it wasn't pathetic."

Ash cut a wide grin. "Welcome to my existence. Now if you'll excuse me?"

"Wait!" Sam stopped him from leaving. "We still don't know what to do to get there. You said it's another dimension?"

Ash nodded. "Drive to the end of Elysian Fields where it connects to UNO. There's a circle there. Stand at the outer edge, facing Pontchartrain and—"

"Won't the Research and Tech Park interfere with the view?" Fang asked, interrupting him.

"Not for long."

Dev was still baffled. "But there's nothing in the circle. It's empty."

Ash held his hands up in surrender. "I didn't create the hole. I'm just telling you how to access it. Face the park and the moment the sun sets below the horizon, the way will be shown. It'll only last for sixty seconds. Move fast. Once the door closes, it won't be open until the next sunset."

"Which is out of time for us," Sam said under her breath.

Ash nodded. "Good luck, guys." This time he vanished before they could ask him anything else.

Fang blew out an elongated breath before he looked over at Dev. "Since there's nothing we can do for the next few hours, I'm cutting out of here to spend time with my wife . . . just in case I don't make it back."

Sounded like a good plan to him. Fang left the room through the door. A weird move for a Were-Hunter but sometimes in their chaotic paranormal existence you just needed to be normal.

Now alone with Sam, Dev wished he could touch her. She looked so sad that it made him ache for her and all he wanted was to see her smile again. "We'll get the girdle, babe. Trust me."

Sam wanted to believe him, but she couldn't get her premonition out of her mind. Over and over, she saw Dev dead. It was so clear. So torturous. What would she do if he went down?

Would she be able to survive it?

"I wish you hadn't made this bargain with Thorn."

Dev offered her the kindest, gentlest smile she'd ever seen. "We're both fighters. You know what I do. We won't go out lightly and we'll find some way to defeat her. Believe in me."

If only it were that easy, but she knew the ferocity of her people. Yes, the Amazons were women and physically weaker than men. However there had never been a more skilled set of warriors assembled and Aello had been one of their best.

As the old saying went, it wasn't about the size of the dog in the fight. It was the fight in the dog.

And even in the body of a Chihuahua, an Amazon was a Rottweiler.

She reached out to brush a strand of his hair away from his eyes, only to feel nothing. Her fingers affected nothing. She felt the absence of his warmth all the way to her missing soul.

I wish I could touch you, Dev.

Not wanting him to know how much that thought made her ache, she offered him a smile. "Well, the good news is in this incarnation, I don't have anyone's emotions haunting me."

"See, there's always a bright side."

And he always saw it, but not her. While she lived life to the fullest and grabbed it with both hands, she'd never really seen the beauty of it. She'd lost that ability.

Until she'd seen Dev standing outside of Sanctuary.

Dev reminded her of the things she'd learned to ignore. With him she actually felt the happiness—the exuberance—that life had to offer.

"I wish I could make love to you."

He sucked his breath in sharply. "You talk like that, you're going to kill me." He moved to stand just before her. "I wish I could *smell* you."

She pulled back sharply. "Smell me?" What a repugnant thought.

He nodded. "Your scent makes me drunk. I love having it on my sheets and on my body."

Yeah okay, not gross. That was actually a thought that made her hot and needy. "I really hate Thorn right now."

"Me too. You think we should kill the prick?"

She laughed. How was it that he always made her laugh no matter how dire the event or circumstance?

Dev dropped his hungry gaze down to her lips. An action that made her stomach contract with wanton heat. "We can look on the bright side though."

"I don't have to look for parking spaces in New Orleans?"

His laugh was deep and rich, and it sent a shiver over her. "There's a perk I didn't think about. But I was referring to the lack of Daimon attention. It's actually quiet for once."

Sam wasn't willing to concede that to him. "Yeah, that would be a big bonus if I could have sex with you."

His brows shot up in surprise. "Now who's being the horn dog?"

She wrinkled her nose playfully as her hand ached to feel his hair in her palm. "Definitely me, and only because I know how torturous it is for you."

"Well, I could surf online and you could read a novel on the bed while we ignore each other, then we could pretend we're a happily married couple."

She laughed again. "Is that really what you'd do with your wife?"

"Absolutely never. I've lived hundreds of years alone. If I were ever lucky enough to find my mate, I'd spend the rest of my life letting her know how grateful I am to have her."

"How totally *un* horn dog of you."

"I know," he whispered. "So don't tell anyone. You'd ruin my rep." He reached for her, then dropped his hand as he remembered he couldn't touch her. "What about you? Did you ever ignore your husband?"

A knot choked her as she remembered Ioel and his charming smile. She could count on one hand the number of years she'd been lucky enough to know him. "I didn't have him long enough to grow bored. Maybe it would have happened eventually, but I doubt it. It's ironic really. We both knew when we agreed to it that we'd have a short marriage. With both of us being warriors, the odds were never in our favor. It was just a matter of the wrong blow during the right battle. So from the moment we came together, we knew to value every heartbeat because it could be our last."

Dev ached for the pain he heard in her words and the torment he saw in her eyes. "I'm so sorry for what happened."

"What? That my sister was a selfish bitch? That definitely wasn't your fault."

"No, but families are supposed to hang together in every adversity. It sickens me when they don't. I wish I could kill your sister for you."

Sam had to catch herself before she told him how she felt about him. No good could come of that. They could never be together and she knew it. No matter how much she wanted it to be. . . .

Some wishes just weren't meant to happen and all the desire in the world couldn't change that.

I love you, Dev.

Unfortunately, her love wasn't selfish. She only wanted the best for him and the best wasn't her. It was a woman who could have his children and stand by his side here at Sanctuary. Not one who'd sold her soul to a goddess.

The song "You" by Fisher played through her head. Those words had always choked her up but never more than right now when she understood them in a way she never had before.

"You don't know it yet, but you're everything. . . ."

Why did her life have to be a study in losing the things she cared about? It was so unfair and yet how could she complain? She'd chosen this life. She was a defender to the world. There was no higher calling than that. No job more honorable or noble.

Trying to reinforce her resolve to let him go, she cleared her throat. "You ever think about having kids?"

"All the time. I'd love to have a houseful. Then one of my nieces or nephews turns Exorcist on me and spews the most disgusting things imaginable out both ends—things that make the demon snot feel like a bubble bath. That usually cures me of that stupidity for at least a day or two."

She laughed so hard her eyes teared. She'd never quite thought of it that way, but he was right. Kids had a tendency to explode. A lot. "You're so bad."

He shrugged with an innocence he definitely didn't possess. "You asked. I answered."

She shook her head. "Seriously though, don't you want Dev cubs?"

"Honestly? I don't know. It's a lot of responsibility. It's scary and unpredictable. I think about it sometimes. Not that it matters. I'm not a single cell organism capable of mitosis so without a mate it's a moot topic and I don't believe in torturing myself over things I don't have. I'd much rather focus on and be grateful for what I do have."

Gah, he made it so hard to hate him. So hard to push him away even when she knew it was the only practical thing to do.

Most of all, he made her want to reach out and touch him. Just to hold him for one moment.

If only . . .

Dev felt the sudden awkward silence between them like an iron cloak. "Did I do something wrong?"

"No."

How did women do that? Say a word that was the exact polar opposite of what they meant. Obviously he'd said or done something to destroy her playful mood.

If only he knew what it was.

Whatever. He couldn't make it better unless she told him what he'd done to offend her. But that was the one thing about the female gender that made him insane. For a group who prided themselves on communication skills, they could be remarkably silent when it came to things that really mattered to them.

It was the old if-you-knew-me-like-you-should-then-you'd-know-why-I'm-mad game. Well, how was he supposed to learn her if she didn't tell him?

Vicious cycle and it was one he didn't have time for. Not when they were about to launch themselves into something that could get all of them killed. An image of her lying dead seared him. Her current state was a lethal reminder of what could happen if he failed.

And Fang . . .

Aimee would never forgive him. But there was no way to leave him at home. Fang wasn't that kind of wolf. Bastard.

He had a sick feeling in his stomach that things weren't what they should be. There was something in the ether around him that wanted to warn him.

If only he knew what . . .

The seen and the unseen. Things were about to get hairy as hell for them all.

ETHON COCKED HIS head as he heard the spirits of the fallen whispering to him. It was a talent that had served him well for the last five thousand years. It enabled him to see his enemies coming and to hear the souls that had been lured by the Daimons.

But what they told him right now left him cold.

Dev and Sam were about to kill themselves.

Two against Aello was a fool's errand. While Ethon had never faced her himself, his grandfather had been with Herakles when Herakles had defeated her. When Ethon had been a small boy, his grandfather had spent hours detailing the vicious attacks of the Amazons as a tribe and Aello in particular.

No one escaped them unscathed without divine inter-vention. Which both Sam and Dev lacked.

This was going to get bloody and if no one helped them, they wouldn't live through the stupidity.

Reaching for his phone, he made a quick call.

If they were going to battle, they weren't going alone. *I won't let you die again, Samia.* This time he wouldn't fail her. And if he had to lay down his own life for hers, so be it.

DEV MET FANG in the hallway. By Fang's grim visage, he knew the wolf would much rather be tending the bar tonight than joining him on a suicide run. Not that he blamed him in the least. He'd rather be downstairs himself.

But not at the cost of Sam's freedom.

"You know you can stay here," he said to his brother-in-law. "I'd actually prefer it."

Fang shook his head. "I would never leave you to do this alone. You didn't shirk at going into hell to help me, Dev. I've not forgotten it."

Which was why Dev had grown to appreciate his unique family member. Fang had proven himself worth the risk Dev had taken to save him and he was glad to call him brother.

Sam cleared her throat. "We better hurry. We don't have much time until dark."

Dev inclined his head. Just as he was about to teleport himself and Sam to the circle, he saw two people coming up the stairs.

Ethon and Scorpio.

And they were dressed for battle. Both in solid black, Ethon was dressed in a pair of slacks and a button-down shirt. His long coat hid a full weapons arsenal. Knives, at least one gun, and most likely a sword. Scorpio on the other hand was much more overt. He wore a short-sleeved shirt with leather vambraces Dev knew concealed steel spikes he could shoot out and use to punch through just about anything.

Dev scowled at them. "What are you doing here?"

Ethon gave him a shit-eating grin. "Covering your back, Cochise."

Interesting comparison. Cochise had been resourceful and clever, escaping death time and again. Dev only hoped that when this war was over, he was as lucky as the Apache chief to die at peace.

Sam drew up short as she saw the Spartan there. "Ethon—"

He held his hand up to stop her protest. "It's all right, Samia. Scorpio and I have run it past Ash. The Dogs stand together. You know this. Warriors to the end."

"Fools to the end," she snapped.

Ethon's grin widened. "Always."

Sam wanted to argue with him, but she knew it would only waste time they didn't have. Ethon was every bit as impossible and stubborn as Dev. "Fine. Make sure you keep up."

Fang stepped toward Ethon. "I'll take this one."

"I got the other." Dev met her gaze. "I'll see you in a minute."

Sam watched as they teleported from the hallway to the park. She took a moment to glance around the old house as she felt a strange tremor of foreboding go down her spine. Evil was at play here.

She only hoped she was the sole target of it.

Closing her eyes, she teleported to where Fang and Dev were standing in the fading sunlight. There was no sign of the Dark-Hunters.

Her heart stopped beating. Had they burst into flames?

"Did you get hungry and eat my colleagues?"

Dev pointed down to the dark green wool blanket at his feet that she'd somehow missed seeing. "There's still enough daylight to blister you guys so we hid them fast."

But oddly the sunlight wasn't hurting her at all—most likely because of her ghostlike form. Amazed, she watched the first sunset she'd seen in over five thousand years. The sky was absolutely breathtaking with ribbons of pink and orange twisting through the darkening blue.

If only she could feel the rays on her skin.

But seeing it was enough. She wanted to cry over the sight she'd missed all this time. "It's beautiful." But that tender swell in her breast died as she glanced down to the blanket and realized what it looked like spread out over the grass.

Two dead bodies.

And it was painfully obvious there were bodies under that blanket.

A car slowed down as it drove past them, raising the hair on the back of her neck. The driver stared at them until Fang looked over at her. Then the driver gunned the engine and sped away as fast as she could.

Sam let out an elongated breath. "Sheez, guys, I think we better hurry before someone calls the cops and tells them you're trying to hide bodies in the Pontchartrain."

Ethon's laugh rang out from under the blanket.

Dev kicked him. "Sorry. Accident."

Ethon growled low in his throat. "You better be glad I'm pinned, Bear."

Dev flashed her a grin before he turned his attention back to their task. "Sun's setting. Anyone see anything?"

Just the research building and Lake Oaks Park across the street. The parking lot on her left for the university and fitness center and the houses behind them. It all looked completely normal and the traffic was getting heavier.

We are so going to jail. . . .

Would Ash bail them out?

Fang turned around slowly.

And true to her prediction, she heard police sirens in the distance, drawing closer.

Crap.

"Gods, I hope that's not for us," Fang mumbled.

Dev snorted. "Oh, you know it is. That's our luck, *mon frère.*" He glared at the horizon. "C'mon sunset. Don't fail us."

Fang scoffed at his words. "Fail us, hell. The police show up and I'm flashing home. I say we leave the Dogs here to get their own butts out of the sling."

"Screw you, Wolf," Ethon snapped.

Dev held his hand up to silence them. "Look."

Sam didn't see anything until the last ray vanished. Then there was a slight shimmering just a few feet in front of them. The kind that most would dismiss as a summer haze. Heat coming off the pavement.

But it wasn't that.

"Dev . . ." Fang's voice was stern as the sound of speeding cars drew closer.

Sam saw the police lights.

"Hunters, rise!" Dev ordered.

Ethon and Scorpio rolled out from under the blanket at the same time the police shouted at them to freeze. Ignoring them, they ran forward.

Sam heard the sound of guns firing. One second she was shouting at Dev to dodge the bullet headed at his back, the next everything was different.

The terrain remained the same. But the street and buildings were gone. A bright, piercing light bathed everything in an overexposed glow. Whatever the source, it obviously wasn't sunlight since neither Scorpio nor Ethon were blistering from it.

Sam lifted her hand to shield her eyes as she looked over the men to make sure they were all right.

They stood like fighters in front of her. Dev with his hip cocked and the others ready to battle. Only there was nothing to fight.

Dev walked a slow circle, taking in their new landscape. "Anyone want to hazard a guess as to which way we should try?"

Ethon wiped his hand over his chin. "I'd say we try GPS tracking, but I'm going to bet we don't get any satellite reception here. What do you think?"

Scorpio answered by releasing the spikes in his vambraces so that they stood out like a porcupine's quills. Without a word to any of them, he headed for the black water that lapped against a light gray beach.

"Guess we're going north," Dev said slowly. "Everyone, follow Lassie. Timmy's in the well."

Scorpio raised his left arm. Interesting that with the blade extended, it looked like a vicious "FU" to Dev.

Ethon clapped Dev on the back. "Careful, Bear. I think you made Lassie mad. Remember in his case the bite is definitely more fatal than the bark."

Just as they neared the water, the ground under their feet started shifting. Fang cursed as it split apart and he started to fall into a ravine. Shifting forms from human to wolf, he leapt clear while Dev and the others ran to stable ground.

With her current form, Sam was in no danger. She floated over the shifting ground to hover near the men who were watching their feet suspiciously.

"That was close."

The men ignored her.

Frowning, Sam waved her hand to get their attention. They all four acted like she was invisible.

What in the world?

Irritated at them and scared that she was becoming even more of a ghost than she'd been before, she opened her mouth to chastise them. But the moment she did, she heard a deep, vicious growl coming toward her.

Turning her head, she gasped. It was a herd of leucrotae. Ferocious wolf-dogs who could feign the voice of people in order to lure their prey into closer range. The Greek historian Photius had once described them as "brave as a lion, swift as a horse, and strong as a bull. They cannot be overcome by any weapon of steel. . . ."

And they were headed straight for them.

Chapter 15

Ethon passed a friendly grin to Scorpio. "Hey, *cabrón*, they're not really dogs. You can kill these without guilt, I promise."

Scorpio pulled two swords out from the top of his boots and extended their blades. *"Lo que son?"*

Ethon unsheathed a sword of his own. "They're what happens when the gods get frisky with the wolves. Their offspring make all kinds of sickening things. Right, Fang?"

"Blow me, Greek."

"You're not my type."

Dev rolled his eyes. "The leucrotae were created as guardians to the gods. Their hide is supposed to be so thick it's impenetrable to just about everything."

Fang made a sound of utter annoyance. "I guess it's too much to ask if anyone happens to know a way to kill them?"

Ethon laughed evilly. "Yeah, I think so. Ever play the old arcade game Joust?"

"Yeah?"

"Remember the invincible dragons?"

Dev grimaced. "The ones you had to stab in the mouth when it was open to kill them?"

"Exactly." Ethon saluted them with his sword. "May your stab be straight, my friends. If not, I'll see you in Tartarus . . . remember to avoid the grapes."

The first hound to reach them went for Scorpio's throat. Hairless and bloodred, the hounds had small heads and a bony ridge that ran all the way down their spine to the tip of the burred tails that looked like a pointed mace—a mace they brandished with evil intent. With the teeth of a saber-toothed cat, the leucrotae were a force to be reckoned with.

Sam felt completely helpless as Fang and Dev turned into animals to fight. Scorpio and Ethon hacked at the leucrotae and tried to drive them back into the dark abyss. One of the dogs came at her. Instinctively she tensed in expectation of the fight. But the hound went right up to her, sat on his haunches, then barked twice and returned to the fight.

Two more hounds repeated the gesture, before they went on to ignore her while they attacked the others.

How weird . . .

"Lucky you." Ethon growled as he tried to pound the one off his forearm where its teeth were shredding his flesh.

"Are they made of armor?" Scorpio asked in Spanish.

Ethon cursed. "Not supposed to be. I think their flesh is just that strong. Remember, their weakness is their eyes and the soft tissue of their mouths."

Sam felt completely helpless as she watched them fighting the hounds. What could she do? She kept trying to hit them, but her arms were worthless.

Wait . . .

An idea struck her. She summoned her telekinesis. Throwing her hand out, she mentally grabbed a nearby rock and held her breath, hoping this would work. She concentrated and tried to lift it.

It did!

Her heart pounding, she threw it at the hound that was on Dev's leg. The rock hit it hard enough to knock the hound sideways. It yelped and growled, then returned to the fight as if nothing had happened.

Now that she had a way to fight against the hounds, she joined the fray. She was even able to pry the jaws open on the one that had Ethon.

"Bless you," he breathed, wringing his arm out of its bloodied razor-sharp jaws. But as soon as he threw that one off, three more latched on. "Gah, whoever heard of piranha Cujo? I am *never* going to own a dog again or anything that even remotely resembles one."

Scorpio laughed. "They're not dogs, amigo. Is that not what you said to me?"

"I lied and now the gods are punishing me for it." Ethon would be funny if they weren't all in the process of getting maimed.

Sam used her powers to pull one off Dev. "You should have brought Chi for this."

Ethon scoffed. "Oh, now why would I want to bring a demon expert into a demon realm to fight demons? Where would the challenge be in that?"

Sam glared at him. "Bite him, Cujo. Right there in the fleshy part of his thigh where it'll really hurt."

"Aigh!" Ethon cried as the dog did just what she told him to. He curled his lip at her. "That was wrong. Another inch and I'd be falsetto."

She ignored his anger as she realized something . . . had that been a coincidence?

Or did the dogs actually understand her?

"Leucrotae, heel!"

It did nothing to stop them. They kept gnawing, biting, and attacking her friends.

Maybe they don't understand the command.

So she tried something that should make sense to them. "Leucrotae, *stamata*!"

The hounds let go of their victims and stopped just like she'd ordered.

Holy Zeus . . . it actually worked. *"Ela!"* She snapped her fingers to emphasize the "come here" command.

Like clockwork the hounds withdrew to her side. Several of them jumped up as if trying to reach her. *"Kato!"* True to the word, they settled down.

Incredible . . .

Ethon's jaw hung wide open. "I can't believe it. Sam's queen of the Damned."

Neither could she. It was a miracle.

Dev shifted back into human form. Her stomach clenched at the sight of the bleeding wounds on his body. Still, he was gorgeous with his cheeks flushed from the fight and his muscles rigid from the blood pumping through them. "What else can you tell them to do?"

Before she could answer, the ground under their feet began shaking again. The hounds howled, then bolted.

Fang gave a low whistle as he manifested back into a human. "Anyone else think it might be a good idea to follow them?"

Dev nodded.

Fang returned to his wolf body to chase after the hounds.

In human form, Dev started after him, then slipped as the dirt under his feet parted and sent him sliding sideways. A sharp, pointed boulder shot up from the ground, gouging his side while the black soil under him literally evaporated. There was nothing to hold on to. No way to catch his fall. He was going down.

He knew it.

Sorry, Sam . . .

Suddenly something wrapped around his wrist. Something that stung like a scorpion strike and jerked his arm so hard, he was amazed it was still attached. He dangled precariously over a deep cavern where flames danced, licking at his boots.

Looking up, he saw Scorpio's determined grimace as he held tight to the whip he'd used to catch Dev before he'd fallen too deep to be saved. "Hold tight, Bear."

Even though his wrist and forearm were bleeding and burning, Dev wrapped one hand around the coarse, braided leather and grabbed tight with the other. He wasn't about to let go.

Sam came running. He saw the panic in her eyes that warmed him. Until the ground started shifting under Scorpio's feet. Gasping, Sam jumped back out of habit.

Ah, shit . . .

He heard the sound of the hounds screaming after they fell into the pits and were consumed.

Sam wanted to cry as fear ripped through her. She had to do something. Closing her eyes, she reached deep into her powers to pull Dev up. Because he had his own powers and he was a living organism, it wasn't as easy to lift him as it had been with the rock. It took a lot more power and she wasn't used to it.

"Ay Dios," Scorpio breathed as his feet started slipping. "I can't hold him."

The ground under Scorpio crumbled, sending dirt all over Dev. Sam wanted to scream as she saw images of Dev dying in the flames.

There was nothing she could do.

Out of nowhere, Fang shot forward. He knocked Scorpio sideways so hard that it cleared the shattering ground. But the jolt caused Scorpio to let loose the whip.

"Dev!" she screamed.

Ethon dove at the pit.

Sam couldn't breathe as she closed her eyes. But she couldn't be blind to Dev's suffering. He was in this because of her.

I've killed him.

Her premonition came back tenfold as bile rose in her throat. Tears scalded her eyes.

"Damn, Bear . . . what did you eat? How much do you weigh? Ever heard of Weight Watchers? Dude, diet is not a four-letter word for someone who weighs in at a solid freakin' ton."

She forced herself to look while Ethon continued berating Dev. To her complete shock, he had the whip and was trying to pull him up.

Fang and Scorpion grabbed Ethon by the waist and added their power to his.

She bit into her knuckle so hard, it bled. *Please, please, please* . . .

For the first time in centuries, she felt like the gods were on her side as they hauled him up.

Dev slung his leg over the edge. Ethon grabbed him by the shirt and hauled him clear of the ravine. Then all of the men sprawled out on the ground.

Ethon let out a sinister laugh. "I think I need a vacation."

Fang groaned. "I need a new backbone that doesn't feel like someone did a two-step down it with steel-plated razor cleats."

Scorpion sucked his breath in sharply between his teeth. "I need a *belleza* well tutored in massage."

Dev rubbed his bleeding wrist. "I'm going with Scorpion. Except my *bonita* is unfortunately intangible at the moment, which doesn't do me any good."

Everyone went silent as they became aware of the fact that Dev had just proclaimed her his. Publicly. Sam was stunned by his words.

"Oh, c'mon, people," Ethon said in a mocking tone. "We're all adults. Not like we didn't know what was going on between them. You know Dev isn't risking his jewels 'cause she plays a mean game of pool, for Zeus's sake."

Fang turned his head to pin Ethon with a gimlet stare. "That explains Dev. I'm here to keep his sister from beating on me if I let him get hurt. Neither of those explain why you two are signed up for this."

Ethon scoffed. "Mine's simple. Brain damage."

Scorpion shook his head. "I just like to kill things."

Ethon rolled over and pushed himself to his feet. "But not dogs."

"*Sí*. No dogs."

"Why?" Sam asked.

Scorpio didn't answer as he flipped straight up into a fighting stance.

Dev got up and helped Fang to his feet. "You think there's a rhythm to when the ground breaks on us or not?"

Sam shook her head. "It's random."

Ethon wiped at the blood on his forearm. "At least it got rid of our four-legged piranha problem."

Yeah, but Sam wasn't so sure it was a good sign. She glanced around the overexposed landscape. It had such a weird orangish hue to everything. It looked like hell had been superimposed over New Orleans. She could see the street that had surrounded their circle. Only instead of a road, it was a burned-out hole. A blistering wind swept against them, making her hair sting her cheeks as it slapped against her face. Weird that she could feel that when she could feel nothing else.

The men were on their feet now, moving toward the bank where water boiled against a dark purple shore. She had an overwhelming urge to hum a spooky tune. But she didn't think the guys would appreciate it. Plus, they were a little jumpy and on edge as all of them waited for the next attack.

A whistle rent the air.

Dev reached out toward her instinctively. It was an action that made her heart catch. But she wasn't the one in danger.

He was.

And all she wanted to do was wrap her body around his and shield him from harm. If only she could.

Fang turned around looking for the source. "What is that sound?"

Scorpio tucked his whip back around his waist and pulled out his swords again. "Is it just me or does that sound like wings?"

Sam fell quiet to listen.

He was right. It did have that swishing wing sound. Only these had to be huge wings to make the noise she heard.

This wasn't good.

Dev ground his teeth as he looked for the next threat that was coming for them. His entire body was aching all the way to the marrow of his bones. All he wanted was to find the damn girdle and get out of here before one of them was killed. Most of all, he wanted to go back to when it'd been just him and Sam in her house. To that moment of perfect bliss when there had been no danger. No goal. And they'd been naked in each other's arms.

Weird how he didn't want to leave anymore and start over. He was perfectly content to stay, so long as she was with him.

But then life was insidiously evil in that it seemed to always be a study in how hard it could kick you down. Like the king Tantalus that Ethon had mentioned earlier. Life dropped you neck-deep into the water you craved most, then the minute you stooped to drink, it evaporated. It let you starve while succulent grapes hung over your head, so close your fingertips could brush them, then the instant you reached out for one, a phantom breeze would blow them right out of your grasp. All the while you could see your desires so clearly, you could reach out and almost touch them, but you could never have them.

That was what he hated most about it. Life was anti-happy.

He glanced to Sam. Right now, he couldn't even touch her. She was completely intangible and yet there she shimmered in all her beauty. Calling out to him when he knew he couldn't have her, couldn't touch her. And right now, her features were pinched and strained with worry. Of everyone here, he knew exactly how much torture it was for her to not be able to really help them, and all he wanted to do was make it better.

"Mommy? Mommy? Where are you?"

Dev felt sick as he heard the voice of a little girl and saw the devastation on Sam's face.

"Mommy? I'm so scared. Why did you leave me?"

She started forward.

"Sam!" he snapped at her. "It's a trick. You know it is."

Sam wanted to believe it, but the voice . . .

It was Agaria. She would know that sweet, precious voice anywhere.

"Sam? Is that you? See, Ree, I told you Mommy hadn't forgotten us. I told you she'd be back."

Dev's heart clenched, especially when he saw the pain etched on Ethon's features. "Damn you, bastards!" Dev roared. "Stop with the cruelty."

"Devereaux? Is that you, brother?"

Pain lacerated Dev as he heard Bastien's voice in the strange shadows around him. Before he could stop himself, he'd taken a step toward it.

"Fang? Is that you?"

Fang swallowed hard. "Anya?"

Dev cursed at the name of Fang's sister who'd been killed by Daimons. . . .

Ethon was the first to come to his senses and completely reject the voices. "It's the manticore, guys." He moved to stand in front of them so that they couldn't head toward the voices. "People, wake up! Listen to me. You're under a spell. It's the—"

His words died under an assault of arrows.

Dev hissed as one grazed his arm and laid open his biceps. "Take cover!"

Unfortunately, there wasn't much cover to be had. One arrow landed deep in his shoulder.

Sam cursed as she saw Dev go down. Her powers dipped, but before they vanished completely, she raised the stones from the ground, giving her friends a modicum of shelter as the arrows rained down on them with such ferocity, she understood how King Leonidas had felt against the Persians. She controlled her rising panic as she heard the manticores drawing closer. They were growling like lions now as they continued to shoot arrows at them from their tails. It was the wickedest of weapons and one that was long range. Damn the gods for that.

And while the manticores had the bodies of lions, they all had the head of a human, which made them some of the deadliest of Greek monsters because they weren't mindless animals. They could think and deceive and use their voices to mimic others.

Most of all, they could kill up to five hundred feet away. It was why so few people ever saw them. By the time you looked one eye to eye, death was already rattling in your chest.

True to his Spartan nature, Ethon laughed. "We should feel flattered that the gods sent these after us."

Dev passed him a sneer that said he thought Ethon had been inhaling fumes. "Flattered?"

"Yeah. It means we're bad ass even to the gods." He pulled out a handful of shurikens. "C'mon, you bastards! Let's dance." He dodged out from behind the rocks to throw them.

Sam ignored him while she studied the arrow in Dev's shoulder.

"I've got it," Scorpio said, coming to tend the wound.

Dev hissed as Scorpio touched the arrow that was buried deep while Ethon fell back against a rock that shielded him, laughing in triumph.

Dev looked from Ethon to Sam. "Please tell me his brother had better sense."

"Not really." She laughed. "He just wasn't as enthusiastic about his stupidity."

Ethon tsked. "Ah, Sam, that hurt my feelings."

She gave him a droll stare. "What are you talking about, E? You don't have any feelings."

"Oh yeah. I forgot. But if I did, they'd be aching right now."

And still the manticores came closer.

"How do we defeat these things?" The words had barely left Fang's mouth before the ground rumbled again.

With one clean, powerful yank, Scorpio pulled the arrow out of Dev's shoulder and used his powers to heal the wound. "I'm growing bored with this ground trying to swallow us every few minutes."

The ground must have heard him. Because this time, it didn't open below their feet. It rose up like mountains, trying to spear them.

"Head north." Fang returned to his wolf form.

They ran forward, but it was hard. The earth acted like a dirt geyser, spraying them with rocks and soil. Fang yelped as one foul spewage threw him into the air. He landed a few feet away on his side. Panting, he made no move to get back up.

Dev ran to him. The ground started rising. Tucking Fang under his arm, he pulled him to a safe area.

"Thanks, Scorp." Ethon curled his lip. "Next time, could you wish for us to be attacked by cotton puffs or something?"

The ground heaved one more time, throwing all of them into the air before it calmed again.

After slamming down hard, Dev lay on his back, panting. Fang was a few feet away. Groaning with a pain they all felt, Scorpio pushed himself up and went to Fang to examine his left leg, which had been injured.

Sam was ill over everything that had happened.

Because of her.

She walked slowly to Dev and sank down beside him. "I'm so sorry I got you into this."

"Oh please." He sat up with a light groan. "It's risk my life here or pick my nose at the door, waiting for some dumbass human to think he can punch Remi or pinch Aimee on the ass. Don't apologize. I haven't had this much fun in centuries."

Sam laughed even though she thought he was insane. "You are so not right."

Dev smiled at her, wishing he could brush the curls back from her beautiful face. "True, very true." Only an idiot would fall in love with an Amazon Dark-Hunter.

Dev was startled by that random thought. At first it terrified him until he realized just how true it was.

He loved her.

It defied all logic. It made no sense. And yet it was absolutely true. All he wanted was to protect her. To keep her from harm and make sure nothing in the world ever hurt her again.

No wonder Remi's insane.

For the first time in his life, he fully understood his brother and why Remi was so angry at the world. Only Remi had it worse. While Dev would have to be man enough to watch Sam go her own way and leave him, he wouldn't have to see her mated to his own identical brother. See her every day of his life and know that but for a freak accident of mistaken identity she would have been his.

The worst part?

Quinn didn't love Becca. They were friends and mates, and they took care of each other and their children, but nothing more. There was no passion between them. None of what Dev felt for Sam whenever he looked at her.

What a sick twist of fate that had been.

Too young to know the differences between them, Becca had waylaid Quinn, thinking he was Remi. In Quinn's defense, he had no idea Remi loved her—Remi never shared things like that. All Quinn had seen was a warm body pawing at him and he'd done what most men would do when a woman showed up naked in their bed.

He'd slept with her. Within the hour and just after Becca had realized her mistake, their mating marks had come in and Remi had been forced to step back and watch his brother claim the woman he'd fallen in love with first. The woman who loved him with everything she had, who'd been trying to mate with him and not his identical brother.

Remi had never emotionally recovered from that tragedy.

And while Dev had thought he understood Remi's pain, it was only now he really got it. The strength of Remi's character was unfathomable. To have stayed with the family and witnessed their relationship all these years. To have never once cheated on his brother with the woman he loved . . .

That was what real love was. The ability to put someone else's happiness above your own no matter how much it killed you to do so.

It was the sacrifice his mother had made. She'd died to keep Aimee from losing her mate.

Remi made that sacrifice every day. While a Were-Hunter male could never cheat on his mate, women could. It would have taken nothing for Remi to cuckold Quinn. And Dev knew for a fact Remi never had. As big of a bastard as his brother could be, Remi had honor and he loved his family even though he still wanted to break Quinn into pieces.

How do you do it? How could Remi have walked away and not killed Quinn? Because right now the thought of not having Sam was more than he could bear.

All he wanted to do was kiss her, even though they were one step away from death.

"Incoming!"

Dev looked up as a pack of manticores launched out of nowhere to land all around them.

The men pushed themselves up, then put their backs to each other as the manticores circled them while barking and hissing.

"Why aren't they attacking?" Fang asked.

Ethon shook his head. "It's like they're herding us for something."

Yeah, but what?

Sam moved to hover by Dev's side. The manticores flicked their tails as they eyed them warily. She swallowed as she watched the arrows swim up their tails. The arrowhead would peek out of the ball of fur on the tip and then slide back down only to head back to the tip as if waiting for it to be flung at a target.

With the faces of men and women, they were creepy-looking.

"You should not be here," one of the females snarled.

"We'll be happy to leave." Ethon flashed a grin at her. "Just let us pass."

The female hissed at him.

Dev inched closer to the manticores until they turned on him. He stepped back and they retreated. "What do you want with us?"

"They want nothing with you."

Sam looked up to see a beautiful woman in the leather and gold armor of the Amazon nation. Her flaming red hair glowed in the overexposed light. Her hair was braided and held back from her face by a feathered leather headband. Matching feathers made up the white and brown mantle she wore over her armor as she eyed them with a warrior's gleam.

This was Aello. There was no doubt she was the girdle's protector.

"Why do you come here?" Aello demanded.

Ethon held his hands up. "The scenery. My God, have you ever? I mean really. I had a choice. Spend a day in Rio or come to the back door of hell. What can I say? Hell won out."

Aello angled her spear at his throat. "Are you mocking me?"

Sam used her powers to push the spear away. "Don't take it personally. He mocks everyone."

That brought Aello's stare firmly to rest on Sam. Her green eyes glowed in the strange light. "I know you."

"No. You died before I was born. I'm the granddaughter of Hippolyte and I'm told I favor her."

Suspicion hung heavy in her eyes as she measured Sam from the top of her head to the tip of her feet. "You want the girdle." It was a statement, not a question.

Sam nodded. "It belongs to me. It's part of my inheritance."

"And are you Amazon?"

She lifted her chin in pride and indignation that Aello would dare to question her heritage. "I was queen."

Aello lowered her spear. "Then you know nothing in our tribe is ever freely given. You must earn the right to wear your grandmother's girdle."

Ethon scoffed. "Couldn't we just buy a Playtex?"

"Silence!" Aello jerked the spear and would have beheaded him had he not ducked.

Ethon grabbed the lance and jerked it from her hands. "I'm not—"

Before he could finish, the spear turned on him and beat him down without anyone touching it. It swept his feet out from under him and once he was on his back, it kept slapping the ground on each side of him until he stopped moving. Then it hovered threateningly right above his neck.

Aello called the spear back to her. With a feral grimace at Ethon, she returned her attention to Sam. "Do you accept my challenge?"

Like she had any choice? "I do indeed, but I have no corporeal form, which puts me at a disadvantage." Something no self-respecting Amazon would accept. There was no dignity in winning over a lesser opponent. Only in defeating the absolute best.

Aello grabbed her and jerked her forward.

Sam's breath caught as she was transformed back into her body. Not just that, but she no longer wore a T-shirt and jeans. She was now in her warrior's battle armor.

She'd forgotten how heavy it was. Still, it was a good weight. A familiar weight. And it came complete with all of her weapons.

Oh yeah . . . with this she could do damage.

Bring those mutant lions forward now and she'd show them the business end of her toys.

Aello nodded in approval. "Now you look like what you claim."

The armor invigorated her as it reminded her exactly who and what she was. "I *am* what I claim."

"We shall see."

The manticores pushed the men back as Aello moved forward to pull Sam away from them. "The test is simple." She gestured toward the water.

The dark boiling waves receded. From the sand a pedestal arose. On top of it, in a glass case that held a nest of cobras, was Hippolyte's shimmering gold girdle.

Aello's smile didn't reach her eyes. "You race me to the girdle. She who dons it, owns it."

"And if I lose?"

Aello didn't hesitate with her answer. "You all die."

The manticores laughed happily.

Sam looked at Dev and she saw the concern in his beautiful blue eyes for her. She had no choice in this. If she refused the challenge, Aello would still kill her.

And them.

She met Aello's gaze without flinching and delivered the code of their people. "I am the steel and the hammer that forged a nation never defeated. My arm is without equal and my judgment pure. My heart is fierce and this challenge is met. I will not be defeated. Not by you. Not by anyone. I am Amazonia."

Aello smirked at her. "Spoken like a true queen. But let's see if your skills match your tongue."

Sam gripped her spear with her right hand and her bow with her left. And as Aello sprang forward into the obstacle course without notice, she remembered something crucial about her people.

Amazons always cheated.

Chapter 16

Dev held his breath as he watched Sam run to catch up to Aello. He'd known Sam was a fierce fighter, but this was without a doubt the most impressive display of skill he'd ever seen from anyone.

The first test was an open pit that had arrows shooting up from it in random spurts that had no pattern whatsoever. Aello hit it at a dead run. She launched herself into the air and flew to the other side as several of the arrows grazed her, but none did any real damage.

Safely across, she brushed at the bloody patches on her skin and kept going.

Sam took a second to put her bow over her head and shoulders so that it lay diagonally across her back. Tossing her spear to the other side where it embedded itself in the soil, she ran up a side bank and, jumping up, backflipped over to catch four of the arrows that the pit shot out before she landed on the far edge, facing him, right beside her spear. In one fell swoop, she winked at him, put her gathered arrows into the empty quiver on her back, and yanked her spear out of the ground. With a grace that the gods would envy, she turned and ran for the next obstacle.

"Damn," Fang breathed in awe.

Dev beamed as a wave of fierce possessive desire tore through him. "That's my girl."

Ethon scoffed at both of them. "Trust me. You ain't seen shit she can do. That was child's play"—something she proved well at the next challenge. There, they had to launch themselves up from a small springboard made of moss to land on single poles jutting out of the ground that were barely as big around as their feet. In fact, they had to stand on their tiptoes to fit. The only problem was the poles weren't stable and the moment their weight hit the tip, they wobbled, requiring superb balance to keep them from slamming down and crashing into sharp rocks lining the ground.

If that wasn't difficult enough, Aello attacked her as soon as she was on one, using her spear as a staff. With her own staff in hand, Sam countered the rapid blows that came so fast, Dev heard them more than he saw them. Sam shoved Aello back, then moved to jab her with the tip of her spear.

Aello danced to the next pole and renewed her assault.

Sam followed and the two of them created a frightening ballet of lethal skill as they moved down the line while fighting like juggernauts.

Dev's heart pounded as he feared for her. One sneeze . . . one subtle miscalculation and she would slam onto the rocks below and be killed.

Aello jabbed at her feet, requiring her to dance to one pole, then jump to the next. One pole crashed to the ground, splintering into pieces as the rocks rose up literally to devour it.

Without thinking, he took a step forward, intending to lend a hand.

The manticore in front of him reared up and forced him back. "Help her, Bear, and she forfeits."

And they would all die. . . .

But it was hard to sit back and watch as she risked everything for them.

Sam landed a vicious blow to Aello's side. The Amazon wobbled and just when Dev was sure she'd go down, she flipped to the ground on the safe side. There, she ran to Sam's poles and used her spear to start knocking them down before Sam could reach them.

Cursing, Sam ran as fast as she could while maintaining her balance. As Aello knocked over the last, Sam caught it with her foot and literally rode it to land beside Aello.

With a cry of fury, Aello tried to stab Sam. Sam caught her wrist and head butted her, driving her back. She sliced at Aello's throat. The Amazon barely dodged it before she swung around with a cut Sam countered like a pro. Then Sam lifted her leg and kicked Aello back.

Realizing Sam was the better swordswoman and fighter, Aello threw a dagger at her and ran to the next obstacle.

Sam caught the dagger and automatically moved to toss it at Aello. Dev saw her barely stop herself before she threw it. Most people wouldn't have had the integrity to do that, especially given the way Aello had been cheating.

But Sam was better than that. She refused the cheap shot and he couldn't be prouder of her.

Go baby . . .

The next obstacle had them climbing up a thick vine into a copse of trees they had to run across. The only problem was the trees were thin and some kind of prehistoric bird of prey that looked like a cross between a pterodactyl and an eagle kept attacking them.

Sam reminded him of a gazelle as she leapt through the trees with a sure foot that a satyr would envy. When the bird dove at her, she fell to her knee and pulled an arrow from her quiver. With perfect aim, she let fly the arrow that embedded in the place where the bird's wing met its body. Not a mortal wound, but one that forced the bird to land and leave her in peace.

Aello paused to stare agape at the shot. But as soon as Sam was on her feet, Aello returned to the competition. Unlike Sam, she hacked and stabbed at the birds until she made her way across.

The final challenge was to reach the girdle's case.

Sam hesitated.

What was she waiting for? She'd be first if she'd just run straight to it.

But Sam stayed back. And when she put the back end of her spear into the ground and it instantly disintegrated, he understood why. It was redsand. So named for the lives that had been lost to it. Unlike quicksand which was seldom deep or inescapable, redsand had been created by Hades to keep the damned penned in Tartarus. In the highly unlikely event one of them escaped, the sand would make sure they didn't get far. It was like an acid that would eat through any form. Living. Dead.

Or in between.

All that would be left behind was your blood. Hence the name, redsand.

Aello laughed. "You give up?"

"Never." Sam cupped her hands around her mouth and let loose a strange bird call. It came in pulses of three and was followed by a whistle.

Aello duplicated the sound.

Dev exchanged a scowl with Scorpio and Fang. Ethon however was grinning.

"What are they doing?" he asked the Spartan.

"They're calling for Ares's *arpaktiko pouli*."

Dev rolled his eyes at a term he couldn't even begin to wrap his lips around. "Dude, that's all Greek to us. You ever notice there's a reason why people pick on Greek?"

Ethon scoffed. "Only because they've never tried to speak Welsh. Trust me, we've got nothing on them." Then he moved back to the important topic. "They are the war birds of Ares and were special to the Amazon nation." He jerked his chin toward the women. "The Amazons used to keep them as pets."

Dev looked back and sure enough there was a flock of giant black birds headed toward them. Yeah ... that would be like keeping Nessie in a wade pool. How in the name of pickles could they have ever domesticated something bigger than a semi?

Fang sucked his breath in sharply. "This can't be good. They won't even have to chew before they swallow us. And I have to say that being wolf jerky sucks." He slid a look over to Ethon. "I bet Dark-Hunter jerky is chewy though."

Ethon shoved him.

267

Ignoring them, Dev prepared for war as the birds swooped down. Manticores or not, if those things went for Sam, he was going for them.

Sam picked up the bone necklace from around her throat. She placed it in her mouth and blew it sharply in a distinct pattern.

One of the birds cawed then ducked down and glided on the wind. Sam held her hand up as if summoning it like an old friend. The huge bird landed in front of her on the ground. Spreading its wings, it snapped its head back and made one last cry before it settled down. It leaned forward, brushing its beak against her cheek.

Sam caught it against her and gave a light pat.

There was no missing the gleam of respect in Aello's eyes as she watched Sam swing herself up onto the bird's back. The bird bristled ever so slightly before it became acquainted with Sam's foreign weight.

"Ya!" Sam shouted, kicking the bird into flight. Spreading its wings, it shot to the sky with a velocity that made Dev's stomach draw tight. He didn't know how she stayed on its back, but she managed well.

Aello duplicated the gesture. Unsheathing her sword, she went for Sam.

Fang let out a low whistle. "Anyone know that Amazons could ride a giant bird?"

Ethon gave him a *duh* stare. "Those of us who fought them, yeah, we know. How you think they kept kicking our asses?"

"Cause you're pansies. Everyone knows that."

Ethon went for Fang, but Scorpio caught him. "He was joking, Ethon. Grab a sense of humor." Especially since

Fang's sense of humor was close enough to Ethon's that they should be relatives.

Ethon growled at Fang before he stood down.

Dev stayed focused on the fight in the sky. It was incredible to watch. Aello attacked and Sam countered as they circled in the air over the pedestal. How they could remain on the back of the birds and fight was beyond him, especially since neither had a saddle nor bridle. They guided their mounts with their knees and held on with one hand.

Dev glanced down at the manticores. He still wanted to help Sam, but he knew better than to try. They looked a little too eager to kill.

Aello circled around, then dove for Sam. In a maneuver that Dev would have called impossible, Sam twisted with the bird and went straight up, parallel to the ground, letting the blow miss them entirely.

However, it overextended Aello's reach and unbalanced her. With one sharp cry, she slipped from the back of the bird and went tumbling toward the ground.

Sam jerked her bird around and headed for her. Tucking its wings to its body, the bird looked like a black torpedo moving through the sky. They cut though the air, trying to catch Aello before she hit the ground. Just as Dev was sure Aello was a stain in the dirt, Sam caught her by the wrist and pulled the Amazon on to the back of the bird, draped on her stomach, in front of her. Sam guided the bird to the shore, then set Aello down in a safe area before she headed back to the pedestal.

At first Dev thought Aello would summon another bird and go after her.

She didn't.

They watched as Sam guided the bird to the pedestal and knocked the glass case from over the girdle. It landed on the sand and shattered, then dissolved. The cobras hissed and reared in protest at being disturbed. Sam diligently hovered above them, out of striking range. Using the tip of her spear, she very carefully hooked, then pulled the girdle up, taking care to shake off the cobras that tried to cling to it. Several of the snakes launched themselves at her and the bird from the pedestal. Sam had the bird pull back so that the cobras missed and fell to the ground. They were quickly devoured by the sand.

A minute later, it spewed out their bones which were quickly dissolved into a red puddle.

Dev grimaced at the gory mess.

Sam ignored it as she draped the girdle over her lap, then turned the bird back toward them. She flew over Aello's head to land just in front of him.

Her smile was wide as she dismounted and held her grandmother's girdle high. Dev couldn't have been prouder for her win.

Aello came running at her back.

Before he could warn her, Sam turned around, prepared to fight.

But that wasn't the intent. Aello skidded to a halt, then dropped to one knee in front of Sam. Clapping her right fist to her left shoulder, she bowed her head reverently. "My queen."

Sam froze at a title she hadn't answered to in so many centuries that it seemed odd to hear it now. And it along with the contest she'd just won awoke vivid memories, good and bad, of a time and place she'd never have again. A past that burned inside her.

At one time, she'd lived for competitions such as this one. They had invigorated her. Had proven her honor and her skills as a warrior. How important all of that had been to her then.

Now she knew that things like that, while they were nothing to shirk at, were not the most critical things in life.

Family. Friends.

Love.

Those were what people needed to battle for. To hold tight to until their knuckles blanched. Everything else was just an icing and while it tasted good, it wasn't filling and it couldn't sustain a person.

A life alone was hell itself.

Dev came up behind her and wrapped his arm around her shoulders. She trembled as foreign emotions swept through her. He was her present, and right now she needed him to ground her to reality. All she wanted was to feel him there, against her forever.

This was what mattered to her.

He nuzzled her hair before he laid a chaste kiss on her cheek that set her on fire. "You were amazing."

Funny, she didn't feel that way. She'd done what she had to. Nothing more. Nothing less.

Aello looked up at her. "Why did you save me?"

How could she not? How could she have allowed a woman like Aello to perish so horribly over something so petty? "We are sisters. Why would I allow my family to die over a difference of opinion?"

Even though her own sister had killed her for something that in the end amounted to nothing more than table scraps.

Aello took her hand and kissed it. "You do honor to Queen Hippolyte and it is with honor that you take her girdle. May you live a long, happy life."

If the poor woman only knew. . . .

Not wanting to taint her heartfelt wishes, Sam inclined her head to Aello before she turned to look up at Dev. "Anyone know how we get out of here?"

Aello rose to her feet. "You must fly the birds as far south as possible. Once there, when the ground breaks, let it take you home. But you must keep your thoughts focused on where you want to go or it will take you where they drift."

Ethon scoffed. "Who says that's a bad thing? I hear the south of France is incredible this time of year."

Fang gave him an arch stare. "It's also daylight there. Can you say Krispy Kritter?"

"Well there is that." Ethon shrugged. "Fine. Take all the fun out of my dreams. You bastard."

Sam summoned enough birds for all of them. Once they were mounted, she took flight. Something that wasn't that intuitive to the men. Fang was the first to slide off. Then Scorpio.

Dev kept his seat. . . .

Barely.

Ethon held on, but only because he was low and had his legs locked like he was a terrified toddler.

Laughing, Sam circled back.

"Do these things have training wheels?" Fang asked.

"Unfortunately not. Just do what Ethon's doing. Wrap yourself around them and they'll fly on their own."

Fang's expression was filled with doubt. "What if it gets spooked?"

"You would be screwed," Sam said in a dry tone. "Royally. Pray that doesn't happen."

Fang hissed at her before he pulled himself back up onto the back of the bird. Before he mounted, Scorpio used his whip to make a bridle. His bird fought it for several minutes, then settled down to take it.

He flashed a cocky fanged grin at her.

"Show-off," Ethon sneered.

Laughing, Sam headed south with the men following behind her. It didn't take too long to get to the border. There was a red haze around it that was so thin she could see the spot in New Orleans where they'd been.

Darker now on the human side of the veil, the haze made it look like infrared.

Sam urged her bird down so that she could dismount. The men quickly joined her as she fastened her grandmother's sword belt around her waist.

Ethon tapped his fingers impatiently against his thigh. "Why is it when you want the ground to swallow you whole, it decides to stop trying?"

Fang sighed. "Watched Pot Syndrome."

"Yeah."

Sam ignored them as she heard something odd in the background. The birds chittered and danced, then flew off abruptly.

Dev met her gaze. "That can't be a good sign."

No, it couldn't.

Sam glanced around as she tried to find the source of the sound . . . a sound that was steadily getting closer.

"Oh. My. God."

She looked over at Ethon who was staring up at the sky to his right. Following his gaze, she gasped.

"It's the attack of the flying monkeys."

Only these weren't the cute little bluish-gray monkeys from *The Wizard of Oz* that were dressed in adorable hats and jackets. These were huge with fangs that made hers look like plastic Halloween wear. With dark-gray leathery skin, their eyes were yellow and their tails were razor sharp.

They all drew weapons as the fire-breathing monkeys attacked.

Ethon dodged one that tried to blast him, then whirled and slashed at its wing. "You know, there are just some things you never expect to face even on this job. A flying primate that shoots fire out its nose is one of them."

Scorpio snorted. "Yes but are they cercopithecoid or platyrrhine primates?"

Ethon glared at him. "Get your head out of the Discovery Channel and on the attack."

"At least they're not farting flames that would stink in more ways than one." Fang ducked one monkey only to have another one attack him.

Sam threw her knife, catching the monkey between its shoulder blades before it could bite Fang. Shrieking, it fell to the ground.

That attack seemed to set off something fierce that called in more reinforcements.

Her stomach hit the ground. Yes, the men were fighting like demons and holding their own, but this was about to get ugly. The sky above them was darkened by the wave of incoming primates.

We're dead. . . .

Just as that thought went through her mind, the ground below her shook. She started sliding.

"Think home!" Fang shouted to remind them.

Dev wrapped himself around her right as the ground below her opened and she plunged straight down. Sam held on to him with everything she had, grateful he was with her. She focused on his room in Sanctuary.

One minute they were plummeting and the next . . .

They were naked in Dev's bed.

A wicked grin teased her. "You thinking what I was thinking or were my thoughts just that intense?"

Heat exploded over her cheeks. Honestly, this was exactly what had been in her mind. Laughing, she went to kiss him only to have her body fade back into her ghost form.

Dev cursed in anger. "I'm going to kill Thorn."

"I would say it's okay, but right about now, I'm with you one hundred percent." She rolled over onto her back and stared at the ceiling. "It's so unfair."

Dev ached to kiss her. But he had to get her back into corporeal form first. "Let me take the girdle to Fang and then to Thorn. I'll see you shortly." He ran his hungry gaze over her body. "And I want you just in this position ten minutes after we get back."

She laughed. "Yes, sir."

Dev got out of bed and dressed himself in his jeans and a shirt before he went to find Fang. He pulled his phone out and rang Ethon.

"You make it back?" Ethon asked him.

"Yeah. Where are you?"

"Don't ask. It's too embarrassing. I'm headed back to Sanctuary as soon as I get cleaned up."

Not that that brought up all kinds of images in Dev's mind. "Exactly where are you again?"

"I told you not to ask. Cause I'm not going to say. Asshole." Ethon hung up.

Dev called Scorpio.

"I'm in the bar. Where are you?"

Dev was impressed. "I'm at Peltier House. Is Fang with you?"

"No."

Fang stepped out of his bedroom and jerked his chin toward Dev's door. "Looks like you had the same thoughts I did."

God, he hoped not. The thought of Fang with his sister made him sick. Not that he was stupid enough to think they weren't having sex, he just couldn't mentally handle the concept of his baby sister with any man.

Get out of my head. . . .

"Take me to Thorn." Dev hung up on Scorpio.

Fang placed his hand on his shoulder and teleported him from the hallway to the door outside of Thorn's office.

This time when Shara answered, her expression was impressed. "You're not dead."

"Not yet."

Shara withdrew from the steel and opened the door to admit them into the room, which seemed unearthly chilly given the fact that the fire burned even brighter in the fireplace than it had earlier.

Thorn was on his feet, waiting for them. Still impeccably groomed and dressed, his hands clasped behind his back. He glanced to the clock that was still ticking.

Dev's jaw dropped as he saw the time. No. It couldn't be.... One minute more and he'd have missed the deadline. "What the hell trick is that? It hasn't been twenty-four hours yet."

Thorn arched one perfect brow into the most arrogant and disdainful expression Dev had ever seen. "Oh? Did I fail to tell you about the time? It travels differently on the other side. You've missed an entire day here while you frolicked with some of my friends."

Anger erupted inside him. "You bastard!"

Thorn's eyes glowed vibrant red. "Don't push me, Bear. You have your belt and you've won. For now. Take your prize and be grateful I didn't change the rules on you." He turned his attention to Fang. "Get them home."

All of a sudden he and Fang were in a small room where Sam was pacing. The sight of her there ... of her safe and sound and in corporeal form again.

Those feelings slammed into him so hard, he was amazed his legs didn't buckle. It was only now that he was with her that it hit him just how much he'd expected Thorn to keep her in spite of everything they'd done.

But now that she was with him again ...

Her face lit up in a way no one's ever had before and it turned his emotions inside out. If he could have anything in the universe, it would be to always have her look at him like that. It was obvious she was as delighted to see him as he was to see her. She ran and launched herself at him.

Catching her leap, Dev staggered back as he held her close and inhaled the scent of her soft hair. The warm floral smell made him hard and aching. It was all he could do to not take her right here and now with Fang watching them.

But he would never shame her.

Sam knew she shouldn't be doing this. Especially after everything Thorn had told her about Dev's future if they stayed together.

She had to let him go.

Yet right now, she just wanted to feel him close to her. To have his arms soothe her fears and uncertainties. Gods, she'd forgotten just how good it felt to hold him like this.

"You okay, baby?" he breathed in her ear.

She laughed at that deep, precious voice that sent a shiver over her. "Yeah." It was only then she realized just how she'd wrapped him up in her body. Her legs were around his waist and he completely supported her weight. Heat stung her face at what she'd instinctively done, especially as she became aware of the sizable lump under his jeans that was pressing into her and making her wet.

Fang cleared his throat. "I think it's safe to say she's glad to see you, huh, Bear?"

Dev gave her a quick kiss to her cheek as she unwrapped her legs and slid to the ground in front of him even though that was the last thing she wanted to do. "I don't mind it in the least. Kind of nice to feel welcomed."

Fang cleared his throat. "Especially after what we just went through.... Everyone still have all their fingers and toes?"

Sam held up both hands and wiggled her fingers. "Think so."

"Good." Fang gestured to the door over his shoulder. "Let's all head home before Thorn changes his mind and decides to keep us here where time apparently has no meaning to anyone but him."

Sam couldn't agree more. Like Fang, she wouldn't be surprised in the least if Thorn stopped them.

Or sent another round of flying monkeys after them—just for shits and giggles.

Dev took a minute to secure her grandmother's girdle around her waist. Sam looked down at it. Originally designed to hold a sword, it looked like any thick belt with heavy embossing. She had a sword at home that was kept in the matching scabbard that would hook onto the girdle. Without that piece, no one would ever guess it to be of any real significance—that it was the prized belt of the Amazon nation that Hercules had crossed a sea to claim for a foreign princess. Never mind know that it was something people would kill to possess.

Including her own sister.

"You ready?" Dev asked.

She nodded even though it wasn't entirely true. Her earlier encounter with Thorn had been brief, but traumatizing. He was one scary SOB. And his warning about Dev stood loud and clear in her mind. If she stayed with him, he would die.

And she couldn't be responsible for his death. Not after she'd killed Ioel.

Dev held her hand as Fang took them not to Sanctuary or the Charonte Club as she expected, but to a room she'd never seen before. All the windows were shuttered closed and there was a massive plantation style bed in the room with an antique styled blue silk comforter over it.

She looked at Fang with a frown. "Where are we?"

Before he could answer, Nick Gautier materialized in front of them. The dim light cast an evil shadow over his face. His whiskers were thickening, like he'd gone several days without shaving, and his eyes held a wicked gleam to them. "Welcome to my nightmare, Princess."

By the look on Dev's face she could tell he wasn't expecting to be here any more than she was.

She scowled at Fang "Why did you bring us here?"

Fang shrugged. "It's what Ash told me to do when I talked to him before we went questing for you. I figured Mr. Omniscient knows best about keeping his people safe—" those words were interrupted by Nick giving a rude scoff that Fang didn't even pause for—"so I didn't argue." He inclined his head to her and Dev. "Now if you'll excuse me, I have a Lady Bear I haven't seen in a day and I don't want her to kick my ass for leaving her high and dry."

He left before anyone could say another word.

In the silence that followed, Sam felt suddenly awkward. True it hadn't been the real Nick who'd tried to kidnap her out of Sanctuary, but still.

There was an aura of pure evil around this man and it set her hackles on edge. Whenever Nick looked at her, she had the feeling he was sizing her up for a body bag and it made her blood run cold.

"Relax," Nick said in a soothing tone as if he felt her unease toward him. "I don't want *your* blood. Since it's a rogue demon after you, Ash and I decided this would be the best place to hide you where the fewest lives would be threatened by your enemy." He gestured to the room. "Make yourself at home. Everything's been sanitized so it shouldn't give you nightmares or images to touch it." Something Nick knew about since she'd told him that when she'd started guarding him. How ironic for the tables to now be turned. "If you need anything, there's an intercom on the wall." He gestured to the unit that was just inside the door. "Call and I'll answer. And . . ." he pointed to the nightstand. "Ash sent over your cell phone so that you wouldn't be without it. There's a message from Chi who's been worried about you and pissed off that the guys didn't invite her to rescue you. I don't envy them. Ethon in particular was promised a major ass-whipping."

Sam frowned. Nick didn't look well. When she'd first met him on this assignment months ago, he'd been well coifed and gorgeous—except for the bow-and-arrow mark on his face. Now he looked pale and exhausted. Shaken. Like something had him in a vise grip and he couldn't breathe for the pain of it.

If not for the fact that Dark-Hunters couldn't get sick, she'd think he was about to hurl.

"Are you okay?"

"I'm always okay." His bitter tone denied those words.

Sam wanted to touch him and see what the truth was, but her inner alarm told her that she didn't want to see whatever demon had its claws into him. *When you stare into the darkness, sometimes it stares back. . . .*

And those mirrored images were often the most terrifying and threatening.

Nick paused in the doorway to look back at them. "By the way, I should warn you. It's almost noon here and Stryker's mounting his attack to take you into Kalosis. I don't know when he's planning to strike, but I'm sure it'll be before dark since you'll be at a disadvantage in the light. My house is technically shielded, however Stryker's powers are such that I don't know if it'll hold against him."

Sam narrowed her gaze dangerously as her suspicions about him mounted. "How do you know what Stryker has planned?"

When Nick answered, it wasn't with his mouth. She heard his voice loud and clear in her head. *The same way I know you love Dev, little girl. And if you do, send him home before nightfall. He won't survive otherwise.*

And with that he walked out of the room and closed the door without touching it.

Chapter 17

Sam watched as Dev went over the room making sure nothing would harm her even though Nick had assured them it was safe—neither of them trusted him.

The care Dev took as he reviewed it all was adorable and it reminded her so much of the image she'd seen of him protecting his sister when they were young. He was so protective and sweet. . . .

Worst of all was the compunction she had to brush his hair back from the nape of his neck and nibble his skin until he made that little growl in the back of his throat that sent shivers over her. She wanted to walk into his arms and just have him hold her until everything else vanished.

Love them. Leave them. That was the Code she'd lived by. As an Amazon and a Dark-Hunter. In her ancient world, men had often been seen as an impediment to the Amazon social structure. Amazons would go, have sex, and then never tell the men they'd fathered children unless they had to. They raised the daughters independently and brought them into the Amazon nation. Sons would be given to their father or his family.

It was rare for an Amazon to marry. Her sister had tried to use that to undermine her authority, but the Amazon code was actually more versatile than that. The point of their nation was for women to have the power to make their own choices about their lives and their happiness.

In an ancient world were women had less autonomy than male slaves, it was up to the woman to determine if she wanted domesticity or not and the rest of them had vowed to support their sister in whatever decision she made. Yes, most chose to live without a man. But not all. Sam wasn't the first to marry and she hadn't been the last.

For that matter, not all Amazons gave up their male children. Their world had been about respect and support. It was why she'd loved her nation so much.

As a Dark-Hunter, she'd had the same freedoms. Much like her people, they supported each other. Very rarely was a male Dark-Hunter chauvinistic—Ash kicked that out of them during training. The most important thing about being a Dark-Hunter was their vow to protect humans.

Be a part of the world, but not in it.
Let no one know who or what you are.
*   Take care of carnal needs when you have to so*
that you can stay focused, but never take a lover or a
significant other. They will distract you and weaken you.
Most of all, they become a target to be used against you.

Ash's rules. They all knew them and as she looked at Dev, she wished she'd listened.

Because right now, she didn't want to leave. She wanted to snuggle. Most of all, she wanted to wrap her body around his and make love to him until neither of them could walk straight.

But she had to get him out of harm's way before it was too late.

"Why don't you head back to Sanctuary?"

He looked at her with a fierce scowl. "Why?"

Because I don't want to see you hurt. It would destroy me. "I was just thinking they might need you there. The Daimons might come back for retaliation against your family."

Grinning, he scoffed at her dire tone. "I think my family can handle it."

"I don't know. Aren't Were-Hunters supposed to be extra special nubby treats for them?"

"When they can get us, yeah. But the problem is we have the same powers they do so getting one of us isn't easy. We bite back and we have clans who tend to attack en masse whenever they dare attack one of us. As a rule, they leave us alone." He moved to the window to make sure there was no smidgeon of daylight escaping.

He would have to make this difficult.

Don't make me hurt you, Dev. The last thing she wanted was to stomp on the one person who had finally made her feel alive again. It took every part of her sanity not to walk into his arms and hold him.

Her mind flashed to the sight of Ioel going down. The sound of him calling out to her to run.

I can't let you die, Dev.

But she didn't want to live without him.

"I really wish you'd go home."

He turned sharply and the look of hurt on his face cut her soul deep. Maybe that was her punishment for having made her bargain with Artemis. Hate had brought her back, and now she found something more sustaining than that, and couldn't have it because she'd been reborn from that hatred.

The gods were twisted that way.

Let him go.

"What are you saying, Sam?"

"I'm saying what I'm saying. I want you to go home now." When he started to argue, she knew she had to come up with something stronger to get him out of the line of fire. Something that would offend him and make him go even though neither of them wanted that.

Gods help me. . . .

She choked on the words that stung her throat and her heart, but forced herself to say it. For his sake. "Look, I'm not used to having people hang all over me and it's starting to get on my nerves. I need my space."

The look on his face shredded her and it almost succeeded in making her cry, but she was stronger than that. She was an Amazon and they didn't weep, no matter the pain.

Dev clenched his teeth over her unexpected verbal bitch-slap. It left him reeling. What the hell was her problem? What had he done other than risk his life to take care of her?

He cramped her space? Oh yeah, that pissed him off to a level he hadn't hit in awhile.

"I didn't realize I was getting on your nerves. Forgive me for trying to help." He walked over to her and had to bite back a resounding set down. But he wouldn't be that way.

Not with her. He refused to kick her with the same gut punch she'd just delivered to him.

"Fine." He took a step away from her. "I'm not one to stay where I'm not wanted. Have a nice life. Maybe I'll see you around sometime."

Sam didn't move until he'd vanished. Then the sudden absence of his presence tore through her. It was like someone had ripped out her heart and left her vacant. The room seemed to shrink down to nothing and yet at the same time it left a hole in her life so large, it swallowed her whole.

Her eyes watered as tears gathered in her throat to choke her. "I'm so sorry, Dev." But he'd never hear that apology. Not now. Not after she'd effectively cut him off at his kneecaps and left his ego throbbing.

She tried to tell herself that it was for the best. That she was doing this to save him.

None of that mattered to her heart. It ached and it begged her to call him back. "I can't." He was gone and she had to leave it that way.

Even if it killed her.

THORN DIDN'T MOVE as he felt a powerful presence behind him. Normally he'd be blasting anyone who dared to intrude on his sanctum.

But to do that to Savitar would be tantamount to suicide.

Well, not really.

It would, however, result in one seriously bloody battle that, while it would alleviate his boredom for a bit, would ruin his favorite suit.

"What could have possibly gotten you off the beach and brought you to my dark domain?" He turned his head to see Savitar standing behind him.

Dressed in white cargo pants and an open Hawaiian shirt, Savitar looked like any surfer right off the beach. Right down to his Birkenstock sandals, dark wind tossed hair, and opaque sunglasses.

Thorn arched a brow as he saw Shara frozen mid movement behind Savitar.

"You're tampering with my Were-Hunters again. You know how I feel about that."

Thorn scoffed at the ire in his tone. "Didn't realize you owned them. Not sure they've realized it either."

Savitar gave him a droll stare as he moved forward to stand in front of him. "You're lucky I didn't fight you when you grabbed Fang without my permission, but Dev . . . I want you to stay away from him."

"Why? This town not big enough for the two of us?"

A muscle ticced in Savitar's jaw. "Don't push me, Thorn. Don't forget that I know why you did what you did for Dev and Sam. Unlike them, I know you're not the asshole you pretend to be."

"There you'd be wrong, beach bum. I assure you. Every day I live is a study in how not to give in to the powers that beckon me . . . like you. We're creatures of destruction."

"Then you should remember that. Leave Dev alone."

"And I repeat . . . why?"

Savitar gave an evil laugh.

Chapter 18

"What are you doing here?"

Dev paused as he met Remi in the living room of Peltier House. In deference to the Dark-Hunters and other nocturnal creatures who visited them from time to time, this was the one room in the house where sunshine was allowed to flood in.

It had been their mother's favorite room and one Dev had spent many hours in, playing with his nieces and nephews.

Today, however, he didn't see the beauty of the room or his mother's impeccable decorating taste. Today, it was gloomy even with the sun shining bright.

And Remi's tone chafed him like a knife down his spine. "What? I can't come home?"

"Don't bark at me, asshole. I just thought you'd become the internal kidney for your new honey and since she's not here . . ."

"She's not my honey." Dev started for the stairs, but Remi stopped him.

For once there was actual concern in Remi's eyes. "What's wrong, *mon frère*? Really?"

That succeeded in making him feel like a jerk. It was easier to take Remi's eternal barbs than to deal with his brotherly affection.

That alone weakened him.

"Nothing, Rem. I'm just tired."

He saw the doubt in Remi's eyes. "If you say so."

Dev took a step, then paused as Sam's words about his surliest brother went through him. It was so incongruous with everything he knew about Remi and yet curiosity sank its evil claws into him so that he had to have an answer. "Do you really listen to the Indigo Girls and watch *Just Like Heaven*?"

Remi's face blanched. "What are you talking about?"

Dev would have burst out laughing, but the sheer shock of having Remi confirm Sam's absurdity kept him from doing it. Dear gods, it was true. His brother had a whole tender side he'd have never guessed at.

Remi probably even cried while watching *Bambi*. . . .

Damn. What was next? Dobermans nursing kittens? The whole concept messed with his entire view of the natural world order. It was so screwed up. . . .

"Nothing. It was just a little bird I heard in my ear."

Remi curled his lip and his eyes blazed with murder. "Yeah, well, you know me better than that. I watch gory horror movies and I listen to death metal."

And he listened to Amy Ray and Emily Sailors. The thought was hilarious because his brother denied it.

Honestly, he liked them too. But he'd never admit it either.

Dev bit back a smile as he headed upstairs to his room. But the moment he opened the door and his gaze fell to the rumpled bed, his amusement died under a bitter reminder of Sam making love to him. Every sense he possessed was suddenly filled with memories of her and it slammed into him like a fist in his bread box.

How could she have come to be so important to him when they'd only just met?

And yet he couldn't deny the pain he felt over not being with her.

I loved your father the first moment I laid eyes on him. I couldn't believe that one so precious was cut from the blood and bone of my enemies and yet . . . he was the only one I could ever see myself with and I'm grateful that the Fates saw it the same way I did. I would be lost and bereft without him.

That was the only conversation he'd had with his mother about mating. His parents had been one of the rare Were-Hunter couples who'd been mated the first time they'd had sex.

For the rest of them it could take dozens of encounters. Or never.

He looked down at his bare palm. When he'd been younger, full of stupid dreams, he'd tried to imagine what his mating symbol would look like. While clan symbols were similar for the species, each one was unique to the couple. And as a kid, he'd actually painted one on just to see.

As a man, he'd been grateful that no one had marked him. While it was a bonding of two people, it also came with a heavy commitment. One they could never back out of.

He closed his fist tight. *I don't need a mate.* He was happier alone.

But as he thought of Sam, he knew that for an absolute lie. He would be happiest with her.

And she had no use for him at all.

URIAN WAS SUPPOSED to meet his source at Sanctuary so that he could gather more information about Stryker's plan for Acheron. He and Davyn had always tried to pick spots where there was no chance of any of Stryker's people seeing them together. If Stryker ever learned that Urian still talked to his old friend, he'd kill Davyn immediately.

And it wouldn't be quick.

He rubbed his neck where his father had cut his throat in a fit of rage over the fact that Urian had dared try to be happy for five seconds. The bitter memory of that night was never far from the surface and it was carved in blood on his heart. He'd worshiped his father his entire life—had committed all manner of atrocities to please him.

And for what?

So the bastard could kill Urian's wife and then cut his throat the first time he displeased him?

One day I will have my vengeance.

If it was the last thing he did, he would kill Stryker for what he'd taken from him.

"C'mon, Davyn, have something good for me." Urian went over to the bar to order a beer while he waited.

Colt handed it off to him. Without a word, Urian drifted around the game area.

He checked his watch. Davyn was late. Something highly unusual for him.

Had Stryker found out? The mere thought made his blood run cold.

Suddenly, a familiar tingle went down his spine alerting him that there was a Daimon on the premises. Urian scanned the semicrowded bar, looking for his friend.

He saw a flash of white blond hair in the far corner and headed for it.

It wasn't until he was within sight that he realized it wasn't Davyn. This was a woman and when she turned toward him, he felt like someone had sucker punched him.

No, it couldn't . . .

It wasn't possible.

"Tannis?"

The woman frowned at him as if the name and his face meant nothing to her.

But to him that name had meant everything.

Time froze as he was taken back to the day his little sister had died. Unlike him and his brothers, she'd been too gentle and kind to take a human life in order to live. And so she'd withered away into dust on her twenty-seventh birthday. The pain of her decay had caused her to scream until her throat had bled. And still she'd had no peace. No mercy. It had been the most agonizing death imaginable.

One given to her by her own grandfather's curse.

After they scooped up her remains and buried them, they never spoke her name out loud again.

293

But Urian remembered. How could he ever forget the little girl he'd protected and championed? The one he would have killed to protect.

Before Apollo had cursed them, they'd called her Diana to honor their great-aunt Artemis. And then after his grandfather had cursed their race, Stryker had refused to ever call her Diana again. He'd wanted no reminders of his Olympian family who had betrayed them all. Especially since Artemis was the one who'd created the Dark-Hunters to hunt and kill them.

Diana had been more than happy to change her name.

But this wasn't Tannis.

She's dead. He'd seen her decay into dust with his own eyes. Yet this woman was a complete physical copy of her, except for the way she moved. While Tannis had been hesitant and dainty, this woman was sure and determined. Fluid. She moved like a warrior ready to kill.

Before he could think better of it, he closed the distance between them.

Medea turned as a shadow fell over her. Expecting it to be her informant, she was stunned when she looked into the face of her father.

But this man was different. Instead of her father's short dyed black hair, his was long and snow white—pulled back into a ponytail. He was also a hair taller than her father. Not obvious at first, yet undeniable as he came closer.

Still, there was no denying the similarity of their features. This was her father's doppelganger.

"Who are you?" they asked simultaneously.

Medea hesitated when he didn't answer right away. Why was he being reserved when it was obvious he was a relative she hadn't met? Maybe a cousin even her father didn't know about?

Curiosity got the better of her so she answered first. "I'm Medea."

"Medea . . ." He seemed perplexed by her name. "I'm Urian."

Urian.

She gasped at the name of her mysterious half-brother she'd heard about, but never expected to meet. He was now a servant of Acheron. Enemy to all of them after he'd betrayed her father.

"Filthy traitor!" she spat.

He didn't take that well as he gripped her arm and yanked her toward him. "Who are you?"

She wanted to see the shock on his face when she delivered the truth. "*Your* sister."

Urian blinked twice as that news sank in. He'd only had one sister. There was no way he could have another and not know it. "How?"

"Stryker married my mother, then divorced her to marry yours. She was pregnant with me at the time and he never knew."

His jaw went slack. Why hadn't Davyn told him about this? Davyn had told him about Stryker's first wife returning, but a sister . . .

A living, real sister. Why would Davyn have kept that secret? Suddenly he remembered Acheron telling him. . . . Shit! The bastard had removed that memory. Why would Ash have done that?

And with that thought came a really bad feeling. "What are you doing here?"

"Sightseeing."

He knew better, especially with someone sired by his father. "You're spying for Stryker."

She jerked her arm out of his hold. "Don't take that tone with me, little boy. You served him too and for many more centuries."

The thought made him ill. "And I paid the ultimate price for that blind stupidity. Trust me."

She scanned his body. "I don't know. You look pretty healthy and happy to me."

"Yeah, right. Let me tell you something, *little girl*, I was his favorite. His pride and joy above all others. For *thousands* of years I served at his side, doing everything he asked me to. *Everything*. Without question or hesitation. And in the blink of an eye, because I dared to marry without his permission, he cut my throat. Literally."

"He cut your throat because you married his enemy."

Yeah, right. It had nothing to do with whom he married and everything to do with his father's ego. Stryker couldn't stand the thought of anyone questioning his authority.

Not even his own son.

"I married a kind, gentle woman who never hurt a soul a day in her life. She wasn't a warrior. She was an innocent bystander whose only mistake was falling in love with a monster." And making him human. Making him care for someone other than himself and he would sell his soul if he could have one more moment with her. "Don't delude yourself for one minute. Stryker will turn on you, just as he turned on me."

"You're wrong about that."

"For your sake, sister. I hope to the gods that I am." But the bad thing was, he knew better. It was just a matter of time before their father went after her, too.

SAM FELT LOST in Nick's house. It was huge. But luckily he had all the windows closed even though she knew from her protection detail that for some reason, *he* could walk in daylight. No one was sure why and Ash refused to comment on it.

They had hazarded guesses of everything from he was really a demon to a Daimon plant. To the fact that he was sleeping with Artemis. The Dark-Hunter scuttlebutt could be as creative as it was entertaining.

Personally, she believed it was the result of the fact that he hadn't been murdered like the rest of them.

He'd killed himself for vengeance. Somehow, she was convinced, that had altered his Dark-Hunter powers and made him something more than the rest of them. She suspected that Acheron knew what he was and was afraid to tell the rest of them.

Perhaps the people coming for him, that she was charged with protecting him from, were a result of his unnatural rebirth. Whatever the truth, both Ash and Nick were keeping it close to their vests.

Sam sighed as she pushed those thoughts away. No matter how much she pondered it, she wouldn't get an answer. And right now, she should be sleeping. But she couldn't seem to manage it. Her emotions were too raw and bleeding.

She wanted Dev and it was the one thing she couldn't have.

Without thinking, she reached out and touched one of the photos on the wall of Dev and Nick playing pool. The moment she did, her powers surged and she saw that moment occurring in crystal clarity.

"Come here, you little hustler." Dev laughed as he pulled Nick around the table for his shot. "You beat that and I'll pay you a hundred dollars."

Nick gaped at him. "Dude! You're so on . . . um, do I have to pay *you* if I lose?"

Grinning, Dev shook his head and ruffled Nick's short hair. "Nah, but you will have to wash dishes for a week."

"That sucks."

Dev tsked at him. "You a coward?"

"Oh you're going down, Bear. Open the checkbook. Daddy's going to show *you* how it's done." Nick lined up the shot.

Dev danced around the table, trying to distract him. "Your mother was a hamster and she smelled of elderberries."

Nick scoffed at the Monty Python reference. "I don't know what you're talking about, Grizzly Adams. You're the one whose mom is covered in fur. My mom just wears sequins." He let fly the cue stick and the balls scattered across the table. Unbelievably, he made the shot into the upper left hand pocket like a pro.

"Ha!" he shouted triumphantly.

Dev snorted. "Lucky shot." But it hadn't been lucky. Dev had used his powers to put the ball in the correct pocket. Nick had no idea.

Feigning disgust, Dev had pulled his money out and handed it over to Nick. "Next time, kid, it's double or nothing."

"Bull. Next time I'm not taking the chance that I could miss."

Dev jerked his chin toward the money in Nick's hand. "So what are you going to do with all that?"

Nick folded it up and slid it into his pocket. "I'm going to take my mom to Brennan's to eat for Mother's Day. She's never been there before and she's always wanted to."

Dev clapped him on the back. "All right, Pool Shark. Have a good time. I better get back to work before you completely clean me out."

Nick had reset the table while Dev went back to his station at the door.

Sam swallowed at his kindness that made her ache deep inside. Dev, unlike Nick, hadn't changed a bit.

"What are you doing?"

She jumped at the sound of Nick's deep voice behind her. "I was just looking at your photos."

Nick moved forward to see the one of him and Dev. There was a sadness in his eyes that actually brought a lump to her throat. "We had a lot of good times back then. My mom used to save and frame everything she could."

And she'd put them on the wall and then rotate them out at random times—it'd been a game she'd played with Nick to remind him of the things she thought were important in his life.

Friends. Family. Smiles.

His mom had been a great lady.

Sam cleared her throat. "You and Dev look pretty tight."

"He was always a good friend to me which is why I'm glad you sent him home."

His words didn't match the feelings she got from him whenever he was near Dev. Nor did they match the emotions she was picking up from him right now. "Then why do you hate him?"

Nick stiffened. "I don't hate him. I'm just mad—basically at the entire world. Dev let my mom leave Sanctuary with a Daimon disguised as a Dark-Hunter."

"Dev would never—"

"I know, Sam." She felt his pain as he said those words in a trembling voice. "He had no idea he'd put her in harm's way and I know he'd have never done it intentionally. But I can't get over that night and I can't forgive anyone who had a hand in her death. I just can't."

She could understand that. "It's hard to live with that kind of guilt all the time."

"You've no idea."

"You're wrong, Nick. I know exactly what it's like to watch the people I love more than anything be slaughtered while I was powerless to save them. I, who trained my entire life to fight, couldn't save the very people I'd vowed to love and protect. How could I not be there to save them?"

A tic started in his cheek. "How do you live with it?"

She answered honestly. "Angrily. Every single day. Every single night. I want blood and all the killing in the world never changes it. Never eases it."

He let out a tired sigh. "So this is how I'll feel forever?"

"Unless you can find another reason to live. Find something that gives you peace."

He looked down at her. "Have you found that peace?"

Yes, she had. But it was so corny and cliched that she couldn't bring herself to admit it.

"A wise man once told me that peace has to come from within. We have to learn to like ourselves before we can find our place in the world."

Nick curled his lip. "Acheron."

She smiled. "He's said it to you, too?"

"No. We don't talk much these days, but it sounds like something he'd say." His gaze turned dark. "Don't trust Acheron, Sam. He's not what he seems."

She sensed. . . .

Sam concentrated, but she couldn't get a handle on it exactly. There was something Nick knew that none of the rest of them did. It was like he was hating Acheron for the same thing he protected about him.

It made no sense, but there was no denying what she felt. Nick did know a major secret about Ash.

And he knew one about himself that he would die before he gave up.

"How do you mean?" she asked, trying to get him to verbalize what she was sensing.

He refused to elaborate. "Believe me, there's a lot more to him and he's not really on our side." With that, he walked off to leave her alone.

Sam scowled at his hostility. Part of her knew there was a lot more to Ash than he let others see, but she didn't believe for one instant that he could ever hurt any of them.

Nick on the other hand . . .

She didn't trust him at all. He was infected by evil. She was sure of it.

Her heart heavy, she started back to her room, wishing Dev were with her.

I did the right thing.

He was safe and that was all that mattered.

Sam had just reached her room when she felt her hand beginning to burn. Hissing, she blew air across her palm, trying to soothe it.

Just when she was ready to scream from the pain, it stopped burning.

To her instant horror, she watched as a design drew itself across her flesh. There in her palm was a mark that looked like a tribal bear claw.

Oh shit.

She was mated. . . .

Chapter 19

Dev came awake to a scorching hot pain. At first he thought he was under attack, until he realized it was only his palm that hurt. Scowling, he shook his hand, then looked at it to see what he'd done to it.

His stomach drew tight. No . . .

It wasn't possible. It just wasn't possible.

Yet he couldn't deny what he saw. There in his palm was the one thing he'd waited a lifetime to see.

His mating mark.

And there was no doubt who his mate had to be. He hadn't been with anyone else in months. *How could this be?* Sam was a Dark-Hunter. How could he be mated to one? No Were-Hunter ever in their entire history had been mated to a Dark-Hunter.

"You bitches are crazy." The Fates had to be. Why else mate him to Sam?

Artemis would have a fit when she found out.

Incredulous, he wanted to go to Sam, but he knew better. She'd tossed him out and she wasn't the kind of woman a man went to. At least not without a Kevlar cup.

His phone rang.

He reached for it and flipped it open without checking the ID.

"Dev?"

He went hard at the sound of Sam's voice. "Hey."

She hesitated before she spoke again. "I . . . There's . . . um . . ."

He understood the panic he heard in her voice. He felt it too. Closing his palm so that he'd feel closer to her, he licked his lips. "You have a mark on your palm that looks like a bear claw."

"Yes. Does this mean what I think it does?"

He took a long, deep breath before he answered and tensed in trepidation of how she'd react. "Yeah."

She sucked her breath in sharply. "We can't do this, Dev. You know we can't."

He winced at the determination he heard in her voice. "You know I can't force you." Mating was always up to the female. "But if you reject me, you might as well kill me."

"Dev!"

He clenched his teeth. "I'm not a eunuch, Sam. I don't want to live in celibacy for the rest of my life. I'd rather be dead."

"Don't be so fatalistic. It's just sex. You can live without it. Trust me."

She didn't understand what he was trying to say. It wasn't just the sex. It was knowing that she was his mate and that he was forbidden to be with her that would ruin him. Were-Hunters were always insanely protective over their mates. They never liked to be apart.

Knowing she was out there alone . . .

It *would* kill him.

Sam let out a tiny breath. "How long do we have to decide this?"

"Three weeks." After that, he'd be impotent. Gah . . .

"Okay. I need to think about this."

Take your time, by all means. Not like you're the one who's going to be impotent. Whatever you do, think about yourself first. He had to bite his tongue to keep from saying that out loud. But if he did, then he'd be as selfish as he was accusing her and that he'd never do.

"You know where I am, Sam."

"Okay. I'll talk to you later."

He turned his phone off and hung his head in his hands as his emotions overwhelmed him. The bear inside him wanted to go over to Nick's and take her whether she wanted it or not. The man knew he couldn't. The Fates didn't work that way. This was completely in her hands and there was nothing he could do except wait.

I hate you three bitches. May you rot in Tartarus.

THE GREEK GODDESS Atropos pulled back from the loom where she and her two sisters wove the lives of those they were responsible for. As the three Fates, each of them had a job to perform. Her sister Lachesis was responsible for assigning the length of a person's life. Clotho spun the events that shaped and broke those lives.

And Atropos was the one who ended them. She had the final say. . . .

At least so long as their brother didn't interfere. Bastard.

Not wanting to think about that, she looked up at Lazaros who watched her in silence. "It's done. They're mated."

Lazaros smiled in satisfaction. "I can't thank you enough, little cousin. You are truly a lifesaver."

What an ironic thing to say to the one whose prime responsibility was death. "I don't see how. But if Artemis has anything to say—"

"She won't. I promise. And if she should, I will take care of it." He kissed her hand. "Now I have one last favor to ask."

"And that is?"

He plucked at the strand on the loom that represented the Dark-Huntress Samia's life. "Don't cut this thread until I tell you to." Because Sam wouldn't be able to die until Atropos cut it. So long as it was unsevered, he could torture Sam to his heart's content.

She inclined her head to him. "As you wish, coz. I'll leave it until you've had your fun."

He squeezed her hand before he released it. There were times when being related to the Fates was a good thing.

Today it was more than good.

DEV COULDN'T STOP staring at his hand. It was so strange to see it there after all these centuries of wondering if and when it would happen. Even though it was a girly thought, he'd always expected his mating to be really special. Like there would be the sound of trumpets or fireworks or something. People cheering. His family fainting in disbelief. Remi's head exploding.

The reality ...

It was remarkably anticlimactic.

Just another day.

Nothing had changed and yet everything was different. Closing his eyes, he summoned an image of Sam's face. *Please don't leave me hanging, babe.* She had to accept him.

What was there not to love?

He really didn't like the voice in his head that began cataloging the answer to that. *Yeah, I'm a pig-bear. I leave my wet socks on the floor. I like to fight and I don't listen as much as I should ...*

I'm such a schmuck.

"Hey Dev?"

He sighed as he heard his brother Kyle's voice in the hallway. Rolling over on the bed, he landed his feet on the floor and went to see what Kyle wanted.

He opened the door.

It wasn't Kyle.

Stryker was on the other side, smiling snidely. "If Mohammad won't come to the mountain ..."

He shot Dev in the chest.

SAM HAD HER phone clutched in her palm. She was trying to tell herself why calling Dev would be a bad idea. Why she didn't want to be his mate.

But everything kept coming back to one thing.

How Dev made her feel. How much she loved to see that cocky grin of his even when it annoyed her.

I am so messed up.

307

She traced the image on her palm that marked her as a bear's mate. She should be horrified by what had happened, yet it somehow seemed right. In a weird way she felt like Ioel was happy about it too.

But if she went ahead with this, there would be a major problem. She didn't want to be human again. Ever. There was no need. To be human wouldn't get rid of her powers. They would remain, but she would be mortal.

She would die.

Yes, she could have children, but that was the only benefit. And having died while pregnant ...

She *never* wanted to be that vulnerable again. And if she didn't have children, she'd be robbing Dev of that pleasure.

You could always adopt.

Could she? She would still be a Dark-Hunter who owed her service to Artemis. Would the goddess understand or would she demand Sam's head for this?

The entire thing was giving her a migraine as she tried to unscramble the mess.

She jumped in startled alarm as her phone started ringing. It was from Dev. Smiling, she opened the phone and answered it. "Yes?"

"In the heart and in the soul,
"Evil takes its wicked toll.
"When moonlight shines like flowing blood,
"Over the earth the demons will flood."

Her blood ran cold as someone in a demonic voice whispered over her phone. "Who is this?" she demanded.

"Someone who misses you. Isn't that right, Bear?"

"Don't come near me, Sam. Don't—" Dev's words broke off into a sharp growl that sounded like he wanted to go for someone's throat.

"If you want to see your mate again, leave the house right now, tell no one, and go down the street to Lafitte's Blacksmith Shop Bar and I'll be waiting for you outside."

"How will I know it's you?"

"You'll know, Dark-Hunter. And you better come alone. Dev's life depends on it." The demon hung up.

Fury and fear mixed inside Sam and it made her want to kill something. But worse, it brought out her nightmares and shredded her confidence.

How had they captured Dev? How had they known to go after him?

I jeopardize everyone I love . . .

Tears gathered in her eyes, but she blinked them away. She would not cry. She would not go down without a ferocious battle.

And right now, she wanted blood from Thorn and Nick. Had they known he'd be captured? Was that what they'd been trying to tell her?

Would Dev have been all right had she stayed with him instead of listening to them? They'd promised her that she was getting him out of the line of fire and instead, she'd handed him over to her enemies.

This isn't your fault.

Dev's a big boy.

Yeah and Ioel had been one too.

Right up to the moment they'd killed him.

Her heart hammering, she dressed in her warrior's garb and had to sneak out of the house without Nick seeing her. It was just after dark as she crept down Bourbon Street toward the corner where it intersected with St. Philip's. There was already a nice crowd there. Friends and couples drinking and laughing.

How she wished she could be so carefree.

Sam looked around for her contact, but all she saw were humans. Tons of humans which would make for a lot of collateral damage in a fight. And right now, all their residual emotions and thoughts were playing havoc in her mind.

She stopped on the corner, scanning the people at the tables while she debated what to do.

A dark shadow fell over her. "Keep walking, Huntress."

Her blood ran cold as she turned to see the lethal killing machine.

It was Stryker.

She wasn't about to let him know how he affected her. Putting up her guard, she sneered at him. "So you came yourself."

"I'm not here to talk." He jerked his chin to her right. "You go through my bolt-hole or I'll feed your mate to a mob of hungry Daimons who would kill to dismember a Were-Hunter. Literally."

She lacked all appreciation for a joke he was proud of. And she had to force herself not to attack him. "Do I have your word that you'll release him if I obey you?"

"Would you accept my word?"

That was a tough call. How could someone trust evil incarnate? And yet Stryker was an ancient warrior—like her.

Sam flinched as that thought triggered her powers. She saw Stryker in a home she'd never seen before. He was with another Dark-Hunter. . . .

Ravyn Kontis.

Stryker had him and his woman trapped and outnumbered.

"Do we kill him, my lord?" one of the Daimons asked.

Stryker cocked his head as if considering it. "Not today, Davyn. Today, we show a bit of mercy to our worthy opponent. After all, he taught me that you don't trust the human cattle. Only other immortals understand the rules of war."

And in another flash, she saw Stryker battling with Nick and Acheron. . . .

For them against a common enemy to save everyone.

Even though Stryker was her enemy and didn't shirk to commit heinous kills on innocent people, he was strangely a man of honor and he followed a very screwed up code.

Once he gave his oath, he would abide by it.

Even so, it was hard to utter the words she knew he wanted to hear. "I'll trust you, Daimon."

Stryker inclined his head to her. "Then yes. I will release both of you once this is over . . . *if* you obey."

Sam knew from her powers that she could trust him. But that was easier said than done. Not to mention one small fact, he was the one holding Dev.

So while her common sense screamed at her to run, she did what he said and stepped into the bolt-hole. The force of the vortex ripped at her skin and clothes. It was painful and terrifying as she spun and fell without anything to give her any sort of orientation.

I'm going to be sick.

No wonder the Daimons were always in such a foul mood when she ran across them. If she had to travel like this, she'd be grouchy too.

She finally fell out of the vortex and slammed into the ground where she landed unceremoniously as a lump on a cold, black marble floor. She hit it so hard, it knocked all the wind out of her. Groaning out loud, she looked around to find herself in the hall she'd seen through the slug demon's eyes. Dozens of Daimons were there, along with Zephyra. All of them eyeballed her like the top sirloin on a hamburger buffet.

Stryker landed beside her in a powerful crouch. Without so much as a grunt, he rose to his feet to stare down at her with one arched brow.

Effing show-off.

Sam pushed herself up and stumbled. Yeah, she still didn't have her vortex legs.

Stryker stepped past her to his throne where a small orb that reminded her of the sun was set on the right arm. It hovered just above his hand—no bigger than the size of her fist. It was so bright, that she could barely look at it without flinching.

His dark eyes gleaming, Stryker danced his fingers under it. "This belongs to my father. I want you to touch it and tell me his weakness. Tell me how to break our curse so that my people don't die. And most of all, I want to know how to kill that bastard."

His hatred radiated to her.

But the sad thing was, she couldn't help him. "It doesn't work that way."

Fury poured from his glare. "For your sake, Huntress. For Devereaux's sake, it better."

A shiver went down her spine. This had the making of a royal disaster. She had no idea if she could hone her powers that way. . . .

C'mon, don't fail me now. It wasn't just her life on the line. It was Dev's.

Sam looked around at all the Daimons who were gathered and as she did so, she picked up bits and pieces from them about their lives. Most of all, she picked up their hope that she could free them of their curse.

I have to get Dev and get out of here.

She was a powerful fighter, but she wasn't good enough to win against this number. If Stryker was lying, there really wasn't much she'd be able to do except die painfully at their hands.

But she'd go down fighting. To the bitter end.

Taking a deep breath, she closed the distance between her and his throne. Her gaze locked on his, she reached out and touched the orb. The light that emanated from inside it arced and filled her palm with warmth. She saw so many images all at once that she couldn't understand any of them.

Until one became more prominent than the others.

It was Artemis dressed in a white gown and looking just as she did the night Sam had sold her soul to the goddess. Artemis was furious as she confronted Apollo in his temple. "What have you done, brother?"

Apollo's golden hair gleamed like pure sunlight. His features were beyond perfect. He sat on an overstuffed gold chaise with his sister beside him. "They betrayed me. They killed my son, my baby son. Was I supposed to forgive them that?"

Artemis shook her head. "Why would you curse *all* of them?"

He sneered at her. "Like you have never acted impulsively? This is all *your* fault. Had you not been sleeping with a human whore none of this would have occurred!"

313

Artemis glowered at him. "And you've killed him too and damn near all of us in the process. Would you destroy this entire pantheon over *your* dead whore?"

He stood up to tower over her. "Why not? You risked it for yours!"

Artemis refused to back down as she faced him. "Leave Acheron out of this, brother, or so help me—"

"What? You won't do anything to me, Artemis. If you do, I'll tell every god here how you, the virgin goddess, spread your legs for a common piece of human filth."

Sam reeled from that revelation.

Artemis didn't flinch as she fisted both of her hands as if she was one step away from punching Apollo. "I hate you."

"And I return that to you tenfold, sister. Now leave me."

"I can't. Your people are feeding on the humans because of *your* curse."

Apollo bristled. "Not *my* curse. Apollymi was the one who taught them how to steal human souls. She's the one housing and protecting them now. I have nothing to do with it."

"Then lift your curse from your people. Apollymi won't be able to control them if they don't need to take human souls to live."

"I can't."

Artemis shook her head. "Can't or won't?"

"Can't. If I take it back, it will kill me and undo the entire creation of the world. I *can't* fix this."

Artemis let out a long sigh before she raked him with a repugnant sneer. "You're pathetic, Apollo. Pathetic." She turned and left him alone in his temple where he stared into an orb similar to the one in Sam's palm.

Apollo's hand shook as he conjured an image of Stryker in his orb. His eyes swam with tears. "You were ever disappointing to me, but I never meant to hurt you. I was trying to make you strong." He choked on a sob. "If I could undo this, Strykerius, I would. I would. . . . I am so sorry for what I've done. . . ."

Sam pulled back from the scene as her head whirled with everything she'd learned.

Especially about Acheron. Was that what had made him the first Dark-Hunter?

He'd been Artemis's lover?

A whore . . .

Surely Apollo hadn't meant that Acheron was really a whore, whore. Had he? Or was it just his anger at Acheron that caused him to say that?

"Well?" Stryker prompted. "How do I kill Apollo?"

She blinked at Stryker's impatient tone as her mind replayed everything in sequence.

Zephyra sat forward on her throne. "What did you see? Can we break the curse?"

Sam shook her head. "It can't be undone."

Rage contorted Stryker's handsome features. "You lie!"

"No, I swear. There is no way. Apollo would have undone it in the beginning had he been able to."

Stryker cursed. "And his weakness? What will bring him to his knees?"

Oh he wasn't going to like the answer to that question. She knew it. "The same thing that caused him to curse the Apollites to begin with."

"His whore, Ryssa?" Stryker asked.

She shook her head. "The death of the son he loves more than anything."

Scowling at her, Stryker sat back. "I don't understand. What son?"

She licked her dry lips and braced herself for his wrath. "You, Stryker. You're his weakness. You're what he loves above everything else. . . . You're the only thing he loves."

Zephyra put her hand on his shoulder as Stryker sat there completely stone-faced. "She's telling the truth."

Stryker grabbed Sam by the arm and jerked her to him. "Are you playing with me?"

"Why would I?"

Snarling, he threw her away from him. One minute she was in the center of the hall and in the next, she was being sucked back into the vortex.

Sam fought against it with everything she had. Stryker had lied, there was no Dev. He was sending her back empty-handed.

Screaming, she tried to stop falling. Tried to get back to Kalosis so that she could hunt for him.

It was no use.

She found herself on the street just a few feet from where she'd gone into the vortex earlier.

"No!" she screamed as it closed right behind her and left her alone. She got up and ran around trying to find another opening.

There wasn't one.

She was here and Dev . . .

Oh God, Dev . . .

Tears blinded her as that old helpless feeling ripped her apart. "You lying bastard!"

Guilt and grief tore through her. Dev was dead and it was all her fault. She'd caused this. Had she not thrown him out, she would have been there to protect him when Stryker came to get him.

How could she have let him go?

You're a fool. Twice now she'd lost the man she loved.

And as she wept, she felt her Dark-Hunter powers waning. *I don't care.* Nothing mattered to her anymore. Let them kill her.

Yet again the Daimons had taken everything from her. Only this time, she couldn't blame her sister.

She could only blame herself.

Sick to her stomach, she didn't know where to go or what to do. Aimless, she found herself back at Nick's house, walking through the gate and then the back door.

How do I tell Dev's family what I let happen? They would be crushed. All of them . . .

Nick stopped her as she reached the bottom of his staircase. "Where did you go?"

She ignored Nick's question as she stepped past him.

"Sam?" Nick snapped. "What are you doing?"

Numb, she couldn't think straight. "I need to be alone for a minute."

Or a millennium.

I just want to die.

She stumbled up the stairs, wishing Stryker had killed her too. How could she have ever been so stupid as to trust a Daimon?

Her heart breaking, she opened the door to her room and froze.

No way . . .

Was it possible?

She blinked her eyes in disbelief as she saw Dev standing near her bed.

It couldn't be.

"Dev?"

He was looking around as if he was as dazed as she'd been in Kalosis. "How did I get here? I swear I'm not stalking you, Sam. I didn't—"

Laughing, she launched herself at him and wrapped her body around his while she kissed him over and over again.

Dev staggered back as Sam assaulted him. He'd expected her to be mad for his breaking her "space," but there was nothing even remotely angry about her giddiness as she kissed him senseless.

Yeah, the woman was nuts. But as she rained kisses over him, he was getting harder by the minute and forgetting why he wasn't supposed to be here with her.

"I thought you were dead."

"Not yet."

She squeezed him so tight, he could barely breathe. "I'm so sorry if I hurt you, Dev. I'm so sorry." But for someone apologizing, she got more aggressive as she shoved him back onto the bed and pinned him there under her body.

Then she gave him the hottest kiss he'd ever had in his life.

But he wasn't playing this. As much as he hated doing it, he shoved her back. "I'm not your yo-yo, Sam. And you're not going to play head games with me."

Sam swallowed as she saw the fury in those precious blue eyes she'd never thought to see again. "I don't want to bury you, Dev. I don't. I love you and it terrifies me."

Those words hit him like a vicious punch to his gut. "What did you say?"

"I love you."

He cupped her cheek in his hand as he stared at her in disbelief. Those were the three words he'd never expected to hear from someone he wasn't related to. "I don't want to live without you, Sam."

Tears glistened in her eyes. "I haven't been alive in over five thousand years. Not until some bear made a smart-ass comment about my bad driving and followed me home."

He bristled under her accusation. "You invited me."

Her smile blinded him. "And I'm inviting you in again."

"Are you sure?"

She nodded. "I know this is fast, but—"

A loud knock on the door interrupted her. "Clothes on, people, quick," Nick said from the other side of the door. "Buckle up, buttercups. We have incoming and it's about to get bloody."

Chapter 20

Dev opened the door to find Nick in the hallway, dressed for battle. "What's going on?"

"My Spidey sense is off the radar. There's a massive demon migration and it's charting a course straight for us. Since I don't want my house destroyed, I vote we take it where we're least likely to be seen and where we have an advantage."

"And that would be?" Dev asked.

"The St. Louis Cemetery. This time of night, it'll be closed and empty."

Sam shook her head. "I can't go there. I'll get possessed."

Nick rolled his eyes. "Better you than my house."

"I thought you had it shielded?" she shot back.

"I do, but this—"

A loud pop downstairs cut his words off.

Nick cursed as he stepped back and tilted his head. "Looks like we waited too long. Gird your loins, people, join the fight." He vanished.

Dev sighed irritably. "That's so not what I want to do with my loins right now."

Sam laughed. "Don't worry, baby. I'll take care of your loins later. Right now, we fight."

By the time they reached downstairs, Ethon, Chi, and Nick were standing with their backs to each other. Sam could hear the demons scratching, trying to break the shield around Nick's house.

She looked back and forth between Chi and Ethon. "What are you two doing here?"

Ethon winked at her. "Nice seeing you, too. Thanks for the gracious welcome."

Chi ignored him. "We came in at sunset to help guard you and Nick."

"Thank you." Sam turned to Nick. "Where's Ash?"

Nick curled his lip. "He's not welcome here and I refuse to have him in my home."

Dev looked at him like he was crazy. "Is that a good idea given what we're facing?"

"My vote is double hell no," Ethon said, swinging his sword around. "But I think we can handle them."

Sam gave Captain Suicide a droll stare. "How did you die again? Oh wait, I know this. 'I can take 'em. I don't need to wait for reinforcements. I can do it myself.' How'd that work out for you again?"

Ethon glared at her. "It wasn't that cut and dry and I would have won had my best friend not stabbed me in the back. Literally."

Nick growled at them. "They're breaking through. You guys might want to get your heads out of your asses and pay attention for this."

The sound of glass shattering echoed through the house an instant before it began crawling with demons.

Lazaros manifested in the center of the room. Ten feet tall and in the form of a twisted one legged serpent, he faced them. "Give me Samia and I'll leave the rest of you in peace."

"Why do you want her?" Nick asked.

"She killed my brother."

Sam frowned as she searched her memory. "I've never killed a demon."

"Liar!" Lazaros snarled. "Your sister sold her soul to him to kill you and your family so that she could be queen in your place. When you became a Dark-Hunter, you hunted him down and killed him."

Frowning in confusion, she shook her head. "No, I didn't. I killed a Daimon."

"You killed an empusa, you moron. And I would have killed you then but I was told you were dead and then I was captured before I could confirm it." He narrowed a blood red stare on her. "Tonight my brother will finally be avenged and I will bathe in your blood." He lunged for her throat.

Dev caught him and drove him back.

The other demons attacked en masse. They swooped in like a dark cloud that wanted to consume them. Sam put her back to Dev's as they fought with everything they had.

She cut the head off one, then drove another to Ethon who quickly dispatched him.

Lazaros whipped his tail, catching her across the back. It felt like a razor slicing through her flesh and it brought out agonizing memories of his brother killing her and her family.

Cursing, Sam stumbled.

Dev caught her and the memories instantly faded so that she had total clarity again. He blasted a shot with his powers straight at Lazaros who absorbed it and sent it back to him. It knocked Dev flying.

Sam caught herself, then gasped as she saw Dev bleeding on the floor. Her powers drained out of her immediately.

Please don't die. Please don't die . . .

Running to him, she saw that his eye and nose were cut. He had a gash in his side. But he was alive. Bloodied, but alive. Relief swept through her.

He moved to stand.

Over and over, she saw the premonition images of him lying dead in this room. Normally she took power from such things as her rage went through her like the Hulk, but right now . . .

Her fears paralyzed her. She couldn't lose him.

Dev saw Sam's eyes turn green and his breath was sucked out of his body as his fear mounted. She was human which meant she could die.

Terrified for her, he flipped to his feet and put himself between her and Lazaros. There was no way he was going to let her go down.

Not tonight.

The demons had Ethon and Nick pinned. Chi was completely out of sight. And more demons were coming in.

Lazaros rushed for Sam.

With a battle cry, Dev lunged at him, but just as he reached the demon, it darted and swiped him with its tail.

323

One minute he was about to stab it, in the next he was flying through the air, ass over tea kettle.

Sam snarled as she found her human power. Screw the Dark-Hunter crap. She didn't need it.

The lioness in her roared to life and all she could focus on was saving the people in this room who meant the most to her. And Dev topped that list.

She picked up the fallen sword that Ethon had dropped and true to her Amazon nature, she attacked with every instinct and skill she possessed. She dodged and swerved, hacked and sliced. Lazaros blasted her and she ducked, letting the blasts fly past her and hit the couch, walls, and tables which started burning.

"I hate you bastards," Nick snarled as he saw the damage. "Couldn't you have attacked at Ash's house?"

Not paying Nick's outburst any attention, she completely disengaged herself to keep Dev safe.

Dev was impressed by Sam's prowess as she met every attack with a counter. He'd never seen anything like it and when she came up and stabbed Lazaros in his side, his heart stopped.

Lazaros whipped his tail around and pinned her to the floor.

Rage consumed him as he went for the demon. Lazaros turned to confront him. Sam rolled out from under Lazaros's tail and scrambled for the sword she'd dropped. The moment the hilt was in her hand, she threw it at the demon.

She pinned Lazaros's head to the wall like a grisly trophy. The demon screamed out in agony, shuddered, and then died.

Still the others kept coming.

Sam picked up another sword as she met Dev. She kissed him quickly on the lips, then turned to keep fighting.

"How do we stop them?" Ethon shouted.

Nick cursed. "They're not responding to my powers. There's nothing I can do."

Sam had no powers to use. She looked at Dev.

Dev shrugged. "I say we beat them down until they kill us."

All of sudden, there was a bright flash of light as Acheron appeared in the center of the room. He swept his gaze around them and took in everything before he slammed his staff down and sent a shock of something reverberating through the entire house. It was like some kind of weird sonic boom that shook the very foundation and made the demons disintegrate.

Ethon, bleeding and sweating, glared at Acheron. "'Bout time, boss. What kept you?"

Chi appeared beside Acheron. "I didn't want to bother him. But it was getting too close for my comfort level so I went for the big gun."

Ash gave her an irritated smirk. "Next time someone unleashes a herd of demons, an early call would be nice. I don't want to be scraping up my team's entrails. Took too much to train all of you to start over with recruits."

Nick scoffed. "We were handling it just fine. We didn't need *your* help."

"Really?" Ash arched his regal brow. "Let me clue you in on one of your powers, Nick. You can charge off the power of a demon. If you don't, they charge off you and grow in strength."

That took the cockiness right out of Nick. "What?"

"You are the Energizer Bunny for badasses." Acheron looked at Chi. "I thought you were training him?"

"We haven't gotten to that yet. He's a stubborn pupil who doesn't listen to me much."

Acheron let out a sound of deep disgust before he turned back to Nick. "And I thought teaching you to drive sucked." Then he mumbled under his breath. "Hardheaded . . ." the rest was in some language Sam couldn't understand.

Nick held up his hand. "Stop bitching and make yourself useful for once. Clean up my house."

Ash scoffed. "Do I look like a Merry Maid to you?"

"Yes, Bo-Peep. Chop chop. I have blood and entrails on my walls and it's staining the wallpaper."

Sam was stunned Ash let anyone talk to him like that.

Yet he seemed to take Nick's fit in stride. "I should have left you in the coma." He slammed his staff down and everything in the house went back to normal.

Nick licked at his fangs. "Thank you . . . Dick."

Ash ignored him as he moved to Sam.

She swallowed hard as Artemis and Apollo's words about him rang in her head. *Acheron a whore . . .*

In a weird way, she could see it. He did have the movements of a trained courtesan. Slow. Steady. A symphony of movement. Plus there was that unnatural sexual magnetism he put out. It was like a lion in the wild. Something so beautiful that you had an irresistible urge to pet it and yet you knew if you tried, it would tear off your arm.

Yeah, that was Acheron.

He picked up her hand and looked at her marked palm. Dev moved to stand behind her.

Ash didn't speak for several long seconds. He met Sam's and then Dev's gazes. "How do you feel about this?"

Sam bit her lip. "I think it's more a question of how do *you* feel about it?"

Ash's hand actually trembled as he held hers. "I can't get your soul back, Sam. I can't. Artemis won't let me."

Her stomach hit the floor at his news. "You've done it for others."

He nodded. "I know, but things have changed and Artemis won't release any more to me."

Fine, she didn't want to be human anyway. "Can't I be a Dark-Hunter and mated?"

Ash looked at Ethon and then Chi. "The rules were set in place for a reason. Artemis still owns you and she's a jealous goddess. If she finds out about this . . . you don't want to ever see her that angry. And honestly, I don't know what she'd do over this. But in the end, it's your decision. I can't make it for you."

Sam clenched her teeth. "You're sure you can't get my soul back?"

"I'm sure and I'm sorry."

Nick curled his lip at Ash. "You better be glad I'm a better friend to you than you ever were to me or I'd tell them exactly why you can't help her . . . Acheron. But I won't steal from you what you love. My mama raised me better."

Ash's swirling silver eyes blazed. "You know, Nick, but you don't understand. There's a big difference. You have no idea what the world is like when you're completely alone and unprotected in it. Pray to the gods that you never do. The one lesson I can't teach you . . . that neither Chi nor Takeshi can teach you is not to judge others so harshly. As you said, you're mama raised you better and you shame her memory every time you spit at me."

Nick bellowed in rage before he lunged for Ash.

Ash threw his arm out and held him back with an invisible force field. "One day, Cajun, you will have the power to destroy me. But that day isn't here yet." And with that, he vanished.

Nick was so angry, he shook from it. "You're all fools to blindly follow him when you don't know what he is."

Ethon shook his head. "You're wrong, Gautier. I know exactly what he is."

"Yeah?" Nick sneered. "And what is that?"

"My friend. That's all that matters to me."

Nick scoffed at him. "You're a fucking idiot, Stark. He was my friend too and he ruined me."

"For that I'm sorry. But until he betrays me, I owe him my loyalty." Ethon moved to stand by Sam. A sad smile hovered over his lips as he took her marked hand into his.

In that moment, she returned to the day she'd married Ioel. Ethon had been there then too. Standing by her side just as he was now.

He kissed the back of her knuckles. "I'm happy for you, little sister. If Artemis comes for you, call me. I will stand and I will fight for you anytime."

Because he loved her.

Sam's lips trembled at a truth he didn't want her to know but one she'd seen so clearly. He'd been in love with her since long before their deaths. He'd loved her so much that he was willing to say nothing about his feelings for her in order to keep from tainting her happiness. And it was a love she'd never been able to return to him.

He would never be more than a brother to her.

Life was unfair and as Acheron so often said, emotions had no brains. Ethon deserved someone who could return his love with the same passion that burned inside him and she hoped that one day he'd find her.

She squeezed his hand. "I love you, Ethon."

He swallowed. "Like a brother. I know." He held his hand out to Dev. "Take care of her, Bear. I'd say I'd kick your ass if you didn't, but she's a better fighter than I am."

Dev laughed. "Thanks, E."

Ethon inclined his head before he headed to the door. "Time to patrol. There are Daimons on the street and stupid humans willing to feed them. You coming, Chi?"

"I have Nick duty tonight."

"Then good luck. May the gods be with you and don't kill the lippy bastard." Ethon left them.

His gaze bitterly amused, Nick stepped forward. "Congratulations, Dev. Sam." To her amazement, he shook their hands.

And he was actually happy for them.

Chi smiled. "I'm so thrilled for you guys. And I hope Acheron is wrong and that Artemis is understanding about this." She turned to Nick. "You ready to start our lessons?"

He shook his head. "Not tonight. I have something else I need to take care of."

"Nick . . ." Her tone was thick with chiding. "You *have* to learn. You're still extremely vulnerable."

"Yeah, but a good friend once taught me that sometimes you have to put others first. Tonight is one of those."

Sam scowled at the odd note in Nick's voice as he teleported out and left them alone with Chi. "What are you teaching him?"

Chi sighed. "Demonology."

That was impressive and a rare talent. "Does he have your powers?"

"No. His powers make mine look weak. But he has to understand why the others are coming for him." Chi pressed her lips together as she thought about something that troubled her. When she spoke, Sam heard the undercurrent in her voice. "The more I'm with him, the more he scares me. There are times when he's so kind and then something comes over him. Something so evil that it gives me chills." She shook her head. "Anyway, don't let me taint your night. You two have a lot to discuss and decide. Shoo! Go and enjoy. We can catch up later."

Sam inclined her head to her. "I love you, Chi."

"I love you, too, babe."

"You ready?" Dev asked her.

"For what?"

He teleported her to his room.

She cringed as a wave of nausea swept through her. "I really hate traveling that way. It does not like me."

"Sorry. I just couldn't wait to be alone with you and it was the quickest way to get here."

Sam bit her lip as she scanned his lush, scrumptious body. "I know how you feel."

He kissed her gently on the lips. "So what did Stryker want with you?"

"Information on his father and how to break their curse."

"Did you tell him?"

She nodded. "I told him the truth. There's no way to break their curse. And that his father, even after all that's happened, still cares about him."

Dev let out a low whistle. "I'll bet he didn't take that well."

Sam fell silent as she considered that. "He took it better than I thought, but I have a feeling this isn't over."

"How so?"

"The Daimons can still walk in daylight and we're their enemies. Sooner or later, they'll be coming for all the Dark-Hunters and Stryker seems too determined to give up. I think he's got something even more sinister brewing."

"And I hope you're wrong."

So did she. But her gut was kicking and it had never been wrong in the past. They'd won this battle.

The war was still on.

EPILOGUE

Sam paused as someone knocked on the door right as dawn was breaking. She and Dev were just getting ready for bed. "Aimee?" She was the most likely candidate for someone disturbing them at this hour.

Dev shrugged. "Come in," he called.

It wasn't Aimee.

The door opened to show Nick. Once again, he had that sick pallor to his skin like he was in pain or about to hurl. He leaned heavily against the doorjamb as if he didn't have the energy to stand on his own. "Sorry to disturb you guys. But I wanted to give you a mating present."

Sam was touched by his kindness. The Weres had already been spoiling them with gifts and good wishes. "You didn't have to do that, Nick."

"Yeah, I did." He handed her a small wooden box. One that looked ancient.

She took it and opened the lid. There inside was a green amulet that glowed with an ethereal power. "It's beautiful." She reached to pick it up, but Nick stopped her.

"That's your soul, Sam."

She gaped at him as Dev came forward to stand behind her. "I don't understand."

Nick gave her a wan smile. "You don't have to. Suffice it to say, Artemis has agreed to let you go."

She was incredulous. How could this be? "Did you do this?"

That familiar tic started in Nick's jaw again. "Acheron set the terms. But that's not important. I wanted to get it to you guys as soon as possible. Do you know how it works?"

She had a basic idea from what she'd heard as rumors from other Dark-Hunters who'd been set free. "I have to die and Dev has to release my soul back into my body."

"That's an Ash-type explanation. You have to figure out what drains your Dark-Hunter powers and then stop your heart from beating. At the moment of your last breath, the amulet has to be placed over the bow and arrow mark and held there until you come back to life. It's going to burn like fire and if Dev lets go of it even one nanosecond before you start breathing again, you will spend eternity as a Shade." They were frightening ghosts who could never be seen or heard by others. Invisible apparitions who spent eternity in perpetual hunger and agony. It was a frightening thing to be.

Nick replaced the lid. "Good luck to both of you."

As he started to leave Sam stopped him. "I have one question."

"Yeah?"

"Do I have to become human again?"

Nick hesitated before he answered. "No. It's your soul to do with as you please. As of this moment, you're technically free from Artemis and your powers are yours. But if you don't return your soul to your body, you'll have the same limitations as before. You won't be able to have children and you won't be able to walk in daylight. Worst of all, you're off payroll."

She laughed. That wasn't the worst of it. She'd barely spent any of the money she'd made over the centuries so she was flush for at least a few hundred years.

Touched by his generosity, she stepped forward and did the one thing she hadn't done in a long time. She kissed his cheek.

The pain he was in hit her hard and stole her breath. But she pushed it aside. "Thank you, Nick."

He nodded before he withdrew and closed the door.

Dev took the box from her. "What do you want to do?"

"I don't know. I want to mate with you. To bond with you." Bonding meant that their life forces would be joined and when one of them died, they both would. It was something Dev's parents had refused to do while their children had been young—they'd been terrified of leaving them orphans. But once all their cubs were grown, they'd bonded and they'd died in each other's arms.

Sam brushed his hair back from his face. "Your life span is finite. Mine isn't. What say we bond and I stay immortal?" That way they'd never have to say goodbye to each other.

She hated the thought of death. This would be the best of all worlds.

Dev scratched his cheek. "We won't be able to have children."

She bit her lip, afraid of what he might say about her next proposal. "How do you feel about adoption?"

He smiled. "Works for me. All kids need love. But can you stand not being in daylight?"

And that would be different how? "Been five thousand years without it. I'm kind of used to it now and really have no patience with sunblock." She kissed the tip of his nose.

"All right then." He stepped back from her. "Let me go put this somewhere safe. Be right back."

Sam laughed at his urgency as she climbed into bed to wait for him. While she lay there, she turned her palm over to see her mark.

Dev's mark.

She still couldn't believe it was real. That her life had changed so drastically in such a short period of time. But then her birth as a Dark-Hunter had been every bit as quick and dramatic. One moment she'd been bathed in complete happiness and in the next everything had been shattered. It only seemed fair that the reverse could happen just as suddenly.

Dev popped into bed beside her.

Completely naked . . .

She laughed. He was ever a horn dog. "That was fast."

"We have a big safe inside a vault. I hid your soul well and now . . ." He pulled her close.

Sam let out a playful breath. "Why is it everything gets back to you being naked?"

"Nothing gets back to me being naked, baby. It's all about *your* bare skin." He kissed her stomach. Chills spread the entire length of her body. "Now let's see about this mating thing."

"Absolutely."

THREE MONTHS WENT by faster than Dev could blink. Never in his life had he expected to be so happy. Sam was now working night shifts with him and they'd settled into an easy nocturnal lifestyle.

It was 3 A.M. and he was at the door, listening to Sam and Aimee talk over his headset. He was so glad they were friends. It made everything that much easier.

Yawning, he was about to comment on their lame joke when a flash to his left caught his attention. A fissure of supreme power rippled in the air around him.

He stiffened, prepared to battle.

The light above his head went out.

When it came back on again, he saw Savitar standing in front of him.

"What are you doing here?"

Savitar rolled his shoulders into an easy, laid back shrug. "Been hearing some things 'bout your club, Bear."

Aimee, Fang, and Sam came to the door.

"Is there a problem?" Fang asked.

Savitar shook his head. "*Au contraire*. It seems you guys have a lot of friends who've been petitioning the council. Never let it be said that I'm without some form of mercy." He handed Aimee a rolled up piece of paper. "You're license is reinstated. Congratulations. Sanctuary is once again a protected limani. Welcome back to the fold."

Part of Dev wanted to tell him to shove it up the darkest recess of his body. But this wasn't about him. It was about their family.

Their cubs.

So he swallowed his pride and forced out the words he knew Savitar wanted to hear. "Thanks."

"I would say anytime, but I expect you to keep your noses clean."

Aimee inclined her head to him. "We will. Thank you for giving us another chance."

"No problem." Savitar turned to leave, then stopped. He looked at Sam. "The Fates brought you and Dev together out of total malice. I can't express to you how much I hate those bitches."

Sam held her breath as she expected him to revoke their mating. They were bonded. . . .

Could he break that?

Before she could blink, Savitar grabbed her hand. A jolt of electricity ran up her arm and through her body.

For several seconds, she couldn't breathe. "What did you do?"

He let go of her and clapped Dev on the back. "I'm a vain creature. I fully expect you two to name at least one of those cubs after me." Then he turned to Aimee. "You want a shot too?"

"Absolutely." Aimee held her arm out to him.

He took her hand and repeated the jolt. "That should make the three of those bitches scream for a few days. . . . It's the little things in life that mean so much. *Adios, mi amigos.* And don't worry, Sam." He pointed up at the blood red moon over their heads. "Sometimes it's just the light bending around the earth."

337

And with that, he was gone.

Sam stood there, completely stunned for several minutes. Until Dev leaned in and whispered in her ear.

"When you want to get started on making a baby Savitar?"

Laughing, she leaned back against his chest and cupped his cheek in her hand, holding his face against hers. "I love you, Bear. Weirdness and all."

"I'm glad to hear it because my weirdness definitely loves yours too."

And that was the most important lesson she'd learned being with Dev over the last few months. Living was okay, but it wasn't the breaths people took that measured a life. It was the moments that took those breaths away that mattered most.

And Dev did that every time he looked at her.

Naked or not.

If *No Mercy* has left you hungry for more, turn the page
for a sneak peak at Sherrilyn Kenyon's brand new novel
in the Belador series

Blood Trinity

Available now from Piatkus...

TWO YEARS AGO
UTAH ... BENEATH THE SALT FLATS

Similar in height and size, they were different as night and day in skin color and the way they dressed. The one with nothing on but jeans had been conscious when she'd regained her wits twenty minutes ago. Completely still, he hadn't made a sound since then—like a snake lying low until it saw an opportunity to strike. Arms outstretched and legs spread apart, his gaze now cut sideways at a rustle of movement.

The fair-haired guy on his left struggled to reach lucidity.

Being imprisoned with two Beladors would normally fill her with hope for escape because of their ability to link with each other and combine their powers. When that happened, Beladors fighting together were a force only the upper echelon of preternatural creatures could touch. They were damn near invincible.

But linking required unquestioned trust. And right now, she couldn't offer trust so easily. Not after a Belador's telepathic call for help had lured her into this hole—into the hands of Medb warlocks. Her tribe had fought this bunch for two thousand years.

Burn me once, shame on you. Burn me twice . . .

Die with pain.

Even so, could she refuse to help these two warriors—members of *her* tribe—if there was a chance to save them? Beladors were a secret race of Celtic people connected by powerful genetics and living in all parts of the world. She'd only met a few.

Never these two.

But every member of the tribe had sworn an oath to uphold a code of honor, to protect the innocent and any other Belador who needed help.

If a warrior broke that vow, every family member faced the same penalty as the warrior, even the penalty of death.

Evalle had no one who would be affected by her decisions. The only person she'd had was an aunt who'd died that Evalle didn't mourn. Not after what that woman had done to her.

But even without having someone to worry about she'd upheld her vows since the day she'd turned eighteen. Not because she had to, but because she wanted to. And—until now—she'd always supported her tribe without question.

If only she knew which side of the lake those two across from her swam on. Hers or the Medb's?

She had one chance to answer that question correctly.

Live or die . . .

What else was new?

"Anyone know who called for this delightful little meeting?" the fair-haired male grumbled in a smooth voice born of enhanced genetics and a hint of British influence. The sound matched the urbane angles of his European face, which could be Slovak or Russian. He straightened his shoulders as if that would smooth the creases in his overpriced suit, obviously tailored to fit that athletically cut body that James Bond would envy. She'd put him in his early thirties and at close to six foot three.

Bad, black and wicked next to him might be an inch shorter, but he balanced out the difference with a pound or two of extra kick-your-ass muscle.

"Introductions appear necessary . . . unless you two know each other." The blond guy looked in her direction, then at the other male, but she doubted he could see a thing in this blackness.

Then again, who knew what powers he had as a Belador? That thought sent another chill down her spine.

Evalle fought a smirk over pretty boy's dry tone and well-honed nonchalance. She'd never met a Belador male who wasn't alpha to the core. But she had no intention of jumping in first to answer after deceit had landed her here.

One of these two could very easily be a Medb surveillance plant.

Tonight's betrayal had put a serious damper on her "team" mentality, and it burned raw inside her.

"I suppose I shall have to open," pretty boy continued, undeterred by the rude silence. "I'm Quinn."

The other prisoner still hadn't twitched since being hauled into the cave by four Medb warlocks and slammed against the wall. He'd been the last one captured. Blood that had trickled earlier from gashes in his exposed chest had dried . . . and the gashes were gone. Rumors had surfaced that a few of the more powerful Belador warriors could self-heal some wounds overnight, but she'd never heard of one healing so quickly. Odd.

His head was completely bald, which added a lethal edge to his face. Ripped muscles curved along his arms. All that body flowed down to the narrow waist of his jeans. He cleared his throat, and even that sounded dangerous. "I'm Tzader."

"The Maistir?" Quinn's gaze walked up and down the other warrior, sizing him up.

"Yes."

Truth or lie? Evalle had never met Tzader Burke, commander of all the North American Beladors. If he was Maistir, that might explain why *he* was here. He would be a coup in any Medb's career.

She slashed a look at the self-appointed cave host, waiting on Quinn to make the next move.

He shifted his head in Evalle's direction. "I can see another faint aura glowing across from us. A woman, I presume from the look of it."

How come other Beladors could see auras, but not her? What had she done to tick off the aura fairy?

When she didn't pick up the conversation thread, Quinn asked, "You would be?"

"Pissed off." Evalle opened her eyes all the way.

He smirked. "Love the name, darling. Should I refer to you as simply Pissed?"

She ignored his sarcasm. "No offense, I'm going to need a little more information before I'm ready to buddy up to *anyone*. Especially two who could be lying to me."

First again to keep the ball rolling, Quinn nodded. "I had assumed only Beladors answered the call, but your aura is—"

"—not Belador," Tzader interjected.

Quinn's moment of hesitation spoke louder than his words. "I see."

Snubbed again. What else was new? Even though she'd heard the traitor's call for help telepathically just like this pair of full bloods had and felt the sizzle of their tribe's connection on her skin, they still didn't consider her one of them.

Raw fury roiled through her veins. What would she have to do to be considered one of the group? Too bad their hazing wasn't as simple as eating a few live goldfish. But then, why was she surprised or even hurt? Her own family had wanted nothing to do with her. Why should anyone else?

Still, she refused to be discounted so easily. "You two may be able to see *auras,* but I doubt that either of you *see* anything else in this pitch dark. Not like I can."

"That explains it." There was no missing the disgust in Tzader's tone.

"What precisely does that explain?" Quinn allowed his annoyance to come through that time. Not the happy cave host after all.

"She's an Alterant." Tzader stared her way, studying on something. "The only one *not* in VIPER protective custody."

Evalle released a sharp stream of air from between clenched teeth. "Right. *Protective custody* sounds so much more civilized than being *jailed,* which is what really happened to the other four Alterants. I'm not there because I don't deserve to be there and I refuse to live in a cage—just like you would if you were me. So deal with it." She'd been there, done that and burned the T-shirt reminder, and it would take more than the entire Belador race to put her back in one.

And she had no doubt how he'd vote if she shifted into a beast in front of him.

Thumbs down. Hang the Alterant.

Yeah, the pendulum was buried on the side of them being her enemies.

Tzader frowned. "You work for VIPER?"

VIPER—Vigilante International Protectors Elite Regiment—was a multinational coalition of all types of unusual beings and powerful entities created to protect the world from supernatural predators. Beladors made up the majority of VIPER's force, and if that really was Tzader Burke across from her, he'd know the only free Alterant worked with VIPER. Might as well cop to it. "I'm in the southwestern region."

Quinn cleared his throat. "I'm with VIPER as well and was on my way to investigate a Birrn demon sighting in Salt Lake City when I heard the call. What about you two?"

"Meeting an informant in Wendover," Tzader replied, mentioning the small gaming town at the Utah-Nevada border. "What were you doing in this area tonight, Alterant?"

Following a lead I have no intention of sharing with you . . . dickhead.

When she didn't answer, Tzader chuckled in a humorless way that brushed a ripple of unease across her skin. "Listen, sweetheart. We might have another couple hours, or we might only have a couple minutes. The Medb don't ransom. They trap, plunder minds, use bodies in hideous ways and toss the carcasses into a fire pit. I could reach Brina even this far below ground, but I can't get through the spell coating these walls. So there's not going to be a Belador cavalry charging in to save us. You either join up and help us find a way to escape, or prepare for the worst death you can imagine."

As if she didn't know the stakes. . .

And hadn't already lived through a fate worse than death. They had no idea who and what they were dealing with.

"I quite agree, love," Quinn added. "I can understand your resistance to trusting anyone after being caught in this trap. I, too, want that traitorous Belador's head as a hood ornament on my Bentley, but none of us will have any chance to discover his identity if we don't survive, and that endangers all our people."

Evalle would give him that, but hanging here manacled to a rock wall by majik didn't exactly instill a sense of camaraderie in her. More like, it brought back memories that made her seethe.

She held the key to possibly overpowering the Medb—a physical ability to shift into a more powerful form that might afford the three of them the combined energy to fight their way out of here. But using that ability would expose the secret she'd shielded for five years and give the Tribunal, the ruling body of VIPER, all the reason they'd need to lock her up.

Adult Alterants did not get a second chance for any infraction. The four male Alterants with unnaturally pale green eyes like Evalle's had shifted into hideous beasts over the past six years and killed humans—and Beladors—before being imprisoned.